# ACCORDING TO HOYLE

## ABIGAIL ROUX

DIME
10
NOVEL

RIPTIDE
PUBLISHING

Riptide Publishing
PO Box 6652
Hillsborough, NJ 08844
www.riptidepublishing.com

According to Hoyle

Cover art: Simoné, www.dreamarian.com
Editors: Gretchen Stull, Carole-ann Galloway
Layout: L.C. Chase, lcchase.com/design.htm

ISBN: 978-1-62649-215-8

Second edition
December, 2014

Also available in ebook:
ISBN: 978-1-62649-214-1

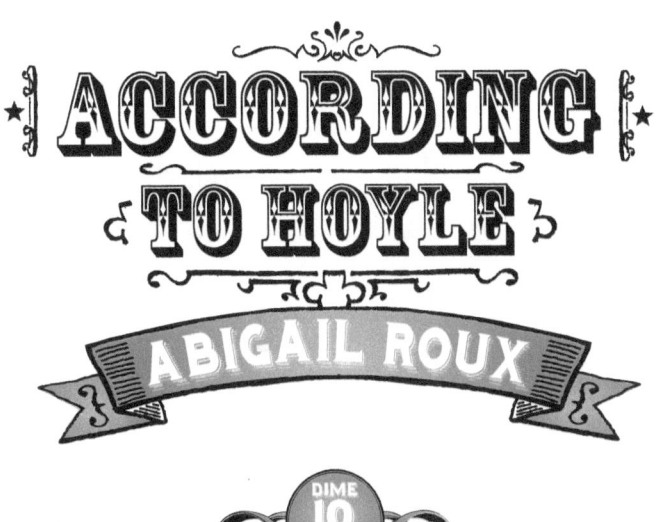

# ACCORDING TO HOYLE

## ABIGAIL ROUX

DIME 10 NOVEL

RIPTIDE PUBLISHING

*For ALR, TMW, and MDT. You make a good posse. Or outlaw band, whatever.*

ACCORDING TO HOYLE: In accord with the prescribed rules or regulations.

Edmond Hoyle (1672–1769) was an English barrister and writer who authored several books on the rules and play of card games. His rule books soon became the authority on all things cards, and the phrase "according to Hoyle" entered the language due to the perceived absolute rightness of the rules Hoyle set forth. The phrase soon took on a more general meaning, referring to any situation in which someone wished to refer to the rules of a higher authority.

It is a similar statement to say we are doing something "by the book," wherein this statement "the book" is often perceived to be the Bible. From the late eighteenth century to the turn of the twentieth century, the phrases "by the book" and "according to Hoyle" were both in common usage. They meant the same thing, only the former venerated the Bible as the highest authority, while the latter deferred to the whims of a deck of cards.

# TABLE OF CONTENTS

# CHAPTER 1

*November 1882*
*Denver, Colorado*

Three men gathered around a linen-covered table in the expansive dining room of the Windsor Hotel in Denver. The great clock on the mantel read well past midnight and candles were all that lit the room, throwing their faces into deep, flickering shadow.

Just two months prior to their meeting, Agent John C. Baird had been in New York, watching as the city's elite unveiled the Pearl Street Power Station and the magic of electricity had lit up the city. He missed that civilized place, and he looked on overgrown mining and cow towns like Denver with disdain he could not and did not try to conceal. There were a few buildings in Denver that had electricity, but the Windsor Hotel was not yet numbered among them, no matter how elegantly appointed it was otherwise.

It didn't matter how uncomfortable the trip was for him, though. He was here on orders, and everything being asked of him hinged on this meeting. It would be worth the trip to this trumped-up little silver town to make certain this mission was done properly.

The room was all but empty, save for a sparse number of diners and the hotel's staff lingering to wait on them. One thing Baird found he did like about the western towns was that people knew how to mind their own affairs. They were in no danger of being disturbed.

"You were late," Baird said to the man just settling into the seat to his right.

"This is a fancy place," the newcomer said in a husky voice. He wore thin leather gloves, but they didn't conceal the fact that one of the fingers on his left hand was missing. His range clothes were dusty, and his hat had left an impression in his black hair when he'd taken it off. It appeared to Baird that he'd just made the trip to Colorado from Texas on the back of a bison rather than in a rail car. The Texan nodded to the grand lobby and the doorman who still stood watching him in distaste. "They weren't going to let me in."

The man opposite Baird gave that a quiet snort. He was handsome and dressed as quite the dandy, in clear contrast to the large Texan. Wiry and of average height, he carried himself with an insolent ease that Baird found both annoying and striking. He certainly wouldn't have been refused entrance to the Windsor Hotel, or any other hotel on the continent. They hadn't let his scruffy little puppy in with him, though, and the beast sat by the window, devotedly watching its master through the speckled glass.

Baird would have sooner dealt with the dog than the shootist. His accent was that of an Englishman, and Baird had instantly decided he neither liked nor trusted the man. This was government business. An Englishman had no right to be involved. Baird's orders were clear, though, and these were the two men he'd been told to contact. Before coming to his current position, Baird had been a Pinkerton agent, and a good one. He knew how to follow orders.

Baird gave the Texan a critical eye. "Fine," Baird said. He wasn't in any mood to deal further with the issue of tardiness. He leaned back in his chair, posture loose and face relaxed, though one hand was on the concealed gun under the table.

The Englishman wasn't impressed. "I'd prefer it if we expedited this meeting."

"If we what?" the Texan asked.

"Expedite. Hurry it along. Make it faster."

"If you mean faster, just say faster."

"Gentlemen," Baird said with a sigh. Both men quieted and turned to him expectantly. Baird inclined his chin and gave them a smile. He looked first at the Englishman and then at the Texan. "You are the men known respectively as Dusty Rose and Bat Stringer, correct?"

Neither man flinched, though Baird had just spoken the names of two notorious gunmen. If either was surprised or concerned at the other's presence, they didn't show it.

"And if we aren't who you say?" the Englishman asked. He kept one hand on the table as a show of respect. The other was, no doubt, in his lap wrapped around a revolver just like Baird's.

"If you aren't who I say, then just who might you be?" Baird asked as he slowly moved the gun in his own lap until it was pointing at the man. It was a misconception that it was easier to kill out West, that no one blinked an eye at murder. The crime was still considered heinous, and prosecuted to the fullest extent of the law. The law, however, didn't reach too far out here. And Baird didn't mind committing a heinous act or three.

Dusty Rose passively returned Baird's stare. The Texan grunted at them both, as if to show he was still unimpressed.

Baird turned an eye on him. He wasn't merely an outlaw and a gunman with a reputation. He was one with something to prove, and that made him even more dangerous.

Baird didn't know much about Bat Stringer other than he hadn't been the first choice for this job. Baird's contacts were supposed to have tracked down Bat's second-in-command, a man known as Whistling Jack Kale. Like Stringer, he'd come to the attention of Baird's superiors after their gang had disappeared from inside a bank under the noses of the very authorities there to capture them.

Kale, however, was rumored to be the brains of the operation. But he was still in the wind, possibly dead. Which was why Bat Stringer was here now instead of him. If they'd wanted a man like Kale for the job, they were almost as well served with his boss. He was said to be a smart man, if not exactly a mastermind, and a fast draw. And if he really had killed Whistling Jack Kale, his best friend, then he was just ruthless enough to serve Baird's purposes.

Dusty Rose sighed softly and glanced away. The Englishman also had a reputation for escaping from the hands of the law. He was famous for his skill at card games, but he was better known as a gunman than a gambler. Clever and charming, he rarely drew the gun he was said to be so adept at handling. He'd also spent a good deal of time with the native tribes, and Baird's sources implied that Rose had picked up certain knowledge that would be vital to this mission.

"I'll get right to the point, gentlemen," Baird finally said. "You don't need to know who I am or who I'm working for. I won't tolerate any questions about either subject."

Stringer sat watching him much like a housecat would stalk a canary in a cage, his dark eyes intelligent and patient. Rose, however, was still looking off to the side, shaking his head as if disgusted with himself simply for being there. Baird's lips twitched into a smile. To lure him to this meeting, he'd made the shootist an offer he couldn't easily refuse. The man had enough trouble with the law, he didn't need any more. And Baird had made it clear that he'd make plenty of trouble if Rose didn't play the game.

Baird waited until it was apparent that neither man would respond before he continued. "At this very moment, there are soldiers working nearby, searching for an Indian artifact."

"Artifact," Stringer repeated with a frown.

Rose sat forward. "It's a trinket, Mr. Stringer. With some sort of inherent value to it, be it regarding history or mankind."

"I know what the damn word means."

Baird rubbed his eyes. He cleared his throat pointedly and both men once again turned back to him. "This artifact, if found, could be very important."

"To?" Rose asked. "Not you."

"What is it?" Stringer asked.

"That is none of your concern, Mr. Stringer."

The man didn't react other than to cock his head and maintain eye contact. It was unnerving. Baird almost preferred Rose's sarcasm and insolence to being the object of such silent study.

"If the Army's already searching for this trinket, why do you need us?" Rose asked, poorly trying to conceal his interest under a hint of nonchalance.

Baird stared at him.

"Because you're not Army," Rose concluded with a slow nod. He looked away again and sighed heavily, as if just realizing how much trouble he might be in if he didn't feel like cooperating. Good. That was how Baird wanted him: scared and backed into a corner.

"The Army is a redundant, stupid beast," Baird said after a moment. "This item cannot be trusted in their hands. It must be taken from them and safeguarded properly. But as you have probably gathered, we cannot have one government agency blatantly stealing from another, and it's best to keep this away from any official avenues."

Rose laughed out loud. He shook his head at Stringer, seeking an ally, but Stringer wasn't laughing. Upon seeing that, Rose cleared his throat and schooled his features into a more serious expression. Baird wasn't amused by his antics.

"You want us to steal this artifact from the Army for you," Stringer said. "So your hands stay clean."

"That's precisely right."

"You want the two of us to attack a battalion of soldiers in the middle of Nebraska, steal an Indian artifact from them in the middle of Indian Territory, and ride off into the sunset without anyone the wiser?" Rose's voice was flat and sarcastic. He leaned forward and put a finger on the table. "Are you insane, or are you just as stupid as you look?"

Baird's shoulders stiffened. "I assure you I am neither," He realized belatedly, as Rose's lips curved into a smile, the trap in the words. His cheeks flushed. He gritted his teeth. "The plan is more complex than that."

"I certainly hope so."

"What *is* the plan?" Stringer asked. He did not appear amused by Rose or impressed with what Baird was saying.

"You will be informed of the details when we come to an agreement on your services."

"On that note, why are my services even required here?" Rose asked. "I am no thief, nor am I a soldier of any description."

"So you say. But you have spent time with the natives."

"And?"

"I believe you have specific information from them about this artifact, whether you are aware of it or not."

"Is that so?" Rose asked, completely unperturbed by the extent of Baird's knowledge about his activities.

"That is so. Your particular services would be required after the initial acquirement of the artifact."

"For?"

"You will be informed of those details when the time comes," Baird answered. "And you have a reputation."

"Yes. For playing cards."

"Playing cards," Stringer repeated, incredulous. He stared at Rose, and Rose returned it warily, as if trying to gauge the threat from the big man. "If you're a gambler, then I'm a seamstress."

Rose scratched at his chin as he contemplated Stringer, then pointed one elegant finger at the man and narrowed his eyes. "Do you darn socks?"

Baird rubbed at the spot between his eyes, feeling an ache in his head coming on. "Gentlemen," he said before the conversation could digress further.

Rose looked back at him sharply, all trace of sarcasm or humor gone. "I believe I made it quite clear in my initial answer to your man a fortnight ago that I am not for hire." His black eyes seemed to glint in the candlelight as he leaned back in his chair and mirrored Baird's stance. "You can threaten me all you please, Mr. Baird, promise you'll make my life hell. It won't change the fact that theft is not my area of expertise and I do not intend to help you rob the Army or the natives."

Baird was no fool. He knew what sort of men he was dealing with. He sat unflinching, returning the intense gaze. "We plan to pay you in solid gold, Mr. Rose. Surely that must pique your interest?"

"No. You know what gold is good for? Weighing you down when you try to run. I have enough trouble on my own. I don't need to go begging it from the Army, the natives, or whatever agency of the government you may be representing. My curiosity into such matters can only lead me so far before my better instincts prevail." He sat forward and put a finger to the tip of his nose. "You smell of trouble I neither want nor need, Mr. Baird."

Baird raised one eyebrow and turned to look at Stringer, who sat watching them silently. "And you?"

"Well, I don't often need to run, so gold being heavy don't bother me. But I'll need to hear your plans before I give my answer."

"As I said, you and I will discuss the finer points of the plan and the vast sums of money you'll be receiving later. And since Mr. Rose doesn't appear interested, I'll consider your offer for employment accepted right after you've taken care of the Desert Flower here."

Rose pushed his chair back and lunged to his feet. Stringer did the same, reaching for the gun concealed under his arm. He didn't draw it, though, perhaps still considering Baird's offer. China crashed at a table on the far side of the room as the handful of late diners dove for cover. Several of the other patrons screamed or shouted.

"Gun!" one of the waiters called out.

Baird sat back, a small smile on his face. There were people all over the country who'd pay good money to see a showdown like this. And he had a front row seat.

Rose hesitated, not drawing his weapon for some reason Baird couldn't fathom. Perhaps he thought he could still convince Stringer not to take Baird's deal. Stringer, though, seemed to make up his mind and slid his gun from its holster with practiced ease.

Suddenly, the floor beneath them began to roll and shudder. The candles shivered and some of them blew out as a terrible rattling and creaking shook the very foundations of the hotel.

Baird gripped the table in front of him, gaping up at the chandeliers and the plaster molds on the ceiling as they began to flake and fall around them.

"Earthquake!" someone shouted, this newer, more unusual threat overriding that of the guns.

Baird looked back at the two combatants and stood when he saw Rose had disappeared. A large piece of plaster landed in the middle of their table, and Baird ducked away from it. Stringer had hit his knees and was covering his head, oblivious to anything but the danger of the falling debris. They both dove for the table and huddled under it.

Several minutes later, the trembling finally stopped. Baird climbed to his feet. His eyes searched around the dining room, and he gritted his teeth.

"Damn the man."

"You want to go after him?" Stringer asked unenthusiastically as he holstered his gun.

Baird shook his head. "He can't hurt us."

"You mean he can't hurt *you*."

Baird eyed him sharply. "If you want to go running through the rubble of Denver to find him, then be my guest. Just be aware he's expecting you now. He won't be quite so easy to kill."

Stringer's full lips curved into a wicked, frightening smile. "Another time, then."

Baird shivered despite himself. At least he knew he had the right man for the job. The information he'd needed from Rose could be acquired in other ways. Harder ways.

# CHAPTER 2

*December 1882*
*Lincoln, Nebraska*

Deputy US Marshal Eli Flynn's boots echoed on the wooden sidewalk as he trudged the last few steps of his trip. He hardly recognized this section of the town; most of the structures had been rebuilt after the fire burnt them all to the ground. When he'd left, this area had been merely foundations and frames. Or rubble.

Lincoln, Nebraska, had grown in leaps and bounds the last several years, trying to become what the residents expected from the capital of a newly formed state. The buildings rose two and sometimes three stories, making the streets feel closed in and dark. Flynn didn't like it. But the Marshal Office remained on the outskirts of town, where the breeze could still reach him and the sun still shone down to warm the cold mornings.

He stopped at the shining new window to the dry-goods store, intending to straighten up a little, to at least seem respectable when he went in. But one look told him it was no use. He was dirty and haggard, and his normally well-manicured goatee was bordering on the wrong side of woolly. But an hour at the bathhouse would fix all that right up too.

He turned away and headed for the Marshal Office. He had to check in before he could even think about trying to remedy any of it, though. It wasn't as if being dirty and tired were unusual west of the Mississippi. Nor was it unexpected after a trip like the one he had taken.

He stopped at the door to the new Marshal Office and wiped his face with his kerchief, took his hat off and swiped at his forehead and eyes, then stuffed the bit of red material back into the pocket beneath his frock coat. He squared his sore shoulders and took a deep breath before strolling into the building that still smelled of fresh pine.

A bell hanging above the door dinged as he walked in. He glanced up at it curiously. The tiny brass bell was just as new as the rest of the construction. A bell there made sense, though. A marshal should have a way of knowing when someone walked in.

The sounds of the bustling street outside reached through the walls of the Marshal Office: horses' hooves clopping along the packed-dirt street, ladies' boots clacking against the raised walkways, men calling greetings to one another in the early-morning cold. It was a comfortable, familiar scene. One that Flynn had missed.

The office, however, was anything but familiar. Flynn looked around at the bright, whitewashed walls and the pristine pine floors. The old office had been sparse and dreary, with scuffed floors, no windows, and very little light. He and Wash had seen fit to fix that when they'd rebuilt. The cells, rather than being all in one room like before, were out of sight in the back of the structure.

Flynn removed his hat and held it at his side, not wanting to knock the dust off his clothing in the clean room.

"Flynn?" The voice boomed from the rear of the building.

Flynn peered into the dim, his eyesight still ruined from the bright morning sun outside.

Deputy US Marshal William Henry Washington, or Wash to friends and strangers alike, emerged from the back of the office, into the light, and surveyed Flynn with sharp, clear green eyes. His sandy hair was shorter than it had been the last time Flynn had seen him. His beard and mustache were gone, with only the sideburns near his ears still present. And for the first time in Flynn couldn't remember how long, Wash wasn't wearing his guns.

"You look like hell," Wash observed with a grin.

"Stillwater to Lincoln is a long trip." Flynn shook the hand Wash offered.

"But it's easier on the return."

Flynn smiled weakly and nodded. Transporting prisoners was never a simple task. Stillwater was one of the better transits because nearly every stop offered a decent place to lock someone up or otherwise restrain them with a minimum of fuss. Other locales weren't so convenient, like when you had to tie your prisoner to a telegraph pole just to get a decent hour or two of sleep. The solo return, of course, was always less stressing.

"Sense of humor is still top notch, I notice," Wash said. He turned away and headed for the desk against the far wall. He picked up a small yellow piece of paper and waved it in the air. "I've got another one for you."

Flynn narrowed his eyes at the telegram with a sinking sensation in his gut.

"They're waiting to be picked up in Junction City," Wash continued as he glanced at Flynn, looking over Flynn's tired face and slumping shoulders. "You ready for another one? I might can give this to someone else . . . Actually, I can't give it to no one else 'cause no one else is around, but I can offer and pretend I care that you're about to yell."

Flynn merely glared at him.

"It's an easy one," Wash offered in a voice that was probably meant to be enticing.

"The last 'easy' one you gave me tried to kill me," Flynn reminded him. "Twice."

"They're outlaws, Flynn. By and large, that's what they do." Wash walked around the desk and held the telegraphed message out to him with a whistle.

"Is this one going to the gallows?" Flynn sighed as he reached for the paper. Prisoners going to their execution always gave the US Marshals escorting them one hell of a hard time. They were fighting for their lives, after all, and more lawmen were killed while transporting prisoners than any other activity they performed. Neither Flynn nor Wash had ever had a prisoner escape on them, though. Not one that they hadn't recovered almost immediately, anyway. Or shot dead during their escape attempt.

"No gallows. There are three in the group you're picking up," Wash told Flynn. "Two are heading to Fort Smith, some sort of military to-do, but you're only taking them as far as St. Louis to meet up with the Army escort. The last is going to trial in New Orleans. You'll have to—"

"Three?" Flynn blurted. "This is an *easy* one? Goddamn, Wash!"

"Taking the Lord's name in vain, Flynn." Wash smirked. "I'm shocked. What would the lady folk say?"

"You ain't no damn lady. And I can't escort three men by myself. Who's going with me to ride herd?"

"You want someone to go with you?" Wash feigned surprise.

Flynn smacked his hat against his jeans and sent a puff of dust swirling into the clean office.

Wash just chuckled and held up his hand. "I'm going with you as far as St. Louis," he said, still laughing. "Then I'm to head to Natchez to convene with the governor, and I'll meet up with you again in New Orleans for the return home."

"You?"

Wash shrugged and nodded. Flynn's attention strayed to the crisp linen sling that hung over Wash's shoulder, supporting his left arm, and then back to the man's eyes in question.

"I can draw a gun with one hand," Wash assured him quietly, suddenly serious as he sat on the edge of the desk.

"You can't restrain a prisoner with one hand," Flynn argued. "You can't chain and unchain them with one hand. You can't expect them to see you as a serious authority figure or anything of a threat with one hand." He waved his hat at Wash's shoulder. "They'll be trying to escape left and right."

"Then I'll be sure to let them know," Wash responded with his customary calm, "that since I can't chain them or restrain them peaceably, I'll just have to shoot them if they cause problems. Will that satisfy you?"

Flynn pursed his lips and blew air heavily through his nose. He didn't want to insult Wash or hurt him, but he also didn't want to be stampeded by a herd of escaping prisoners. "Can you use it at all yet?" he asked, already regretting his criticism. It was bad enough being injured. It was worse seeing that people didn't have much confidence in you, especially for a man like Wash, who had always been so capable.

Wash flexed his fingers against his chest. He tapped his silver badge and smiled crookedly. That was more movement than he had been up to when Flynn had left for Stillwater Prison three weeks ago. But Flynn struggled to keep even a hint of sadness out of his expression as he watched. Would his friend ever get the full use of the arm back?

Wash obviously read him like an open book. He flicked his wrist, producing a derringer attached to a gambler's gauntlet out of the end of the sling.

Flynn blinked in surprise, his body instinctively twitching to reach for his own Colt. He laughed and offered Wash a fond shake of his head.

"You crazy bastard. You're going to get yourself shot."

"Hell, I already done that," Wash said. "And you might find me taking exception to such talk." He turned away, going to the potbelly stove in the far corner and retrieving a tin tray of food that had been warming nearby.

Flynn remained where he was. They'd spent plenty of years together, battled Confederates and Indians together, and become US Marshals together when they'd run out of wars to fight. But since Wash had been forced to take over the Lincoln Marshal Office a year ago due to the untimely death of their superior, Flynn had seen little of him other than the occasional drink or their nightly dinner at the saloon, and that just wasn't the same. It would be welcome, actually, to be able to travel with Wash again and spend some time with him.

"When do we leave?" he asked as Wash retreated into the row of cells with the tray of food.

"After supper. Best you get a bath and some rest," Wash answered over his shoulder.

Flynn hummed. He had slept on the train from Stillwater, and though the thought of a nice soak was highly appealing, he didn't feel like leaving just yet. Escorting prisoners was a lonely task. They weren't much for conversation, and neither was Flynn when criminals and horses were the only things around to talk to.

"When'd they get this finished?" he asked, following Wash back into the darker recesses of the office.

"Last week," Wash answered. "The design we laid out worked perfect."

And one of the newly minted cells was already occupied.

"Who's this?" Flynn asked with a wave of his hat at the man who lay curled on the hard cot within.

"What, you don't recognize Larry Fitz?"

Flynn's lips parted in shock. The man's clothes were thin and tattered, and he was covered in caked mud and blood. His hair was stringy and his face was sunken. Flynn had seen a man dragged by a horse who had looked something like Larry did now. "What happened to him?"

Wash's answer was grim. "He got caught."

Flynn glanced at Wash and saw the familiar hard set of his jaw and the glint in his green eyes. The expression told Flynn that the man inside the cell was lucky to be alive. Larry Fitz, who lay bruised and battered and barely recognizable, was essentially a harmless drunkard. Or he had been, until the night two months ago when he'd gone on a bender and decided to set fire to the Feed and Seed, the building that had shared a wall with the old Marshal Office.

Wash had been inside the jail that night, and he had nearly lost his life trying to release the prisoners from their cells as the building burned down around them. His hands still bore scars from the burns he'd received from the heated metal of the bars as he'd opened the doors. The fire had leaped from the building that housed the General Store and Feed and Seed and the jail beside it, to the buildings on either side of them: the stables and the saloon.

The horses had all been saved, which was a stroke of luck considering their value in a town like Lincoln, but the buildings had burned down like the dry kindling they were, and with them went the livelihood of some of the town's most prominent citizens. The biggest tragedy had been the deaths of three guests renting the rooms above the saloon who hadn't been able to get out in time. The damage to the town and to its reputation hadn't made anyone particularly happy.

The prisoners Wash had risked his life to save had promptly tried to escape as the townsfolk dealt with the spreading fire. That was how Wash's arm wound up in the sling. A bullet from a stolen gun had taken him cleanly through the shoulder as he'd tried to retake the prisoners without violence. Of course, after being shot, violence had not been one of Wash's concerns and the escaped prisoners hadn't made it very far.

The doc was certain he would make a nearly full recovery. Flynn, however, was certain that the doc spent too much time in the saloon, and so he worried for Wash and his arm.

The two prisoners who had attempted to escape that night now occupied permanent spots up in the shady little grove of headstones the local residents had naïvely named God's Acre, thinking an acre would be enough to hold the dead in a town west of the Mississippi.

Fitz, the man who'd caused the whole damn mess, had gone to ground as soon as he had sobered up and realized what he'd done, and he'd been in hiding ever since. Until now, apparently.

"Who found him?" Flynn asked softly.

"Cyrus Beeson, over on the flats," Wash answered. "It's a damn miracle they didn't kill him 'fore I got to him. Just happenstance I was anywhere near when they dragged him in. They were heading for a hanging tree, making a damn mess of it."

"Shame you got to him at all," Flynn muttered.

"Law don't work that way, Flynn."

"It does out here."

"It ain't supposed to." Wash slid his key into the lock and turned it slowly. The man inside didn't move as the hinges groaned. Wash knelt and placed the tray of food on the floor.

"Maybe it should," Flynn argued quietly. "It'd make our lives a lot easier."

Wash eased his way back out of the cell and retrieved his key, locking it and watching to see if Larry would move. When it didn't appear that he would, Wash pursed his lips and turned to Flynn.

"Life's not easy to come by. I don't mind mine being hard, and I don't take it lightly when I'm forced to take one. You shouldn't neither."

"I ain't the one deciding to waste my life by stepping outside the law."

Wash brushed by him and headed back out into the front office. Flynn followed him.

"Even outlaws got their stories, Eli," Wash told him.

"And they can tell 'em to the Devil when they see him," Flynn insisted.

Wash sighed as he sat himself in front of the stove and propped his booted feet on the bench in front of him. "Go get yourself a bath, Marshal Flynn," he suggested with a resigned smile, obviously recognizing the argument as just as hopeless as it had been the last time. "I've ridden horses that smelled better'n you."

*Nebraska Badlands*

A bitter wind whipped through the cottonwoods along the Rosebud Creek. Snow flurries rode the gusts, falling erratically amidst the soldiers from nearby Fort Robinson who labored in the cold. Their breaths were visible in the frosty air even from the ridges that rose above the river. The soldiers were being pushed hard, picking through the rocks that lined the river and piling them carefully into large crates. Some of the rocks contained what appeared to be skeletons; outlines of bones that looked like animals no one had ever seen, trapped inside rocks with no explanation for how they'd gotten there. The soldiers tossed some of these rocks into stenciled crates along with the rest.

Another band of soldiers worked atop one of the high hills above the river, searching the ground for something long buried and digging random holes to find and recover it.

Bartholomew Stringer knelt amidst the scrub ponderosa pine atop the edge of a low butte, his dark eyes narrowed under the brim of his hat. His second-in-command hunched beside him, the man's reedy shoulders bent against the brisk wind that howled down from the Black Hills to the north, into and across the badlands.

"You sure 'bout all this, Cap?" Frank Alvarado muttered as they watched. He was thin and twitchy. His stringy blond hair hung lank around his narrow face, and his deep-set eyes were a pale blue that made him seem weak and sickly. He was anything but. His weedy appearance worked to his advantage more often than not.

Stringer glanced at him. He wasn't used to having his orders questioned. But this was not a normal excursion, so he was giving his band of half a dozen men some leeway. They had traveled all the way from Texas, and most of them had never been somewhere this damn cold. Back home they were known as the Border Scouts, a name retained from ties to the sharpshooters and rogue bands of the now-defunct Confederate Army because of the fear it instilled in those who heard it. Here, they were nothing but another gang of men with guns. It had been a lot to ask of them to give up that esteem and comfort without telling them why they were here.

Stringer's patience with their doubts was reaching an end, though. He was taller than most and wide along the shoulders. His deep voice was often enough to keep order amidst the ruffians who called him Cap, but his size and his piercing gaze helped to remind them just how cruel he could be when they got unruly. It wasn't often he had to resort to actively keeping his men in line.

"You know about Fort Robinson and the Indians, don't you Frank?" Stringer asked in a whisper.

Alvarado shook his head jerkily as he continued to watch the soldiers below. His teeth were chattering.

"Three years ago, there was this Cheyenne Chief named Dull Knife got captured near Fort Robinson and held there. He'd tried to escape with his band of Indians and been massacred, and that was the end of the Indian Wars in the Nebraska Territory."

"How you know this, Cap?"

Stringer shrugged. He hadn't known a lot about the Cheyenne or the Lakota Sioux at the time, and like most in the country, he hadn't cared when he'd heard news about the mass death. But then he'd met John C. Baird in Denver a month ago, who'd told him quite a tale.

"They called Dull Knife an admirable outlaw, whatever that is," Stringer continued. Alvarado gave him a confused frown.

"He hid tribal valuables in the clothes and ornaments of his people as they ran from the Federal troops through the Nebraska badlands. Even their guns got dismantled, hidden in blankets and parts of beads and jewelry."

"Why?"

"I don't know," Stringer admitted. The Cheyenne had been poor, starving, and desperate by the time they'd reached the badlands. Most of the ceremonial trinkets and ancient baubles considered sacred by the elders weren't of any interest to the soldiers who chased them. "Didn't help them much when the cold caught up to them."

Dull Knife, the ill-fated leader of the Cheyenne who'd tried to return to their ancient homeland, had been among the first to be buried, put in the ground atop the very ridge the soldiers now searched, his grave lost to the shifting winds of the badlands. And with it, the goods that had been buried with him to keep them safe.

"What's that got to do with us?" Alvarado finally asked hesitantly.

"Well, Frank," Stringer said with a small, cruel smile. "They say after he was buried, the Rosebud Creek started running with gold."

"Gold?" Alvarado repeated with a dubious lift to his eyebrow.

"Gold."

Alvarado stared at him for a moment, then turned his pale eyes back to the dozens of soldiers laboring below them. "I don't understand."

"Me neither," Stringer told him softly. "I don't believe in magic or no Indian hogwash. All I know is that government man wants whatever these boys dig up, and he wants it bad. Our job is to get it for him."

"If you say so, Cap."

Stringer's men were growing restless. He could occasionally hear the snort of a horse or the cough of a man as they waited behind the ridge amidst the cover of the ponderosa.

They might not be getting a river running with precious ore, and Stringer didn't believe whatever the Cheyenne had buried with Dull Knife had the power to turn anything into gold. But what the government man meant to pay them for whatever the soldiers pulled out of the earth would be worth the wait.

"Mr. Baird, I trust your end of this issue has been taken care of?" the old man rasped.

"I'm afraid there were some complications," Baird reported. "Stringer is well on his way, but Rose refused to work with us. He then escaped before we could dispatch him."

"Escaped."

"Yes, sir. Escaped."

"How?"

"Pure luck, I assure you, sir. An earthquake, in fact."

"An act of God," the old man said in his disconcerting voice. He raised his spotted hand to scratch at his eyebrow. The gold and jewels of the rings on his fingers reflected the light in odd patterns.

Baird fought not to be distracted by it. The silence fell heavy in the room. Dust motes floated by his head in the shaft of light let in by the frosted window. Baird waited for the old man to continue.

"Very well. Can his knowledge harm us? Harm our plan?"

"Certainly, if ever he were to find all the pieces." Baird knew better than to hedge his answers. The truth and only the truth was the thing to give to his employer.

"Will he?"

"He couldn't possibly, sir."

"You believe a man who would be so lucky as to stumble upon an earthquake when one is needed could not possibly have the good fortune to piece together this puzzle you have so artfully taken apart?"

Baird pressed his lips tightly together to hide his frustration. "Point well made, sir. What would you have me do?"

"Kill him."

"It's already in the works, sir." Baird had hired two men to track Rose down and dispatch him. The last telegram he'd received had put them somewhere in Nebraska. Baird was confident Rose would find no earthquakes there.

"And Stringer?" the old man asked without acknowledging Baird's forethought.

"He is quite capable. I have given him the bare bones of our orders and he assures me it will be done."

The old man's thin white hair flew in wisps around his head and his eyebrows seemed to weigh down the skin of his forehead, giving the impression he was constantly scowling. When he offered his snaggletooth grin, he appeared quite ghastly.

Baird smiled politely. He knew how this game was played. He'd begun his lengthy career as a Pinkerton agent during the War Between the States. He and others like him had acted as spies for the Union army, repeatedly going behind enemy lines to do the bidding of those with higher rank.

Baird had risen quickly. After the war, when the Secret Service department had been formed to help handle the workload of the

US Marshals, Baird had been one of the first ones to be recruited. On the surface, the Secret Service were involved with suppressing the counterfeiting of paper money, which had become popular since the currency of the failed Confederacy so many people had hoarded lost its value. But their reach extended much further than that; though they still performed the duties that had been their beginning, now they were also tasked with protecting government officials at certain times, and more importantly, they still acted as spies for the government, on both native and foreign soil.

Baird did not like farming out jobs to untrustworthy and unpredictable outlaws. If they failed, it would be on his head.

"And the information you intended to harvest from Rose. Where do you intend to get it now?" the old man asked.

Baird had no good answer for that. Men who'd spent time peacefully with the tribes were few and far between. "I'm still seeking an answer to that, sir."

"Very well. Inform me at once when you hear of any news."

"Yes, sir," Baird answered as he stood and tipped his head. "A good day to you, General."

"John," the general called after him as he turned to take his leave. "You may see fit to make certain your loose ends are tied. If Rose shows his face in New York, you had better not shows yours."

Baird's polite smile faltered only slightly. "Yes, General," he said obediently, cursing under his breath as the heavy door shut behind him.

The creak of the wagon wheels and the clop of the horses' hooves were the lone sounds that broke the late evening silence as Wash and Flynn traveled south to Junction City. Before setting out the previous evening, they had deputized an extra man they could trust to stay back in Lincoln and hold down the fort until one of the other marshals returned.

They expected to get into Junction City well before nightfall of their second day of trekking, but both men were veterans of plains travel, and knew how unpredictable it could be. They had given themselves plenty of leeway. The only problem with leeway was when you didn't need it. Even with someone to keep you company on the trail, the silence could be oppressive at times.

"Know anything about these boys?" Flynn finally asked to break up the monotony.

Wash glanced over at him. He was guiding the cumbersome wagon over the deeply rutted trail with one hand as if it were easy. "Two of them are soldiers of some description," he answered around the blade of grass between his teeth. When the dry-goods store had burned down, the town's tobacco had gone with it. All the men who smoked for a fifty-mile radius had taken to chewing straw as a poor replacement until the new shipments came up the river. Wash claimed Lincoln had been witness to some very cranky town meetings in the meantime.

Flynn pondered telling Wash that he had bought more tobacco while up in Stillwater, but decided against it.

"Soldiers. Indian Wars? Or War Between the States?" he asked dubiously. Surely they weren't still tracking down deserters and dissenters from the latter.

Wash shrugged and clucked his tongue at the plodding mule pulling the wagon. "I don't think these gentlemen are deserters. I think they're younger. Regular Army, Indian Wars and all that."

"Huh. What'd they do?"

"Telegrams didn't say."

Flynn hummed. Not many soldiers got sent back for trial and hanging. The Army needed the numbers and the guns while fighting the Indians, so for the most part they didn't care about their behavior. And if it was something truly heinous, they were usually taken care of on site, before the bureaucrats got hold of it. These boys must have done something particularly interesting to be sent to Fort Smith. Of course, the Ute and Cheyenne wars had ended almost two years ago, and things had been pretty quiet since. Flynn remembered how soldiers could find trouble during peacetime.

These two unfortunates might be examples to keep order.

Flynn never really gave much thought to what their prisoners had done. He took them where they were supposed to go and then went on with life. He claimed that it was hard to watch a man you'd conversed with hang from the gallows, which it was, but it was also easier to not give a damn about the outlaws they met.

Some of them deserved a noose. Some did not.

"The third is a shootist," Wash continued. "You might've heard of him. Goes by the name of Dusty Rose."

"No kidding?" Flynn said with long look over at Wash. "I have heard of him."

"Everyone's heard of him," Wash said with a laugh. "He's in all those damn dime novels they sell back East."

"Dime novels," Flynn scoffed. "They never get anything right."

Those damn stories made more trouble for people than most anything. If you were unlucky enough to get your name in a dime novel, it was likely you'd have wet-behind-the-ears young guns coming after you from all sides, hoping to make themselves a name by getting the drop on you. Or worse, calling you out across a town square, thinking they were Wild Bill Hickok in *Harper's* magazine. Flynn shook his head, glad that he and Wash both had managed to escape the fate of fame in their wilder youth.

Dusty Rose had not been so lucky.

Flynn hated dealing with rumor. He couldn't help himself when it came to Dusty Rose, though, because the man kind of fascinated him. "They say he's just as fast as Doc Holliday. I heard he dealt faro with Doc out in Colorado for a spell."

Wash laughed softly. It was a low, growling sound that always made Flynn smile. "You curious?"

Flynn glanced back at him and slowed his horse, coming abreast of Wash as the man grinned at him.

Wash looped the reins of the wagon around the toe of his boot and reached into his jacket with his good hand. He extracted a dime novel and offered it to Flynn. "Picked it up at the general store before we left."

Flynn rolled his eyes and snatched the flimsy story papers from him. Of course a new shipment of dime novels would come in before the tobacco. He pursed his lips, reading the title with a frown. "*Best of the West Series: Dusty Rose, the Desert Flower.*"

On the front was a sketch of what the publishers figured Rose looked like. Flynn had found that they were never as handsome or as dashing as the public thought. And they were rarely ever as skilled or heroic. Most were just two-bit horse thieves with catchy names and a knack for dramatics.

"Says he can shoot with either hand," Wash told him as Flynn opened the book and scanned it with morbid curiosity. "Says he's got a dog he trained to take keys out of a man's belt, follows him everywhere he goes. Says he's a bit of a dandy and that he don't drink one lick. Never gambles, never swears, never goes a day without bathing. Can't all be true if he was dealing faro with Doc Holliday. Not if he lived to see the first sunrise after."

"'Always to be found in dapper dress,'" Flynn read with distaste. "'Never a gold button or silk kerchief out of place.'"

"'Nary a damsel in distress or blushing maid can resist his smiling face,'" Wash recited, his voice shaking with laughter.

Flynn grunted and tossed the dime novel over his shoulder. It landed with a plop in the back of the empty wagon. Wash guffawed raucously, obviously having expected the reaction.

"I wouldn't put too much stock in it," Wash said after a while, still snickering. "Kid Antrim down in New Mexico was said to be a dandy too, and you've seen those tintypes of him. Ugly, dirty, little bastard."

"Lots of things was said about Kid Antrim. He's a damn hero now that he's dead and not shooting folks left and right. They'll never call him a hired killer like he really was."

"What is it they're calling him back East now? Billy the Kid?" Wash asked.

Flynn offered that a rude noise. "That'll never stick."

Wash shook his head, smiling as he pulled the mule to the right to avoid a rut that probably would have broken an axle. Flynn watched him as they plodded along, feeling the ache in his chest like he always did when he got a chance to sit back and watch his friend. It was a familiar ache, one that he had lived with since their early days in the Union Army.

"Dime novels never get it straight," Flynn said when the ache became too much to deal with. "I heard that Rose favors the gentlemen over the 'blushing maids,' or whatever the hell they called 'em. Wouldn't that shock the genteel society types?" he mused.

"I've heard that too," Wash agreed. "Might shock the society types, but it ain't uncommon out here. I do wonder how Rose gets by with it being so well-known."

Flunn grunted distractedly.

"That bother you?"

Flynn glanced back at him in surprise and then shrugged uncomfortably. Something about Wash's tone of voice told him that he may have offended him with the subject. "Man's welcome to do what he likes, so long as it don't hurt no one else. I thought Rose was all bluster," he added, irritably shifting his body in the saddle, hoping to change the subject. "All tenderfoot hooey and big talk about how fast he was with iron. Finally turned real outlaw, did he?"

"Word is he killed a man," Wash answered, giving a lopsided shrug. "Two men, actually."

"Word is he's killed lots of people," Flynn countered. "I thought it was all bull."

"Well, the dime novel stuff is bull. But the official reports ain't too pretty. He's been tried twice in New York, was absolved of guilt and let loose both times. Some say his family has big political pull, lots of money," Wash said with another tug on the reins. "But he had to go west after the second trial to save his family's name. Got into more trouble out here. He escaped from a sheriff in Arkansas somewheres, but after the fact it was proved he wasn't even in town when the man he was accused of killing was shot, so they let him be."

"Escaped, huh?" Flynn asked, frowning heavily.

"Seems to be pretty good at it. He's been found innocent of four separate murder charges." Wash grimaced as if the thought of someone getting away with murder caused him physical pain. "They were all self-defense incidents with witnesses and sworn statements and the like. But, rumor has it that in other cases he's escaped from five different lawmen in three territories before ever being brought in front of a magistrate or judge."

"Five," Flynn repeated flatly.

Wash gave a jerk of his chin. "We'll have our hands full."

"Well, ain't that just a treat. I ain't ever hearing 'easy one' from you again, you damn liar," Flynn muttered. "So, what makes this time any different? With the murder, I mean."

Wash shrugged. "Nothing special about it, I don't think. He shot two boys in the street, neither of them yet twenty, then he stuck around until the sheriff showed up, claimed the other men drew first. I guess he was counting on the self-defense thing again. Local magistrate ain't gonna be around for another month and they're worried about him escaping, so he's being sent off to New Orleans for trial."

"Huh." Flynn glanced up at the darkening sky. "He stuck around."

"Yep."

"Peculiar."

"Yep."

"That his real name, y'think? Rose?" Flynn asked after a long moment of nothing but the creaking wagon wheels and the clopping hooves. "Dusty sure as sin ain't his given name."

"Nah, it's an alias," Wash said with a small laugh. "I'm sure there's another name on the papers."

"Guess we'll find out soon enough, huh?" Flynn said as the squat gray buildings of Junction City came into view over the horizon.

"Yep."

"Yep," the old Junction City sheriff greeted drolly. He took the papers Wash handed him. "Yep, yep, yep."

"Good to know we're in the right place," Wash responded, giving Flynn an amused glance and a wink.

Flynn rolled his eyes and then peered up and down the street warily. A smattering of people had gathered as they'd guided the wagon into town, recognizing them as lawmen and obviously aware of who they had come for. Flynn hadn't quite appreciated the fuss this infamous prisoner might cause them as they took him toward the Mississippi. They would have to stay far away from the bigger towns along the route, where word might have already spread. It would make the trip longer, more expensive, and certainly more dangerous.

Flynn's horse shook its head and snorted, sidestepping toward the water trough as Flynn and Wash strode up onto the wooden sidewalk. They followed the sheriff into the tiny jail. It was dark and cramped and dusty. A typical territorial sheriff's jail, as far as Flynn's vast experience went, built out of mud brick and luck.

He stood in the doorway, leaning against the doorjamb and holding Wash's shotgun in the crook of his arm as Wash dealt with the warrants. Men like Dusty Rose had a lot of admirers and a lot of enemies, any of whom might like to catch him as he was being led from a cell in hand irons. It was Flynn's and Wash's job to make certain the prisoners got where they were going alive, preferably without much loss of limb. The government wanted them to still be breathing before they stretched their necks.

But Flynn was of the opinion that if anyone intended to harm Dusty Rose in this particular town, they would have done so already. It would be plenty easy to stick your gun through the bars of the jail cell's window and blow someone away. Lynch mobs were still nearly uncontrollable in these parts too. But, regardless of what his gut told him about the lack of danger, Flynn kept one eye on the street, just in case.

"Just the two of you sent to get 'em?" the sheriff asked as he eyed Wash's sling with rheumy blue eyes that had probably once been sharp and hard.

"You expect them to give us trouble?" Wash asked, obviously not at all concerned with the implication that he wasn't able to handle the job with his injured arm.

The sheriff shrugged and handed Wash back the leather packet that contained their papers. "See for yourself," he invited with a gesture toward the cells in the back partition of the rickety building.

Wash slid the warrants into the waterproof pouch inside his duster and turned to incline his head at Flynn. Flynn gave one last look at the calm street outside and then glanced to the couple of sheriff's deputies who were to keep guard for them. They nodded in unison, and Flynn turned to follow Wash into the back. It took a moment for his eyes to adjust, but soon Flynn could make out two small cells, along with their occupants.

Two men were sitting in one cell. One of them was wearing what was left of a tattered Army uniform and glaring up at them balefully. The other was wearing oilskin pants and a jacket that appeared to be homemade. His greasy hair fell over his face as he sat with his head bowed and his hands hanging between his knees. He didn't look up at them.

Both men were unkempt, long hair and overgrown beards full of dirt and grit. Flynn had been dirty before, the trail always did that, but even he had to wrinkle his nose at the state and smell of the two men.

"How long they been here?" Wash asked with obvious distaste.

"Four days," the sheriff answered from the doorway.

Four days wasn't long enough for them to have achieved the level of filth they had managed, and Flynn glanced at the sheriff doubtfully.

"They was dragged behind a chuck wagon from the Fort. Don't know how long they kept 'em over yon. Ain't our job to delouse 'em," the sheriff explained.

Flynn looked back at the two men. "Great."

The last prisoner sat alone in the other cell, lounging against the plank wall with one foot pulled up onto the cot. A dream book—a packet of papers used to roll cigarettes—sat on his knee. He was rolling a thin, brown cheroot between long, graceful fingers. Flynn examined him as he licked the paper and folded it over with exceptional care.

He was younger than Flynn had expected for a gunman of his expansive reputation. Flynn was certain he hadn't yet reached thirty. He appeared to be about as tall as Flynn and Wash both were, but he was all wiry muscle. It made him appear lanky and taller than he probably was. And, for once, the picture on the dime novel cover didn't really give its subject due justice. He had sharp features: thin lips, an aristocratic nose, and high cheekbones. His black hair had been cropped shorter than was the style, the ends just barely curling over his ears, but because he had been denied any visits to the barber during his incarceration, it had grown slightly wild. His goatee and sideburns were unkempt as well, but he still managed to appear put-together. His black eyes were dancing with amusement as he observed them.

Wash walked over to the other cell and looked in at him. The sheriff had said he'd been in the jail here in Junction City for a little over a week, waiting for transport, but he was clean and calm. His clothing was rumpled, but that was only to be expected; he appeared to be wearing the same clothing in which he had been arrested. He'd either been traveling or having a night on the town. Or he was just a dandy, like the rumors claimed.

He wore a black shirt under a tailored vest that was the color of rye whiskey. A black silk ascot was tied neatly around his neck and tucked into his vest. In Flynn's experience, neckwear was the first thing a prisoner would loosen and toss to the floor of his cell in frustration. The fact that it was still there meant Rose was a cool customer. His boots, Flynn noticed, weren't even dusty. He hadn't paced while in the cell. All in all, he cut a mighty fine picture for a man stuck behind bars.

"Dusty Rose?" Wash asked him in a low voice.

The man looked up at Wash with unreadable black eyes and slipped the cigarette he had been rolling into his mouth. The cigarette jumped between his lips when he spoke.

"I don't really go by that name," he answered in a soft, surprisingly deep voice as he reached into his breast pocket and extracted a match.

"You're an Englishman," Flynn blurted. Nothing he had ever heard or read about Dusty Rose had mentioned that.

"So it would seem," the prisoner murmured as his eyes traveled to land on Flynn and examine him critically. He reached down and struck the match on the side of his boot, carefully lighting his cigarette and then waving the match out without ever looking away.

"What's your real name?" Wash asked, obviously not as thrown by the revelation as Flynn had been. But then, Wash never seemed thrown by anything. Unless you counted that one horse.

The prisoner looked from Flynn to Wash again and lowered his foot to the floor as he leaned forward on the hard cot. "I was arrested under the name Rose," he answered with something like amusement.

"Is that your real name?" Wash asked impatiently.

"Does it really matter, Marshal?"

"Are we sure this is the right man, Sheriff?" Wash demanded as he pushed away from the bars and turned to the sheriff.

"That there's the man known as Dusty Rose back East, Marshal," the sheriff answered with a confident nod. "His real name, as far as we know it, is Gabriel. Gabriel Rose."

"Gabriel," Flynn echoed.

"You didn't think his Christian name was Dusty, did ya?" the sheriff asked in amusement.

"I can't say I've ever given him that much thought," Flynn grumbled with a restless shift of his weight, lying through his teeth.

The prisoner snorted. "Do you give anything much thought, Marshal?" He inhaled from his cigarette as he watched Flynn. He was sitting up straight now, one leg crossed genteelly over the other as he rested a forearm on his knee. He held his cigarette between his thumb and forefinger daintily, and when he exhaled, the smoke formed a perfect ring as it floated away from him.

Flynn watched him with a frown and decided the best response at this point was no response at all.

"I'm Deputy Marshal William Henry Washington. You can call me Wash. And this is Deputy Marshal Eli Flynn. You can call him Sir," Wash announced to the three men. "We're going to be taking you to St. Louis."

"Are you going to bathe them before we get under way?" Rose asked with an elegant wave of his fingers at his fellow prisoners. "Or shall I stock up on more tobacco and papers before we begin?"

"Hey, fuck you, Mary," one of the other men snarled through the bars that divided them. His voice was heavy and sluggish, just like he looked.

Rose's eyes slid to stare at the man. "I prefer my partners willing and *able*."

The man in the buckskin, who had remained quiet, rolled his eyes and let his head bang against the plank behind him, as if he were used to this sort of exchange and was growing tired of it. His louder companion stood and took two steps toward Rose, but his progress was stopped by the chains that attached him to the bars of the cell. Rose raised his chin and, with a smirk, blew another smoke ring toward the man.

The sheriff picked up a carved wooden cane and banged it against the iron bars, shouting at the men like he would at animals in a cage.

"Well," Wash said as he turned back to Flynn and nodded, taking his shotgun and sliding it into the crook of his arm. "Let's get this dog and pony show on the road."

The sheriff ordered a pair of his deputies to move the two soldiers to the wagon as a third stood guard over the crowd. No one in the town knew the two soldiers, though, and they merely looked on curiously. Wash took care of the warrants and paperwork as Flynn carefully set his shotgun against the wall and unlocked Rose's cell. He stepped in with a pair of irons in his hand and nodded at the man.

"Stand up, please," he requested. He had learned that being civil at the start of transports often made things easier. If the prisoner gave him trouble, then he would give him trouble right back. Until then, a please here and there didn't hurt anything. He was probably one of only a few officers of the law who believed that.

Rose slowly stood and held out his hands, his eyes following Flynn unerringly. Flynn met them for a moment, trying to get a read on him.

Putting on irons was the most difficult task involved with arresting or escorting a prisoner. The heavy cuffs had to be unlocked with a key, placed onto a prisoner's wrist and closed, then the key had to be inserted again to lock the two pieces of the cuff together. And that was just one hand. If the prisoner had a mind to escape, he would try it during this process.

Out on the street, the loud soldier shouted obscenities at the gathering crowd and a host of boos and hisses arose in response.

"That man certainly has a way with words," Rose murmured with a smirk.

It was obvious even to Flynn's ears that Gabriel Rose was an educated man. It wasn't unusual for a shootist of any reputation to be intelligent; a man had to either have some smarts or be very lucky to survive long enough to make a name for himself. Flynn once more found himself comparing the prisoner to Doc Holliday, who was not only highly educated, but also possessed a streak of common sense; a rare quality amongst college-educated folks.

Flynn wondered if any of the rumors about Rose were true. He had the soft-spoken confidence of many of the upper-class society types Flynn had come into contact with over the years, but he lacked the pomp and bluster that so many of them had attained from overconfidence or entitlement. Flynn supposed being in jail and accused of murder would do that to anyone, though, no matter how good they were at escaping.

"You got any friends who might be looking to give us trouble?" Flynn asked him as he placed one of the iron loops over Rose's left wrist and clapped it together. He put the key in and turned it, locking it. His eyes stayed on Rose, but the Englishman merely stared back at him, holding his hands out helpfully as Flynn secured the heavy iron handcuffs.

"I've got no friends, Marshal," Rose answered. Flynn slid the second cuff over his other wrist, frowning at him. Then Rose gave him a slow, mischievous smirk. "I wouldn't need friends if I were looking to escape."

Flynn met Rose's eyes as he locked the second iron in place with a small clinking sound. Rose's smirk was still in place, but there was no joke in his eyes.

"Would you be so kind as to hand me my coat?" Rose asked him, his hands still held out in front of him obediently.

Flynn cocked his head, considering him, and then he took a careful step and picked up the thick silk frock coat that lay over the end of the cot. He kept his eyes on Rose as he patted it down, making certain nothing was hidden amidst the pockets, then he draped it over the iron between Rose's wrists. He received a nod of thanks in return.

"My hat as well?" Rose requested just as Flynn started to back away.

Flynn glared at him. A marshal walked a fine line in these instances. You had to show some kindness and decency in order to get cooperation, but you couldn't allow yourself to be walked all over.

"It's a fine hat; I wouldn't want to leave it behind," Rose added with a look of sincerity.

Flynn narrowed his eyes, then reached carefully to the cot and took hold of the bowler hat. He inspected the inner rim, then set it on Rose's head and stepped back to survey the result.

"Makes you look like a tenderfoot."

"And who would want to draw down on some poor tenderfoot in the street, hmm?" Rose drawled.

Flynn raised an eyebrow, nodding in acknowledgment. It obviously hadn't worked too well, though, if Rose had killed two men in a gunfight. He backed out of the cell and reached behind him to retrieve his shotgun, his eyes never leaving Rose. He cradled it in the crook of his arm and gestured with the barrel for Rose to come out of the cell.

Rose obeyed, smiling crookedly as he passed. Everything he did and said made it obvious that he was highly amused by the whole process, as if being considered a dangerous and capable man was something novel to him. Flynn didn't think him a real threat, but he'd misjudged men before. He preferred to err on the side of caution and be thought a fool by his prisoners than be proved one and bleed.

By the time Flynn led Rose out onto the raised wooden walkway in front of the jail, the two soldiers were loaded and chained to the side slats of the wagon. A large duffel bag lay along with them.

"What's this?" Flynn demanded of the sheriff's deputies. They all stared at him.

"Those are my belongings, Marshal," Rose answered in that soft, cultured voice that Flynn was beginning to find both annoying and unsettling.

Flynn turned to question the sheriff and found the old man standing a few steps away and looking at him blankly.

"Man ain't been found guilty yet, Marshal," the sheriff informed him. "If they clear him of these charges down in New Orleans, he'll be needing his things to go on his way."

Flynn stared at the man, nonplussed and vaguely annoyed by the presumption. "If you think he's so damn innocent, then—"

"I think," Rose interrupted before Flynn could go any further, "this is the good sheriff's way of saying, 'Y'all don't come back now, y'hear?'" he drawled with a suddenly affected southern gentleman's accent, then he looked up and down the main street idly and placed his cigarette back in his mouth.

"Shut up," Flynn ordered angrily as he shoved Rose off the sidewalk toward the wagon.

# CHAPTER 3

Flynn walked his horse just behind the wagon as Wash handled the mule with his good hand. He watched the three prisoners, trying to place them each into a familiar peg hole.

The loud soldier, a large man named George Hudson, was little more than a big, dumb animal. He had a shock of thin white-blond hair that fell lank over his forehead, and a scraggly beard, stained brown with tobacco juice and grime. He seemed dirtier than his companion did, but Flynn got the feeling that it had less to do with his recent treatment at the hands of the Army and the law and more to do with a natural grubbiness some men seemed to have. He had narrow pig eyes and cruel, thin lips, and he hunched as if he was always preparing to lunge and attack.

The other soldier went by the sole name of Cage, though he had not introduced himself as such. He hadn't introduced himself as anything. He hadn't, in fact, said a single word. He was smaller than his fellow soldier, but still a larger man than either Flynn or Wash. Tall and powerfully built, sporting several days of facial growth and long brown hair, which was now tied back at his neck with a leather cord because Wash hadn't liked not being able to see his eyes. He would perhaps have been a handsome man in different circumstances, and seemed more bothered by his filthy state than Hudson did. It was becoming more apparent that, though they were being transported together, the two soldiers were not companions in any other sense of the word.

Rose drew much of Flynn's attention, simply because he found the man so peculiar. A true square peg. The Englishman sat leaning against the side slats of the swaying wagon with his back straight and his long legs stretched out in front of him, crossed at the ankles as he rested his restrained hands in his lap. He seemed oddly at ease. His eyes had not yet left Hudson, and the big man glared back at him with a hatred Flynn didn't really understand. They hadn't been jailed together long enough to have grown to hate each other, he thought, but Flynn supposed some men were quicker to that difficult and dangerous emotion than others.

The wagon wheels protested as Wash pulled the mule up short and slowed to a stop. Flynn clucked his tongue at his horse and urged him to trot up to the front of the wagon.

"Want to bed down for the night?" Wash suggested as the dying light tried to stretch across the flat land. "Got the creek right here."

Flynn turned in his saddle, peering into the distance as he tried to remember how far the next small town was. He didn't often make the trip from Junction City to St. Louis, and he'd never made it while attempting to avoid the larger settlements. He wasn't too proud to admit that he was out of his element.

"Next town's another half day's ride, Marshal," Rose said, as if reading his mind.

Flynn turned to glare at the man. "Shut up." The words had become his standard response to anything Rose said. The man's cultured voice just grated him.

Rose chuckled darkly and rolled another cigarette. He had been lighting them almost nonstop the entire trip, trying to ward off the smell of the other two prisoners. He didn't smoke them much, though, just let the smoke waft around his face, which Flynn thought a phenomenal waste of quality tobacco. His chains clanked as his hands moved, and it was an odd thing to see his long fingers deftly making the papers with his wrists bound together. His eyes danced as he ran his tongue along the paper.

Hudson sneered at him, and Cage merely shook his head and looked away with a heavy sigh. The silent man was obviously just as tired of the sniping and bickering as Flynn was.

Flynn dismounted as Wash stood and wound the reins around the wagon brake. They set up the camp methodically, hobbling the horses and mules and building a fire from the store of wood they'd brought with them for the trip, trying to have everything set before the cold of night truly fell upon them. Wash started the coffee brewing and unpacked the grease paper packet of bacon as Flynn rummaged through his saddlebags, looking for the tin mugs and plates.

"We could help, marshals," Rose offered almost tauntingly as he sat with his back to them, blowing smoke up at the emerging stars. "We promise we won't run," he practically sang.

"Why don't you just shut your damn bazoo, huh?" Hudson sneered at him. "I'm gettin' tired of hearing you talk."

"I'm getting tired of watching you breathe, but you don't see me doing anything about it," Rose shot back. "Yet."

"Shut up!" Wash and Flynn shouted in unison.

There was silence as Flynn stoked the fire and, when he glanced back over at the prisoners, Rose was once again chuckling as the big soldier sat and glared at him. The other man, Cage, was still silent. He was eyeing them warily, as if he expected them to begin fighting any moment.

"What's your name?" Rose asked him as he brought his cigarette to his lips. His chain clanked when he moved and Flynn studied him again in annoyance.

Cage sighed softly and then glanced at Hudson with obvious chagrin.

Hudson answered for him grudgingly. "Folks calls him Cage." He didn't indicate whether that really was the man's name or if it was just what people called him.

"Cage," Rose repeated as he lounged in the back of the wagon. "You can call me Gabe, if you like." It wasn't exactly a friendly offer, more like Rose was testing the waters.

Cage looked at him warily, seeming to sense the challenge, and then merely nodded in acknowledgment.

Rose brought his cigarette to his lips and inhaled, holding the cigarette from underneath with his thumb and forefinger. He struck Flynn as completely relaxed as he sized Cage up.

Flynn didn't think he had ever seen a prisoner quite as unperturbed as Rose seemed to be. It made him almost nervous, wondering *why* Rose wasn't worried about his plight. If they found him guilty, he'd hang.

"You've not got much to say, hmm?" Rose commented to Cage between exhalations of fragrant blue smoke. He had given the man plenty of time to respond.

Cage met his eyes evenly and simply shook his head.

"Do you have an issue with me as well?" Rose asked.

"'Course he does," Hudson barked. "Anyone with any sense got a problem with you, Mary."

Rose's head turned as if he was looking Hudson over. Flynn couldn't see his expression, but he stood and waited tensely, wondering if it was about to get ugly. To Flynn's relief, Rose looked back to Cage without committing any violent acts.

"You let him speak for you?" Rose's tone was darker than it had been before. There was a lingering hint of curiosity in it, however, as if he was still willing to give the man a chance.

Cage shook his head again and then lowered it, pursing his lips. His eyes, though, were on Rose. He struck Flynn as a man who was used to being pulled into fights he didn't want. He still hadn't uttered a word.

Rose leaned forward, his irons clanking again as he moved. "Are you deaf and dumb?" he asked suddenly, his tone no longer threatening.

Flynn watched in fascination as Cage shook his head again and pointed to his ear, then covered his mouth with his hand.

"He ain't deaf," Hudson supplied with a huff.

"You're dumb, but you can hear," Rose translated, apparently more for himself than anyone listening to their conversation.

Cage nodded.

"And you were a soldier?" Rose asked doubtfully.

Cage brought his hands up again to place one hand at his forehead, as if he was shielding his eyes from the sun and looking into the distance.

"You were a scout," Rose said with a certain degree of pride in his ability to decipher the man's gestures.

Cage nodded again, with a hint of excitement to it this time. It was the most activity and emotion Flynn had seen from Cage since they had picked them up. He obviously wasn't used to men conversing with him at length. Anyone who wouldn't or couldn't speak their mind was practically invisible out here. Some men liked it that way, and for the most part people rarely pushed if you didn't answer the first question. Flynn found it interesting that Rose had given the man the time of day. Flynn certainly hadn't.

"What did you do as a scout for the Army?" Rose asked. "Tracking and the like?"

Cage nodded and rolled his finger through the air as if there was more.

"He could understand the Injun hand signals," Hudson said grudgingly. "Talk to 'em."

Rose glanced at him and then back at Cage thoughtfully. "That's fascinating," he commented. "Most Army men just kill the Indians they encounter. Consider them savages."

Cage stared at him, obviously not willing to comment on that.

Flynn met Wash's eyes across the growing fire. He didn't know if they should allow this to continue, but Wash shrugged as if he saw no harm in it. Flynn didn't see much harm in allowing them their idle chitchat either, and so he kept quiet. Until they started threatening each other again or devising ways to escape, whatever they talked about was irrelevant to Flynn.

Rose continued to question him. "How did you alert your superiors when you were scouting?"

Cage turned his head to the side and gave a low whistle in answer.

"Can you make your letters?"

Cage nodded and mimicked writing with his hand in the air, the irons on his wrists clanking just like Rose's had done.

"I suppose you have to if you can't communicate any other way," Rose mused. "When those around you can't read, what do you do?"

Cage glanced at Hudson carefully and then back at Rose, shrugging. He lifted his hands then set them back in his lap. Rose nodded as if he'd understood. Flynn wasn't sure he himself had, but then he wasn't really trying to.

"What did you do to land yourself in this wagon?"

Flynn cocked his head at them. That was a question a man just didn't ask another in this country. Especially if you were sitting in hand irons on your way to trial. It was part of the unspoken code of the West. Don't ask questions you wouldn't want to answer yourself.

Rose didn't have any care for the laws of the country, and he didn't seem to adhere to those unspoken rules either, which was probably why he'd been run out of every town he came to.

But Flynn was curious despite himself. The papers on the two soldiers hadn't included much information about their crimes. He could see the bad in Hudson just looking at him, and it was anyone's guess what he'd done to get sent to the gallows. But Cage didn't strike Flynn as the type to be on the wrong side of the law. He was quiet and unassuming, and he didn't appear to want to cause any trouble. Flynn wondered what he'd done to be heading for a probable noose back East.

Cage was licking his lips and frowning, but he didn't seem offended by the question like Flynn had expected him to be. He seemed to be considering how to answer in a way that would be understood.

"Dumb shit," Hudson said with a harsh, ugly laugh. "They catched him burnin' the Army's blankets."

"Is that right?" Rose drawled without ever taking his eyes off Cage.

The scout nodded curtly and diverted his eyes again, peering off over Rose's shoulder.

"Why?" Rose questioned after a moment. Cage looked back at him sharply, as if he hadn't expected Rose or anyone else to care about the reason.

"He writ it on a paper, but no one at the fort gave a care," Hudson told them. He was beginning to warm to the job of translating for them. Flynn thought he simply enjoyed recounting someone else's misfortunes. Hudson sniffed at the aroma of the bacon frying over the fire, and Flynn narrowed his eyes, spitefully hoping the man would give them reason to deny him dinner.

Rose glanced at Hudson in apparent irritation, then back at Cage, who was digging under his filthy oilskin jacket. Flynn could no longer help his curiosity, and he edged closer, leaning over the side of the wagon to watch. Cage finally produced a folded piece of paper and handed it to Rose. Rose reached out and took it with difficulty, their chained hands barely able to reach and make the exchange. Flynn read the charcoal scrawl over the man's shoulder as he held the paper up.

*blankits was making peepel sik*

Rose turned his head to find Flynn behind him.

"Ever heard of such a thing, Marshal? Burning blankets to keep them from making people sick? Sure sounds like a hanging offense to me," he observed in a wry, almost bitter voice as he frowned at Cage. He folded the paper carefully and handed it to Flynn.

Flynn took the paper and looked up at Cage, scowling. He had heard rumors from old soldiers, stories about their grandfathers handing out blankets rife with disease to the Indian tribes back East during the early years of the country. He had never really given it much thought. That was far in the past, and these days the Army just rounded up the Indians and shot them. They didn't hand out blankets to them.

"Who were they making sick?" Flynn questioned.

Cage laced his fingers together nervously and glanced at Hudson, who sat beside him, oblivious. He then looked back at Flynn and nodded his head sideways at the soldier.

The revelation gave Flynn a sudden sinking feeling. "He's sick?"

Cage shook his head and closed his eyes in apparent frustration.

"I believe he means the soldiers in general, Marshal," Rose drawled as he leaned back against the side of the wagon.

That got Cage's attention again and he nodded, pointing at Rose.

"Where'd you come from, Fort Riley?" Flynn asked. Cage nodded. "I ain't heard nothing about soldiers being sick or dying up there."

Cage sighed soundlessly and then gestured to Hudson again.

"The hell I will!" Hudson bellowed. "I answered enough questions already; I ain't your damn puppet!" The bigger man shoved at Cage's shoulder.

Cage's hands moved with the speed of a rattlesnake, wrapping the chain of his irons around Hudson's wrist and capturing him neatly before the man could assault him. He then yanked him closer and jammed his elbow into Hudson's nose in retaliation.

"That's enough!" Wash shouted from behind Flynn. He stood and glared at them from the flickering light of the fire.

But Flynn made no move to stop them. As far as he was concerned, Cage had the right to defend himself. Flynn watched impassively as Hudson put his hands to his face and held his nose.

Cage snorted at him and shoved him further away. He looked back to Rose and covered his mouth with his hands, making a coughing sound to explain.

"Consumption?" Rose guessed, completely ignoring the tussle and the blood pouring from Hudson's nose.

Cage shook his head and put his hand to his forehead, then fanned himself like a lady might do when she overheated.

"Fever," Flynn murmured, ignoring the blood as well. Cage nodded, pointing at him. "Go on."

Cage put his hands to his throat and mimicked having trouble swallowing, then spread his hands out to indicate his throat bulging.

"Diphtheria," Rose said suddenly, and Cage nodded eagerly.

"Wash," Flynn called as he turned away from the wagon and squinted past the light made by the little fire.

Wash was watching him with interest. "I'm listening."

"You broke my damn nose, you savage!" Hudson hollered nasally.

Rose merely chuckled at him in response as Cage shrugged.

"Shut up!" Flynn ordered. "Don't touch him again, and he won't break things on you!"

"You dumb bastard!" Hudson howled.

Rose slouched and kicked the man in the thigh.

"What does it say on Cage's warrant?" Flynn asked Wash, ignoring the bickering prisoners and turning away.

Wash set down the frying pan and reached into his jacket as he stood up again, leafing through the leather packet until he found the right paper. He read it with difficulty in the firelight, then answered in a disgusted voice. "Destruction of government property, undermining morale, disobeying direct orders. For that, they're trying him? He's looking at a hanging if they find him guilty."

"Don't that beat all," Flynn huffed as he handed Wash the note Cage had written and turned to the fire.

Wash remained where he had been, and Flynn glanced at him. He was watching Cage with a thoughtful frown. The man sat in the wagon with his head bowed again. Rose had managed to get all the way on his back and was pushing his boot heel against Hudson's neck, slowly choking the life out of the man, who flailed and gripped at his leg. Wash bent and picked up a rock, then chucked it at Rose and hit him on the side of the head.

"Knock it off!" he shouted in the commanding voice that always made Flynn shiver with delight.

Rose rolled to his side and cursed as he held his head, and Hudson gasped as he was able to get his breath once more. Cage merely sat watching them both expressionlessly.

"That ain't right, Flynn," Wash murmured as he stood examining Cage.

"Your aim's still pretty good."

Wash gave him a dirty look and shook his head. "I mean about Cage. Ain't right to hang him for trying to save lives."

"It's the law, Wash," Flynn reminded gently. The conversation he'd had with Wash several days ago was still clear in his mind. He glanced at Wash carefully. He agreed with Wash on this particular point; sometimes the law was just wrong. Life wasn't always black or white; there were gray areas that needed a human eye to distinguish the lines. The law didn't see those gray areas. But their job was to uphold it as it was written, not decide which ones to follow and who got to follow which ones, no matter how often Flynn thought maybe they should just let justice have its own way with some people.

Flynn had always been a stickler for the rules and regulations, even back in the Union army. He played life according to Hoyle, and that was how he liked it. Wash, on the other hand, was a firm believer in seeing both sides of a story and finding the truth behind them.

Sometimes the two weren't good bedfellows, the law and the truth.

"Law don't always make it right," Wash murmured as he slid the warrants back into his jacket.

Flynn prepared dinner in silence. He didn't know what to say, and so like any smart man, he kept his mouth shut.

John Baird had spent seven rail days of his life traveling to Colorado, and seven on the return to New York, which made a fortnight of wasted days he would never get back. Now he was once again on a train, heading west toward St. Louis and the gateway to the frontier, wasting even more time overseeing an operation that would gain him very little in the end.

Not that he had anything particularly pressing to tend to at home. If this strategy didn't go like it should, his life would be worthless anyway.

It irked him that Dusty Rose had gotten away in Colorado. To this point, Rose was the only hitch in his plan. What sort of unholy fiend could utilize an act of God like an earthquake to escape an otherwise perfectly conceived murder?

The very providence of it grated something fierce, and the train he rode could not go fast enough for Baird's taste. And to add insult to injury, before leaving New York he'd received word by telegram that Rose was being brought to St. Louis by a US Marshal, en route to New Orleans to stand trial for murder.

It was hard not to plot his revenge on Rose, knowing they might very well cross paths in Missouri. Rose had somehow gotten out of a second scrape alive, killing the two men Baird had hired to track him down and murder him, but even a cat only had nine lives. Baird was determined to make sure he took every one of Rose's lives even if he had to fill the man with lead himself. Eventually.

That would have to wait, of course. And it was possible Rose might be hanged before Baird could get to him. That didn't sit well with him. He wanted to do it himself. He hadn't anticipated Rose being captured for the killings. It made it easier to find him, but it would be difficult to get to Rose while he was in custody. It would require a little cunning and even more luck.

Baird had to remind himself again that Rose was a secondary concern. His primary goal was to reach New Madrid in time to see the Oil Cake set sail.

The fire was barely giving off enough warmth to keep the cold from getting to Flynn and Wash, and the prisoners were safely chained to the wagon wheels not far away. The fire popped and sizzled. It didn't have the same cheerful smell that a wood fire emitted, but a man made do using cow chips as added fuel. They were trying to conserve their store of wood in case they hit trouble by using whatever they could find to supplement their fire. It was cold enough that Flynn could pretend he had wrapped his bandana over his nose and mouth to ward off the chill, and not the pungent odor.

The night was quiet and peaceful, but Wash still seemed restless as they hunkered down against the frigid wind.

"You okay?" Flynn finally asked of him.

"My back's cold."

Flynn raised an eyebrow at him and tried not to smile. He refrained from making any comments about Wash living the easy life back in town for too many months.

"I'm not complaining," Wash added quickly, huffing like he knew what Flynn had been thinking. He gave a nod of his head toward the three prisoners. "It's just, if my back's cold, they're *all over* cold."

Flynn glanced over his shoulder. The unfortunate men were curled as tight as a person could get. Rose and Hudson weren't bickering for perhaps the first time since leaving Junction City, and none of them were moving save to shiver. Rose and Cage were chained to the same wheel, and they had scooted together as close as they could, resting their backs against each other and trying to share their body heat.

"They do look cold," Flynn agreed as he turned to the fire. He could feel Wash's eyes on him, and he tilted his head sideways at the man. Wash stared at him with one eyebrow raised. Even behind the cloth he had over the lower part of his face, it was obvious Wash was smirking at him.

"Yeah, all right." Flynn grunted as he tossed the piece of tall grass he had been playing with into the fire and pushed himself up.

He stomped over to their horses and fished two extra bedrolls out of his and Wash's saddlebags, then walked to the wagon. Hudson raised his head eagerly, already anticipating the warmth of the wool blanket without giving so much as a promise of good behavior in return first. Flynn made certain to extract such a promise from the man before handing him the blanket, though he didn't really expect Hudson to honor the agreement.

He then stepped over to the other two with the second blanket in hand. They both looked up at him with the sort of exhaustion that stemmed from the cold and a long day of travel. They were lucky that he and Wash weren't making them walk behind the wagon.

"I only got one," Flynn told them. "You're going to have to share or fight it out."

Rose nodded, and Cage peered up at him as he sat hunched with his hands tucked up under his arms, his back to Rose's. Flynn got the feeling that this tattered Army scout was accustomed to getting the short end of the stick without complaining about it. He reminded Flynn of an abused horse, always keeping his head down and hoping not to get a spur.

He handed Rose the blanket and was slightly surprised when the man wrapped it around Cage's shoulders before tending to himself. He pulled the blanket tight and scooted, putting their shoulders together and getting closer for the warmth. They both lowered their heads again, bowing against the cold prairie night, leaning against the wagon wheel behind them.

Flynn stepped away. They curled together with little regard for the derogatory comments Hudson was offering about their behavior. Hudson, Flynn assumed, had never been out on the plains alone. He didn't know what cold was yet. Flynn had cuddled his horse before for the warmth. He saw nothing wrong with what the two men were doing.

He turned and headed back to the fire before he could admit to himself that he was a might jealous of them as well. Just the thought of touching another man in front of someone else in any way other than a friendly handshake made Flynn blush furiously. Oh, he would do it and had done it if it meant staying warm at night. But he would still be embarrassed about it, worrying if he enjoyed it too much.

How had Gabriel Rose become so comfortable with his reputation for favoring men? Some of the things Hudson had said to the Englishman had made even Flynn want to hit him, just on principle, but Rose had yet to be ruffled. At least not outwardly. Was any of it even true? Or did Rose just play into the reputation to give himself that added touch of mystery or derring-do. He did have an oddly gentle manner with Cage, and the silent man had responded in a way that made Flynn wonder if they had become friendlier while in jail than they were letting on.

He glanced over at the huddle of blankets again. The two men had figured out how to turn their chains so they could lay under the wagon and were now doing so, away from the bite of the wind. Flynn could see nothing but the tops of their heads sticking out from under the wagon. They were curled together under the blanket, apparently sound asleep as Hudson huddled alone and shivered in the cold.

"Kind of cute, ain't they?" Wash said to him.

Flynn examined him in the light of the fire, meeting his eyes with a shiver. He had a sudden urge to blurt out the question he had wanted to ask for ages. It was a perfect opportunity to broach the subject. Over the years, Flynn had built up a sneaking suspicion that Wash wasn't interested in women, but he couldn't even form the question correctly in his mind, much less speak it to Wash.

He pushed it back and merely nodded, looking away and sighing.

"You okay, friend?" Wash asked quietly, his tone somehow soothing.

Flynn glanced up at him and his upper body twitched with nerves as he gave another nod.

"Something happen in Stillwater you need to talk about?" Wash prodded.

"Naw," Flynn answered, unnervingly hoarse. "It's just..." He blew a stream of air out that formed a cloud in the cold and then shook his head. He gave Rose and Cage a glance, hoping to throw Wash off the scent. "I don't quite know how to take that one. Either of 'em."

"Why?" Again, Flynn heard the warning in Wash's tone that betrayed the fact that Wash might be offended, or at least wary of the subject. It was obviously one to be careful of.

"Don't rightly know," Flynn said, his voice gruff. He accompanied it with a shrug, quickly veering away from the topic once more. Wash obviously didn't appreciate discussing such business no matter which way he was inclined.

Flynn settled back into his own bedroll and pulled his hat low over his eyes, signifying the end of the conversation. He crossed his arms over his chest, wrapping his duster tight around himself to ward off the chill of the night.

He could feel Wash's eyes on him, but he sat motionless, willing himself to sleep and praying that his mind would find a new rail to run on by morning.

# CHAPTER 4

It was midday of their second day of travel when Flynn noticed that they were being followed over the grassy plains. After roughly ten minutes, he halted his horse and stood in the stirrups, peering behind them into the distance.

"How many?" Wash asked as he continued to drive the mule along the trail without slowing or turning to look. His shotgun sat in his lap.

"One," Flynn called back. He settled back into his saddle. "Four-legged," he added in bemusement. He urged the horse into a canter that caught him up to the front of the wagon.

"Rider?" Wash asked with a confused frown as Flynn came abreast of him.

Flynn smirked. "I think it's a dog."

Rose spoke up for the first time in hours. "He would appreciate it if you left some scraps along the way."

Flynn turned and saw that the man was watching their back trail avidly.

"He's probably thirsty too," Rose said, sounding worried for perhaps the only time Flynn had noticed.

"What?" Flynn asked with a sigh, almost hating to ask but curious despite himself.

"That's my dog, Marshal."

Flynn had found that he was beginning to hate the way Rose said the word "marshal." He didn't even know why it rubbed him the wrong way. He thought maybe anything Rose did put a burr under his saddle. Just on principle now if for no real reason.

He grumbled and shook his head. "His dog, he says," he muttered to Wash.

"Like it says in the dime novel?" Wash glanced over his shoulder at Rose, who tore his eyes away from the trotting dog in the distance to meet his eyes.

"I wouldn't know," he said coldly.

Flynn's head snapped up. Rose had seemed the type to bask in the limelight of fame, not scorn it. He was becoming increasingly puzzling the more Flynn was exposed to him. It was grating.

"Well, here's the papers," Hudson said as he held up the crumpled dime novel Flynn had tossed into the back of the wagon several days before. He flapped the worn papers around. "See for yourself."

Rose narrowed his eyes at the man as the wagon hit a rut and jostled them all. He didn't seem surprised to see the dime novel magically produced. In fact, Rose didn't seem to be surprised by much of anything.

Flynn found that grating too.

When Rose answered, his voice was quiet and calm, as smooth as honey. "Why don't *you* read it and find out."

Flynn knew the chances of Hudson being able to read or write even his own name were slim to none. He looked away and rolled his eyes before he could see Hudson's response. He heard it, though, and chose to ignore the rest of the sniping.

"Are you going to feel guilty if that dog starves back there?" Wash asked him.

"Puppy, really," Rose called, overhearing the question. "He's just a puppy."

"Shut up," Flynn snapped at him without looking back. He gave Wash a once-over, only to find the man smirking at him. He sighed dejectedly and closed his eyes as he dropped his head. "Yeah, probably."

Wash pulled the mule to a stop, and Flynn slowed his horse.

"It'll give us a chance to water the horses, anyhow," Wash reasoned with a grin he tried to hide. He set his shotgun on the rickety footboard and tied the reins to the wagon brake.

Flynn dismounted with a sullen mutter. "Call your blamed dog, Rose."

Rose put two fingers to his mouth, the irons pulling his other hand up to his chin along with them, and he let out a ringing whistle that carried impressively across the flat land.

In the distance, a delighted yip could barely be heard, and Flynn squinted and watched the lone figure of the dog race toward them. Wash laughed beside him, and Flynn turned away before the prisoners could see his own lips quirk in amusement.

The dog ended up being a medium-sized, run of the mill, long-haired mutt. He appeared to be intelligent. Rose insisted that he could not, as the dime novels claimed, steal a man's gun from his holster, lead a horse with the reins in its mouth, or do anything more than offer companionship and keep him warm at night.

Flynn wasn't sure he believed him.

"And he can stare at you pitifully until you give him your last bit of food," Rose offered as he rested his hand irons on the back of the mutt's neck and rubbed his ears with both hands. The dog's tail banged against the wooden slats of the wagon in agreement. "But I'm afraid he's capable of little else."

"If we start starving, he's the first thing we eat, got it?" Flynn warned in all seriousness.

Rose nodded and gave the dog's rump a pat. The dog leaped from the side of the wagon and trotted over to Flynn, sitting down in front of him and looking up expectantly, tail wagging.

Flynn groaned and turned away. The dog was just as annoyingly charming as his master.

Wash laughed. "He got a name?"

"Koda," Rose answered. The dog whipped its head around when he heard his name and stared at Rose as if waiting for a command. "Hello, darling," Rose murmured to the dog fondly. The dog's long, fluffy tail began to whap the dusty ground at Flynn's feet, stirring up a minor storm.

Flynn took off his hat and waved it at the bits of dust and straw floating toward him. He cocked his head at Rose and narrowed his eyes suspiciously. "You spent time with the Sioux?"

"Why do you ask that, Marshal?" Rose asked. He sounded genuinely interested.

"That's a Sioux word, ain't it? Koda? I've heard it a few times."

Rose gave him a pleased smile. "It is, indeed. I spent some time with the Santee, up near Flandreau," he answered with a touch of wistfulness. "Even the law won't follow you there." The mischievous addition completely ruined any admiration the information may have kindled in Flynn.

"Really," Flynn said.

"That was where I found him. Koda means 'friend' in their fine language."

"Fascinating," Flynn muttered as he finished saddling a fresh horse.

"What were you doing venturing all the way up to Flandreau?" Wash asked.

"This and that."

"How long were you there?"

"Many moons," Rose intoned dramatically. He smirked at Wash. "I find the savages can teach a man quite a lot that's useful in this country."

It was difficult for Flynn to tell when he was being sarcastic and when he was just being English. He suspected Rose was simply dissembling, waiting until they tired of the subject so he wouldn't have to answer honestly. He'd made it very clear previously that he didn't approve of the way the Indians were treated out here, and he obviously didn't think of them as savages, as he'd just called them.

Flynn didn't have much opinion on the matter anymore. He'd seen the aftermath of settlers who'd been massacred by marauding tribes, and he'd seen what a band of soldiers could do to a camp of defenseless Indian women and children. There was never just one side to any story. Wash had taught him that.

Rose continued to talk about the Sioux, his voice losing its teasing tone as he told Wash about the variety of interesting legends and histories he'd learned from them while he was their guest. "During the time I was there, there was quite a lot of talk of something they called *tetlteotl*," Rose was telling Wash as Flynn began paying attention once more.

"That ain't a Sioux word, is it?" Flynn asked.

"No, it's not, Marshal," Rose answered with a serious shake of his head. "I don't know what language it is. Neither did they. Or if they did, they wouldn't clarify it. But from what I gathered, it meant something like 'the wonderful stone.' Or 'the terrible stone,' I wasn't sure. It was very important to them; something they'd lost. They spoke of searching for it in land held by the white man's army. They seemed to think I could help and so they kept me around for a while, trying to determine if I was trustworthy." As he spoke, he seemed to be gauging their reactions for something Flynn couldn't fathom. He almost appeared to be judging whether he could trust *them*, but Flynn couldn't imagine why.

"Did you help them?" Wash asked. Flynn couldn't tell if he was really interested or just making conversation as they waited for the horses to drink.

"I daresay I could now if I ever went back. But I never earned enough trust to try," Rose admitted with what seemed sincere regret.

"Why don't that surprise me?" Flynn muttered under his breath.

Rose merely narrowed his eyes at Flynn and turned around again, no longer willing to talk. Flynn smiled to himself. He'd finally found a way to shut the man up.

They continued on until the sun began to set, the dog happily trotting along beside Flynn's horse. The cool began to settle once more as they pitched camp, and Hudson began to protest loudly about hunger, thirst, cold, soreness, and every other misery he could think up. Interestingly, he didn't complain about being dirty.

Flynn and Wash ignored the man. Rose made several caustic remarks in response to the complaints, but when it became apparent that he was playing above his audience, he tired of the effort. He quieted and leaned against Cage, who was becoming Flynn's favorite prisoner simply because he didn't speak. Rose pulled his hat down over his eyes and Cage settled against him. The dog hopped up onto the wagon, laid itself over their laps, and promptly fell asleep.

Flynn sat awake watching the wagon for a long time, his face set in a frown. He could hear Rose murmuring to Cage, but he didn't strain his ears to listen. The way Rose and Cage behaved toward one another made Flynn's more intimate thoughts turn to Wash, and Flynn was trying his best to avoid that at all costs. He didn't need the heartache caused by lingering over it.

When he finally forced himself to try to sleep, he found himself wondering what the "terrible stone" was, and why it had been important enough for the Santee to keep a man like Gabriel Rose around.

The night was not as cold as the previous one had been, but it was not by any stretch of the imagination a comfortable one, either. Cage lay on his side beneath the wagon, an arm chained to the wagon wheel and his body almost covered by the blanket the marshals had given them. His arm ached, but he'd had worse accommodations.

Gabriel Rose lay next to him, facing him as they shared the thick blanket. The wool smelled of horse and wood smoke, but it was warm against the chill and that was all Cage cared about. Gabriel was warm too, and that was a fact that Cage was beginning to notice more and more.

He was also a talker. Cage found himself smiling despite the discomfort of their situation as Gabriel murmured to him in the darkness.

"Were you born unable to speak?" Gabriel asked him. His breath was warm on Cage's face, which was so close that when Cage answered with a nod, Gabriel was probably able to feel it rather than needing to see it.

Cage had never been asked questions like these. He supposed people had always been too afraid to ask them, or just hadn't cared enough to be curious.

"I bet you find it works to your advantage, sometimes," Gabriel mused. "It took me far too long to learn that keeping my mouth shut was advantageous."

Cage snorted. He wasn't sure Gabriel had learned that lesson in its entirety yet. He raised his hand, placing it on Gabriel's chest carefully. He jabbed a finger against Gabriel's chest and then patted him again. No, Gabriel had definitely not learned the value of keeping quiet.

"Yes, I know," Gabriel murmured in amusement.

Cage nodded, still amazed that Gabriel continued to be able to decipher his attempts at communicating with him. He supposed that was one reason he felt drawn to the man. His hand remained where it had been, resting between their bodies against Gabriel's chest.

"Well I suppose some never do, hmm?" Gabriel whispered.

The silence fell around them for a moment, and Cage soaked in the warmth of Gabriel's body next to his. It had been a long time since he'd shared a bed with another man, even if that bed was on the hard ground beneath a creaky wagon. He was determined to let himself enjoy it.

Gabriel shifted next to him, edging just that much closer as he brought his hand up to cover Cage's. Cage's breath caught and his heart beat faster as Gabriel's fingertips caressed his.

"This is an unexpected consequence of my latest indiscretion." Gabriel's whispered words were barely audible.

Cage swallowed with difficulty, not quite understanding. He recognized the tone of Gabriel's voice though, low and intimate. It hit him hard, stirring a confusing mixture of emotions. On one hand he was thrilled. But they only had until St. Louis to enjoy each other's company, and even that short amount of time was to be had in irons, chained to a wagon under armed guard. But pleasures in life were fleeting. Cage knew that all too well.

"I know what you're thinking," Gabriel said.

Cage shook his head.

"You're thinking, 'Why couldn't I have met this charming Englishman before I got myself arrested?'"

Cage laughed, but he didn't give Gabriel the satisfaction of knowing he was basically right.

"Perhaps not," Gabriel said. "Perhaps you're thinking something more along the lines of what I'm thinking."

Cage blinked at him in the darkness, wishing he could make out more of Gabriel's features. He could just barely see the outline of one prominent cheekbone and his well-defined jaw, the mischievous quirk to his lips when he smiled. His black eyes, though, were in shadow. Cage licked his lips and gave a small, questioning jerk of his chin.

Gabriel edged closer, their noses touching. "I was thinking I don't do poignant good-byes," he answered, just before pressing his lips gently to Cage's.

Cage sighed in approval, and Gabriel pressed tighter, kissing him soundly. When he ended it, he moved back only far enough to be able to speak again. Cage worked his fingers under Gabriel's silk vest and held him there.

"I know you don't know me from Adam's cat, Cage, but I refuse to let them take you back East for a trial you'll never win," Gabriel declared.

Cage's lips parted in confusion. He wasn't sure what it was that had struck Gabriel about him. Perhaps it was the same indefinable kinship he himself felt with the man. Whatever they had between them was strong enough that Gabriel seemed willing to fight for more of it. Cage was too, but not at the expense of escaping only to find themselves on the run in a land where lynching was still the order of the day.

He didn't want to spend the rest of his life a wanted man.

He shook his head vehemently and gave the chain on his wrist a tug.

"I don't plan to escape," Gabriel assured him gently. "Where would we go out here, hmm? There's nothing but wide-open prairie and cow chips."

Cage breathed a sigh of relief.

"We'll have to wait until we reach St. Louis. Make our move then."

Cage groaned and closed his eyes. He could tell there would be no arguing with the man on this point. He would just have to make certain no one got killed trying to stop him.

Flynn awoke in the early hours of the morning with a jerk. He had heard a noise, a faint one, but one unnatural to his well-trained ears. It had been a rustle of clothing, maybe, or the scrape of a boot heel in the dirt. Wash lay beside him, tense and alert as well.

Very slowly, Flynn turned his head to look at the silhouette of the wagon in the moonlight. Two bundles of men, wrapped in blankets, huddled near wheels, just like they had left them. The dog, though, was trotting away from the dying fire, back toward the wagon.

As he watched him, Flynn saw moonlight glint off something in the dog's mouth.

His hand immediately went to the saddlebag where he was resting his head, to the flap where the keys to the manacles were kept, and he cursed loudly when he found them missing.

He jumped to his feet and reached for his gun, but he wasn't wearing his holster. Rose's hands shot out from under the blanket and grabbed the keys from the dog's mouth, then he pushed at the dog to urge him away. Flynn gave a hoarse shout of warning. Wash was already standing, shrugging the blanket off his shoulders as he stood and raised his heavy shotgun with one hand. Rose had managed to unlock himself from the chain that restrained him to the wheel and he rolled under the other side of the wagon before Wash could aim the shotgun.

Next to the wheel, still partly under the wagon, Cage curled into a ball and covered his head as if he expected Wash to fire at him even though he'd missed his chance at a clean shot at Rose.

Flynn scrambled for his holsters and yanked his six-shooter out, whirling and trying to spot Rose in the darkness.

He saw nothing and heard nothing of the wily Englishman, but he did see the dog, loping away from the camp. He aimed his Colt and cocked the hammer.

Rose hit him from the side like a ten-pound mallet. They both went rolling in the dirt, dangerously close to the dying embers of the fire, and Flynn's gun was sent skidding into the night. Flynn struggled to regain his wits before he found himself taking the big jump a little early. He knew Rose was deadly with a gun and even more deadly with a knife. He was just thankful Rose didn't have either at the moment.

What he did have was the advantage of being on top of Flynn. He was stretching the chain between his manacles tight against Flynn's throat, pushing down and strangling the life out of him. Flynn could barely see his eyes in the darkness, shining like some demon in the firelight. He gripped the chain and shoved at it, trying to suck air into his chest as lights danced in his vision.

Then the butt of the shotgun hit Rose right under the ear. He toppled sideways without even a grunt. Flynn gasped and put his hands to his throat instinctively, feeling the indentations the chains had made in his skin.

Wash stood over them both, silhouetted by the moonlight. Flynn stared up at him and struggled to get his breath, speechless and still not quite comprehending what had just happened. He had almost been killed without hardly putting up a fight.

"He got the drop on you, Flynn." Wash's tone was neutral. He rested the butt of the shotgun on his hip and pointed the barrel at Rose's chest.

"I know it, damn you," Flynn gasped. He finally forced himself to move, trying to cover his embarrassment.

"He was going to shoot my dog," Rose muttered, his voice hoarse and broken. He held his hands to the side of his head and curled on the ground.

Flynn lumbered to his feet and coughed, looking down at the man with a sneer. "He was helping you escape."

"He's a dog, he doesn't know what escape is. He was just doing what he's trained," Rose insisted.

Wash huffed. "Yeah? Well, so are we."

# CHAPTER 5

**B**at Stringer sat astride his horse, waiting outside the telegraph office of the newly settled town of Talmage, Nebraska. The Missouri Pacific Railroad was ran right through it, which made it a busy little point of trade for agricultural and mercantile goods. Lots of new people came through every day, and a few men on horseback riding into town wouldn't be given a second glance by the people who called themselves local residents.

Stringer and his men had been all over the damn frozen prairie the last month, following the crates sent from Fort Robinson after the soldiers had pulled something out of the ground near the Rosebud Creek. The crates were marked and guarded as if they carried ore. Stringer wondered about all that rock he'd watched the soldiers load, though. What could the government possibly want with crates and crates of worthless gravel?

The soldiers escorting the shipments were well armed and on the alert, with far too much firepower for eight men to take on, even men as hard and familiar with a gun as the Border Scouts.

The plan from the government man, however, did not require them to take on a battalion of soldiers, as the obnoxious Englishman had believed it would. On the surface it was a complicated plan, one that was taking much more time and manpower than Stringer had anticipated, but underneath it was impressive in its simplicity.

You couldn't just attack a band of soldiers and steal something without the country taking notice, not even in Nebraska. It could be blamed on hostile Indians, but the trouble with that tack was that most of the hostiles in the area had been cleared out and the ones left wanted land and food, not gold.

The operation required some finesse and trickery, neither of which were Stringer's strong points. He was fortunate, though. He knew that he was better served as a blunt instrument. Most men didn't even know that much about themselves. He wasn't the mastermind type, not like Jack Kale had been. He wished Kale were still around, for more than one reason. He missed the man, even though their last meeting had been a violent one. And Kale had possessed the backbone and the brains to pull something like this off without a hitch.

It was a plot Jack Kale would have liked.

Stringer sighed and glanced around as his men loitered about the main street. The telegraph they were sending today was the first step. They just had to make certain the telegraph man wouldn't send it too soon or the entire thing would be blown.

Frank stepped out onto the raised walkway in front of the telegraph office and met Stringer's eyes. His gaunt face was pinched, and his stringy blond hair looked as if he'd been trying to rip it out. He nodded curtly at Stringer—the telegraph had been arranged for the appropriate hour—and made his way to the horse tied to the hitching post nearby.

Stringer turned his own horse without a word, knowing the rest of his men would follow. They had a lot of work to do, finding expendable men in the days that were to come.

The dog was once more following at a distance. Flynn carried a pocketful of small stones with him as he rode, and whenever the dog came too close, he would toss one at the mutt to back him up.

Rose had earned himself a new mode of transportation: he walked behind the wagon, tied to the rear axle, as the mule plodded along. His new station in life and the blood that caked behind his ear seemed to have gone a long way toward silencing him.

Flynn had refused to allow Cage to clean the wound, despite the wordless pleading the big man managed. It was obvious that Rose and Cage had developed some sort of connection in the short time they had been traveling together. Flynn's suddenly spiteful nature made him want to separate them for it.

The only words Rose had spoken that day were to insist that he had not intended to escape and wasn't trying to kill Flynn, only stop him from shooting the dog.

"He's trained to fetch keys," Rose had told them as he'd watched the rest of them eat breakfast. He had not been offered food that morning, nor would he be offered supper if Flynn had anything to say about it. Wash would probably intervene though. He was too softhearted, in Flynn's opinion.

"If you didn't tell him to do it, why'd you take 'em?" Wash had asked. It had always been a trait Flynn admired in Wash, his ability to listen to everyone's side of a story before making a decision. It made him a fair man. It made him a good man. But that morning, it had just made him annoying.

"Because he's also trained to get rid of them after he's done it," Rose had answered. "And if he had done so, we'd never get the damn things off us, would we? I feared he would get confused and run away with them."

"Real saint, ain't ya?" Flynn had growled. He hadn't been in the mood for any of Rose's excuses.

"But you used them after you took them from him," Wash had pointed out before Rose could respond to Flynn. "Tried to escape. Tried to kill a US Marshal."

"I wasn't trying to kill him. He was going to shoot my dog."

"I was going to shoot *you*, but you were off hiding amongst the willows, weren't you?"

"Being shot at is a good reason to duck, Marshal."

Hudson had laughed as he ate his bacon, enjoying the sideshow more than Flynn thought he ought to have. Cage had sat with his head lowered, as if he figured he was somehow at fault and might receive punishment as well. It had made Flynn wonder just what he and Rose had been talking about under that wagon.

Wash had sat and examined Rose for a long time as he ate the rest of his meal in silence.

Flynn still wondered, as they rode on, what his friend had been contemplating as he stared. The possibilities worried him. Wash had already shown that he had a soft spot for the tractable Cage and his inability to communicate verbally. If he started listening to Rose's lies as well—sympathizing with him—then they were in trouble.

They just needed to get to St. Louis before all hell broke loose. After that, Cage and Hudson would be the Army's problem again, and Flynn could always throw Rose in the Mississippi as they headed downriver.

The next two days went by in relative peace. It wasn't until the eighth day of travel that the tensions began to boil over and Hudson finally tried to kill Rose.

Flynn obviously had not given the big man quite as much credit as his intelligence warranted, meager though it may have been. Hudson waited until Flynn and Wash had put the three of them to work, gathering fuel for the fire, before he struck. The three prisoners were chained to each other, walking across the flat plains and gathering bits of old, broken wagon and cow chips for the fire. Flynn and Wash knew that, even if they were stupid enough to try to escape, they would have nowhere to go and very little time to get there.

The marshals hadn't expected trouble, at least not this sort.

Gabriel Rose was exhausted from riding shank's mare behind the wagon, and Hudson clearly knew it. He clearly also knew that Flynn and Wash had been lulled into a false sense of security by the monotony of the travel. And that neither marshal would be close enough to stop him before he could do Rose in. They were probably going to hang him back East anyway; he had nothing to lose. Obviously, a large rock and an opportunity were all Hudson had been waiting for.

Flynn had been squatting, trying to coax the fire to life with the dry kindling he had collected, a job Wash couldn't do with just his one hand. Wash had been following the prisoners with his shotgun, and it wasn't until Wash shouted that Flynn realized anything had happened at all. By the time Flynn got to them, Rose was on the ground with the wound behind his ear bleeding freely once more, and Hudson was on his belly, flailing under Cage's oilskin moccasin, with the barrel of Wash's shotgun at the back of his neck.

"What happened?" Flynn asked breathlessly.

"Went at him with a rock," Wash panted in answer. "Cage took him down."

Flynn looked up to meet Cage's eyes. The man stared back at him sedately, even as he discreetly ground the heel of his foot into Hudson's spine. Flynn couldn't think of a thing to say to him. He merely nodded at the silent scout, who nodded in return and removed his foot from Hudson's back.

They picked Rose up off the ground, and Wash examined his head as the Englishman wavered. Cage stood as far away as the chains would allow to give them space. He seemed to know not to crowd either marshal, sensing his size and proximity would make one or both of them feel he was a threat. Flynn again wondered what sort of life Cage had led up to this point. He certainly seemed used to the short end of the stick.

Cage bent over and picked up Rose's bowler hat with infinite care. He brushed it off and popped it back into shape, then looked up at Rose with a concerned frown.

It was a sweet, almost innocent gesture that Flynn found fascinating.

Wash supported Rose by the elbow as Flynn hauled Hudson to his feet.

"We can't make 'em both drag behind the wagon," Flynn muttered in annoyance.

"Rose'll have to ride," Wash declared as he examined the bloody cut on Rose's hairline. "Let's get these animals tied up."

As soon as Wash stepped away, Cage stepped forward and placed the hat on Rose's head. Rose gave him a weak smile and a nod.

"Cage, you feel like eatin' with the marshals tonight?" Wash asked without even seeming to have considered talking it over with Flynn. Cage watched him warily as Wash unlocked him from the chain. He was suddenly free, without irons or chain or bars to restrain him, and he looked to Flynn like he might be uncomfortable with it.

The man had led a hard life, that much was obvious, but Flynn still didn't like the fact that Wash had just freed him. Especially after he'd just proved what he was capable of.

Cage rubbed at his wrists and glanced between the two marshals uncertainly.

"Come on," Wash said, leading him toward the fire. "Decent man deserves a decent meal."

Flynn watched them sourly.

"Looks like your partner is taking a liking to the good Army scout." Rose snorted. "That can't end pretty for you, Marshal."

Flynn glared at him, then turned his attention back to Wash. He didn't even twitch when Rose staggered beside him and dropped to his knees once more.

"Shut up," Flynn muttered.

Several days of hard travel and five more tussles between Rose and Hudson later, the two marshals arrived with their prisoners in St. Louis. They were all dusty, tired, and slightly murderous. Even Rose, who had remained in a good humor that seemed designed more to irritate his escorts than anything else, had become sullen and silent on the last legs of the trip.

Flynn figured the repeated knocks to his head hadn't helped his mood much.

They had missed the train in Kansas City by less than an hour and been forced to decide whether they would hire a riverboat out of their own pocket or keep on toward St. Louis with the wagon. Finally, lack of funds decided it for them, and they telegraphed ahead about the delay, resupplied, and headed on over the Missouri plains. The hard travel set them behind yet again. When they rolled into St. Louis three days late, they had less than ten minutes to find the Army representatives they were meant to meet to hand over the two men from Fort Riley.

Flynn and Rose had already missed their original paddle wheeler to New Orleans, so Flynn volunteered to handle the prisoner transfer while Wash got Rose settled into a hotel. Flynn and Rose would have to hop the next paddle wheeler available. The cost was troubling, especially since reimbursements were long in coming from the government, but they had more pressing matters to worry about when they limped into St. Louis with their three prisoners, all who were late for their dates with fate.

Wash stopped the wagon in front of the hotel closest to the river, and Flynn dismounted gingerly. He rolled his head from side to side and tried to work out the stiffness. It was the middle of the day and the streets were crowded. Koda trotted up onto the raised wooden sidewalk and plopped himself down in the shade, eyes on Rose and nothing else.

Flynn would give the animal something for loyalty, at least.

"This is cruel and unusual punishment, Marshal," Rose was saying as he lay flat on the planks of the wagon.

"What in the Sam Hill are you doing?" Flynn demanded.

"I'm cowering, Marshal, can't you tell? If you'll recall my sage advice of earlier, you hide when you're about to be shot."

Hudson gave a snort and kicked him in the ribs indiscreetly. To Flynn's surprise, Rose didn't retaliate. He merely eyed the second-story windows of the buildings surrounding them and scooted closer to the sideboard.

Wash looped the reins over the brake, and Flynn stepped over to offer him a hand down. Wash swatted at him and grunted as he hopped off the wagon and landed with a puff of dust.

Flynn glanced over just in time to see Cage stretch across the wagon and take Rose's coat between the tips of his two longest fingers. The chains wouldn't allow him to stretch any further, but he managed to grip the heavy silk and tug. He got a good hold on it and then spread it over Rose's face, covering him with difficulty as his irons got in the way.

Flynn and Wash stood watching, nonplussed, as Cage gave Rose's head a little pat and then sat back. When Cage finally looked up at them, he flushed under his protective layer of sun and dirt and shrugged at them. He gestured to the upper windows and then made his fingers into a gun, aiming it down at Rose and pulling the imaginary trigger.

Wash cleared his throat. "Good thinking."

The man nodded and lowered his head again.

"What, he afeared of gettin' shot?" Hudson asked in amusement.

"Shut up," Flynn warned, jabbing his finger at the man. He watched with a sinking feeling as realization seemed to dawn on the big man's stupid face.

"He's afeared of bein' *seen*," the man crooned as he raised his chained hands above his head. He shouted in a surprisingly loud voice. "Hey! We got Dusty Rose right here!"

Flynn and Wash glanced around in alarm as several passersby stopped and stared. Others had slowed and were looking on curiously as they strolled by.

Beneath the coat, Rose began cursing under his breath and moving as if he were about to sit up.

Wash went over and placed a hand on what Flynn thought might be Rose's shoulder, pushing him down. "Stay down, son," he murmured to the man as he glared over at Hudson.

"Dusty Rose here!" Hudson continued to cry. "He's unarmed!"

More people were taking notice and a buzz of murmured conversation began to circulate through the growing crowd. Flynn darted over the seat of the wagon, grabbing Wash's shotgun as he went. The butt of the shotgun landed with a sickening *thunk* against Hudson's head and he slumped to the side. But folks around them were already watching, whispering to each other, pointing, and staring.

"You really got Dusty Rose in there, mister?" a boy of about ten years called to Flynn.

"Let's see him!" a man called, and several shouts of agreement rang out as the crowd edged closer.

Flynn yelled at the crowd to back up and be on their way, brandishing the shotgun and then pulling his duster aside to reveal the US Marshal's badge on the front of his vest.

"What the hell are we going to do with him now?" he hissed to Wash as the crowd grumbled.

"You could let me go," Rose said in a voice muffled by the coat covering him. "It'll be fine entertainment; we'll see if I'm able to fend for myself. You could place bets; it would be fascinating." Flynn rapped him on the head with his knuckles.

"Ow."

"Shut up," Flynn responded almost without thought.

"Let's get them into the hotel," Wash said as the crowd backed away from them and began to grudgingly disperse.

Flynn was thankful that Cage was obliging. The other two prisoners certainly weren't making life easy. Hudson was just large and ornery and obviously knew that he would be going to the gallows if he did indeed make it to Virginia. He didn't care that he would be tried for attempted murder now as well, because while Rose's attack on

Flynn was arguably self-defense, or so Wash claimed, Hudson's attacks on Rose were pretty straightforward.

It helped that Hudson was still unconscious as Flynn dragged him into the hotel. As heavy as he was, he would have been more trouble if he had been awake. Rose was actually cooperating, but word of his identity spreading didn't make it easy to move him. Some crowded around, just wanting to look at him and be able to say they saw him, while others appeared at the hotel well-heeled, guns slung low and ready to make a name for themselves. There were plenty of men west of the Mississippi that would kill in such a cowardly manner to be known as the man who got the drop on Dusty Rose. Flynn was sure if Rose got shot today, the fact that he was in hand irons at the time would be forgotten in the retelling.

After getting Hudson inside and making certain he wasn't going anywhere, he and Wash guided Rose to the room they had procured, Cage on one side and Wash on the other, protecting him with their bodies.

"I begin to sympathize with Rose's predicament," Wash muttered to Flynn under his breath after they had made it safely into their rented rooms.

"That's what he gets for killing," Flynn said coldly as he glanced out the window at the street below. "They're still milling down there."

"Your life would be a lot easier with just two prisoners, Marshal," Rose said to Wash as he reclined on the bed behind them. He hung his dusty boots over the side of the bed, seemingly reluctant to get the linens dirty.

Wash turned around and scoffed at him. "I suppose you want us to set you free and let you take your chances?"

"Actually, I was talking about my silent companion here," Rose answered with a nod of his head to Cage, who sat beside him on the bed.

Cage glanced at him in surprise and then at Wash with wide eyes, as if he feared being implicated in anything Rose had thought up.

"You and I both know he doesn't deserve whatever the Army will give him," Rose continued in a low voice.

Wash looked over Cage for a long time, his face set in a worried frown. Flynn realized with a shock that Wash was truly considering what Rose was saying.

"Wash," he hissed. "You said it yourself, the law don't work that way. That ain't our decision to make."

Wash cleared his throat and met Flynn's eyes. "I know." He pulled the lace curtain aside and peered down at the street for a long moment. "We're going to have to take them one at a time. We can't leave Rose here unguarded, and can't just one of us handle Hudson and Cage both, not on top of the crowd now."

"I'll take Hudson first," Flynn said with a nod. "You stay with these two." Flynn stopped on the way to the door and turned to frown at Rose and Cage, who were both watching him, then he glanced again at Wash worriedly and found his friend glaring.

"You don't have to worry about no damn escape. Take him," Wash snarled, then turned away and thumped down into the only empty chair in the room.

Flynn pursed his lips unhappily. Nothing about this job had gone right. He turned to Hudson, who was still wallowing groggily on the floor, and gestured for him to stand. "Come on."

Hudson stood with great difficulty, bleeding at his hairline, and sneered at him.

"First sign of trouble from you, and I'll save the Army some rope, understand?" Flynn warned, loosening the strap over his gun.

"See you on the other end, hoss," Rose drawled with pleasure, and Flynn hastily escorted Hudson out of the room before they could start fighting one last time.

# CHAPTER 6

Bat Stringer and his roughly two dozen hired men rode into the city of St. Louis just as an excited crowd was dispersing from the riverfront. Stringer watched the festivities silently from atop his horse, wondering what was going on and if it was important to them.

Finally, he decided it was nothing to concern them, probably just some local excitement over this or that, and he nodded for his boys to disband. They didn't want to attract attention by bunching up near the docks. They were to meet later, after the scheduled departure of a paddle steamer called Oil Cake Jim. Until then, the only thing Stringer ordered them to do was stay away from the drink and keep a wary eye on the extra men they'd recruited. The riverboat pilot they'd found was a drunk, which was why he was located in a saloon and easily cajoled into helping them, and not out on the river piloting a boat. Stringer had high hopes that he'd be relatively sober by the time they needed his brand of expertise.

Stringer dismounted and handed the reins of his horse to Alvarado. The man looked down at him expectantly from atop his horse.

"Head to the docks, hire a skiff," Stringer ordered as he pulled out a leather pouch full of coins and folding money and tossed it to Alvarado.

"Just one?" he asked. He caught the bag and put it quickly into his vest.

Stringer nodded. They would need two, but Stringer intended to steal the other one just before setting off downriver. He told Alvarado as much and the man nodded obediently and went off with the horses.

Stringer watched him go, knowing how lucky he was to have a man he could trust at his right hand. The thought bent his mind toward Jack Kale, and he winced.

He stood on the bustling street alone, looking around at the city. He'd never been to Missouri. In fact, before making the trip to Colorado to take the meeting with John Baird, Stringer had never been farther from Texas than old Mexico. He wouldn't have been tempted to make this trip if the man who'd approached him in San Antonio hadn't said Jack Kale's name. He'd almost hoped Kale would be in Colorado. Most folks thought Stringer had killed Kale and buried him in the Texas desert, a spat between partners or lovers or adversaries, depending on which version you heard.

But that hadn't been the case. Stringer had indeed tried to kill Kale, but only after Kale had informed him he was leaving: just picking up and walking away, without so much as an explanation or even a proper good-bye. Kale had managed to cut off Stringer's finger in the ensuing fight, and Stringer knew he'd lodged a bullet in Kale's ribs in return.

Whether Kale was still alive somewhere, Stringer didn't know. Stringer did know that if he was, he'd sure like to find him. Whether to kill him or kiss him, Stringer hadn't yet decided.

With the amount of gold they were receiving for this simple job, Stringer could afford to pay other men to find Kale if he was so inclined.

Right now, though, he was tired. He didn't want to think about anything but a glass of whiskey. He made his way toward the nearest hotel, rolling his shoulders under the leather duster and working out the kinks.

He nodded to two men exiting of the hotel, noticing the marshal's badge on the blond man's lapel and the hand irons on the big guy he was dragging beside him.

Stringer tipped his hat carefully, holding his head to the side in case his likeness was known this far north.

The marshal merely nodded to him in passing, growling to his prisoner to move along and not cause any more trouble. Stringer turned and watched them go for a moment, his eyes on the chains that restrained the big, dirty prisoner.

"But for the grace of God go I," he murmured to himself wryly before stepping into the hotel.

"Hey, boss," Rose said after about ten minutes of quiet. "How about a bath, hmm? Cage and I both could certainly use one."

Marshal Washington glared at him silently for a moment, then he looked at Cage and his expression softened. Why he appeared to affect the marshal in such a way, Cage didn't know. He had seen many reactions to his muteness: most involved a distant sort of pity, others disdain or outright dismissal.

Marshal Washington's response was peculiar in that he couldn't seem to decide how to react. Gabriel Rose's was even more peculiar in that the silence seemed to intrigue him. It almost felt like Gabriel admired the way Cage was.

Cage cleared his throat and glanced at Gabriel, catching a quick wink from the charismatic shootist. He'd been expecting this ever since they'd rolled into St. Louis. He knew Gabriel had a scheme, he just hadn't figured out what it was yet.

"A bath," Wash finally muttered as he sat straighter.

Cage leaned forward, looking at the marshal hopefully. Whatever Gabriel had planned, he longed for it to include water. He had been dirty for so long, he thought he might actually feel like a person again if he could get clean.

"I've got the money for it, Marshal, if that's the problem," Gabriel offered. "I'd pay a lot more than a dollar for a bath right about now."

Cage nodded vigorously at Gabriel.

"So would Cage," Gabriel supplied.

He had yet to misunderstand Cage's actions, and that in itself made Cage appreciate the man more than he had thought possible. He would miss Gabriel Rose when he was gone.

Wash sighed long and loud, and leaned back in his chair, gazing up at the ceiling speculatively. Finally, he nodded curtly at Cage and Gabriel. "First sign of trying to skin out on me, and I will shoot you," he warned, and Cage believed him.

"You've got little to worry about from us, Marshal. If anything, we'd escape *after* the bath," Gabriel assured him with a smile.

Cage reached over and smacked him on the arm, causing Gabriel to laugh.

Wash stood up and began to pace, holding his chin in his hand. Cage knew that he was trying to figure out how to let one of them bathe while still keeping an eye on the other and not forcing all three of them to remain in the same room.

Cage glanced at Gabriel and met the man's intelligent black eyes. His fingers brushed Cage's wrist under the cold iron, and Cage shivered, attention darting down to Gabriel's hand and back up. He nodded in answer to the unasked question. Yes, he wanted more with Gabriel. Another touch, another kiss. All the time they could beg, borrow, or steal.

He could see the cunning shine in Gabriel's eyes as he looked at him. He wondered if the two marshals understood what sort of man they were dealing with. He almost felt sorry for them.

"Marshal, Cage and I aren't shy," Gabriel drawled, watching Wash closely as he spoke.

The marshal stopped and turned to narrow his eyes at them.

"We don't mind sharing the bath facilities, if it makes it easier on you."

"You're sure interested in how easy my life is all of a sudden."

"I'm interested in a bath," Gabriel corrected. "Easy makes that happen. Hard continues to see us sitting here in a month's worth of filth."

Cage watched Wash hopefully. He was dirty, he knew that. But Gabriel had remained surprisingly clean during their travels, and Cage suspected that he had more pressing reasons to want them together in that bathing house.

"Get up, then," Wash ordered after another few moments of thought.

Cage and Gabriel scrambled off the bed with difficulty and stood, waiting for Wash to decide how best to move them. Cage admired the marshal's grit. It couldn't be a comfortable feeling, being alone with a man of Cage's size and a man of Gabriel's reputation with only one working arm. He was handling himself with confidence and grace, though. Cage respected that, and found he quite liked the man.

Wash followed them down the hall toward the end room that held the hotel's large cast iron tub. He ordered the tub filled and then sat Cage and Gabriel in the corner and examined the room thoroughly as the water was brought in by the two bathhouse attendants. He even stuck his head out the window, looking down at the alley street below, and then back at them critically.

"You don't look like you got wings," he finally decided. He had removed several sharp objects, including a shaving kit, and several heavy things that could have been used as clubs were also sent out of the room.

When he was done, the room contained barely anything but the tub, the water, and some lye soap.

Wash stood them up and stared them down. "I'm trusting you both," he said as he took Cage's hands in his own and unlocked the hand irons. He moved to Gabriel and did the same for him.

"You're leaving us alone?" Gabriel asked in what appeared to be genuine surprise.

"You ain't the only one who was kept up at night out there by your mumbling," the marshal answered with a smile he tried to hide.

Cage found himself blushing as he looked away. The other men had heard Gabriel's soft murmurs to him as they had tried to keep warm under the wagon. Cage had admitted to himself a long time ago that he was attracted to other men, but being unable to speak made life hard enough without the added stigma of preferring men over women, so he had rarely acted on the impulse. Marshal Washington didn't seem to mind.

"I got a heart," Wash told them. "I'm giving you some time together before they take Cage away, understand? Don't make me regret it."

He then backed out of the room, pulling the door closed behind him.

Bat Stringer sat at a table in the corner of the hotel's small saloon, feet propped up on the empty seat opposite him, arm laid across the back of his chair so his coat fell away and made his gun easy to see from anywhere in the room. He wore the weapon border style, with the grip backward so he could draw across his body. If anyone in Missouri recognized it as being specific to men who haunted the dangerous Mexican border, they steered clear of Stringer today.

He smiled to himself as he took a drink of whiskey, enjoying the sideways looks and wary glances he always received in places like this. He could certainly add the sin of pride to his list of transgressions, and he was just fine with that.

Being outwardly dangerous had its benefits. For one, people left you the hell alone. He'd been challenged in the street a time or two, but most young bucks let him be. Every shootist in the West had his own brand of self-defense. Stringer preferred the longhorn method: appear bigger and meaner than anyone else and they'll leave you to it. Others chose to hide, or if they couldn't hide, at least tried to appear nonthreatening. Dusty Rose, for example, dressed like a dandy and used false ineptitude as defense, rather than brandishing his guns.

Stringer sneered when he thought about Rose. The man was a belvidere, quite a handsome man, and Stringer hadn't instantly disliked him. He'd actually found Rose quite interesting, if a little bothersome when he opened his mouth. It was rumored that he openly dallied with men, but Stringer didn't have a problem with that. He'd been involved with other men a few times himself. It was more common in the West than the high society folk back East wanted to think. Out here, the euphemism used when two young men found themselves sharing a bedroll for more than just warmth was "mutual solace." The West was a lonely place; a man took companionship and pleasure where he could get it. Rose didn't seem to mind what people thought of him.

Stringer thought he might have gotten on quite well with Rose if they'd met under different circumstances.

He threw back what remained of his whiskey and stood fluidly. Stringer didn't exactly feel restored by the interlude, but it would have to do. He needed to hunt down one more piece of the puzzle before he could relax, and it was short hours until they would have to set off again. He slid his hat on, ducking his head to hide his face beneath the brim as the blond marshal he'd seen earlier returned, without his prisoner, and headed directly for the stairs.

Flynn joined Wash outside the door to the room at the end of the hall not long after ridding himself of Hudson. He had filled the Army boys in on their situation and had been pleasantly surprised when they allowed for an extra hour to deliver Cage. What Flynn hadn't counted on had been Wash's decision to allow the two burgeoning lovebirds time alone in the damn bathhouse together.

He and Wash stood side by side, restless and silent. Finally, Flynn could no longer stand it and he turned to Wash with some possibly undue hostility. "You know what they're doing in there, right? We ain't running no whorehouse, Wash. This ain't right. It ain't proper."

"Since when have you gave a damn about proper? Give them some time," Wash said with a sigh. "And don't be preachin' to me. If it was you, you'd be thankful for a half hour of peace with someone you thought you might care about. Especially if you thought you was looking at the gallows."

Flynn opened his mouth to deny it, but he knew it was true. It was human nature, the need to be close to someone when you had so little time left. Hell, even knowing he did have time, the idea of spending it all alone because he was a coward was momentarily crushing.

"Hell, it might even make 'em easier to handle. Besides, I don't peg Cage as the type to run. And I don't think Rose will try it without him now. I don't rightly believe he tried it at all before."

"What?"

"You were going to shoot his dog, Flynn."

There was a sudden thump from within the room, and a few seconds later, a soft knock on the door.

"That was quicker'n I expected," Wash muttered as he reached for the door.

Flynn was ready with his hand on his gun, just in case the two men tried anything.

But when Wash opened the door, Cage stood before them placidly. His face was still covered with a few weeks' worth of beard and his long hair was tied neatly at the back of his neck, but he seemed a different man now he had managed to clean all the dirt and grime from his body. His clothes were damp, but they were relatively clean as well. He had washed them in the tub and wrung them dry, as evidenced by the dirty brown water filling the basin. Wash and Flynn stared at him in confused silence, waiting. Cage turned to the side to allow them to see, and he pointed at the window, which was open, its curtains fluttering in the soft breeze. Gabriel Rose was nowhere to be found.

"Damnation!" Flynn launched himself into the room and stuck his head out the window. He looked down and saw nothing but a long drop to the street below, and Rose's bowler hat lying crushed in the dust. He cursed again and brushed past Cage out into the hall.

"Stay here!" Wash ordered Cage, who merely nodded his head obediently and had the door slammed in his face for his trouble.

Cage stood by the door, left alone and unguarded after the flurry of frantic activity. The two marshals had dashed off after their escaped prisoner, trusting him to remain where he was in their haste. The breeze gently tugged at the lacy curtains as Cage counted slowly to ten.

When he was done, he walked over to the tub filled with lukewarm, murky water and brushed his fingers across the calm water. Gabriel's head broke the surface and he gasped. Rivulets streamed down his cheeks and his black hair was plastered to his forehead and over his ears. He ran a hand over his face and then through his hair, making it stick up in all directions.

Cage patted him on the head and offered him a hand. Gabriel peered around the room and then grinned widely up at Cage and pulled himself out of the tub. Cage helped him out of the water and brushed some of droplets off the man's face.

"Did they charge off after me?" Gabriel asked.

Cage nodded, trying not to smile. He didn't want to encourage Gabriel's brash nature any more than he already had.

"Well, that went better than even I could have hoped," Gabriel said to him as water dropped off his curling hair.

Cage gave him a melancholy, affectionate smile and nodded.

Gabriel adjusted the straps of his vest over his sopping-wet shirt. "Come with me," he urged in a whisper.

Cage licked his lips and stared at the man for a long moment, then slowly shook his head in regret.

"Come on, Cage," Gabriel begged. "I'll watch your back, you watch mine. The dog's already smarter than I am, I need someone to talk to." There was a hint of mischief in his eyes.

Cage hesitated, wanting to give in to the desire to go with him. They'd made an instant connection, and that wasn't something Cage was used to or took lightly. Most people just ignored him. He'd had few true friends in life, even fewer who seemed to see past his silence. But in the end, he knew he had to stand trial for what he had done, right or wrong. His conscience wouldn't let him rest otherwise. For the first time in years he wanted to say something, though, to tell Gabriel *why* he wouldn't go with him.

He shook his head again and lowered it, unable to voice his thoughts or emotions.

It surprised him when Gabriel looked crestfallen, and he was even more shocked when Gabriel took his face in both hands and kissed him passionately. He gave a little gasp and grabbed Gabriel's elbows, not certain of how to touch him now that he wasn't restrained by chains, or even if he should. Gabriel kissed him harder for his troubles and then regretfully let him go.

Cage blinked at him, and Gabriel smiled crookedly. "I'll just find you later, then, yeah? After you've served your punishment."

Cage licked his lips again, tasting the other man on them, and he nodded as his mouth curved in a smile. Even without Cage trying to articulate it, Gabriel had understood.

"And if they think they're going to hang you, well, they'll have to go through me first," Gabriel promised with a wink.

Cage nodded. He was willing to serve his time, but his conscience and sense of right and wrong only took him so far. He sure as hell wasn't willing to die for burning blankets that may or may not have been infected with disease. If the Army made an example of him, or if he became the victim of some bureaucratic oversight, they very well could hang him. If Gabriel was planning to help him out of a noose, then Cage wasn't going to argue that point.

Gabriel mirrored the nod with one of his own, then gave Cage a brilliant smile and turned to the door, grabbing his coat as he went.

Cage reached out and snagged his elbow. When Gabriel looked back at him in question, Cage offered a confused frown and shrugged his shoulders.

"What do I plan to do?"

Cage nodded.

"No worries, my friend. I've always got a plan. Just tell them the truth when they question you."

Cage let him go with a raised eyebrow, not quite understanding but willing to trust the man implicitly. Gabriel swung open the door, only to be stopped in his tracks when he found Marshal Washington standing in the hallway, waiting with his six-shooter raised, a grim smile set on his face.

"Howdy," the marshal greeted sarcastically.

Gabriel's shoulders slumped and he looked away from the man with a huff. "Bloody marshals."

Wash swung his arm and hit Gabriel in the temple with the butt of his gun, sending his newly recaptured prisoner down in a heap.

Cage watched him fall without even twitching in an attempt to catch him, and then raised his eyes once more to meet Wash's.

"Did he threaten you if you didn't help him?" Wash growled, pointing his gun down at Gabriel's unconscious body.

Cage swallowed hard. Tell the truth, Gabriel had told him. Cage shook his head.

"If he threatened you, son, then it's all forgiven," Wash said as he placed a booted foot on top of Gabriel's back.

Cage was pretty sure the man wasn't going to be moving for a while. It was the fourth time Gabriel had been hit on the head in the last ten days, if Cage was counting correctly. At some point, you just stopped getting back up. He wanted to check him to make sure he was okay, but with the marshal's good hand still on that trigger, he didn't dare move.

"If you helped him," Wash continued pointedly, "then I'm going to have to charge you with the offense. Helping a prisoner escape is a federal crime, son. Do you understand?"

Cage nodded, his eyes not leaving Wash's.

"Now. Did he threaten you?" He obviously didn't want to charge Cage. Cage could read him easily enough. But Gabriel had said to tell them the truth, and Cage had always tried to be an honest man anyway. It was easier than keeping track of your lies, even if you were mute.

Cage tilted his head apologetically, and then once more he very slowly shook it from side to side.

Wash closed his eyes and sighed heavily, then he looked back down at Gabriel.

Soon Marshal Flynn returned, breathless and incensed over being made to run all over Creation for no good reason. He glared at Gabriel, who still lay where he had fallen in a crumpled heap, and then kicked him for good measure.

"Flynn!" Wash barked.

"I say we kill the little son of a whore now and save the government the trouble," Flynn huffed.

"We've had worse attempts," Wash reminded him, then he glanced over at Cage almost sadly. "And it would appear that Cage is going to be traveling with us to New Orleans now."

"He threatened you," Marshal Flynn said to Cage forcefully. "Just say he threatened you and forced you to help him, son, and you won't be charged."

Cage looked at both men expressionlessly, and then shook his head yet again.

Flynn stared for a beat before turning away in exasperation. "The first goddamn honest outlaw I ever seen. Ain't got sense enough to lie," he grumbled as he stalked back down the narrow hallway.

"That man is property of the United States Army, mister," one of the irate soldiers informed Wash.

Flynn stood back with Cage, observing the confrontation tensely and trying to keep an eye on both their prisoners and his partner. Rose was still unconscious and trussed up in the back of the wagon with a blanket covering him. Cage remained stock-still, scowling at the two soldiers. Flynn couldn't get over how different he looked with a little help from some soap and water. Like someone Flynn would nod to in passing on the street now, even wearing the homemade oilskins.

Cage huffed loudly at the soldier's words. Flynn glanced back at them and frowned. They didn't need trouble with the Army, and Wash would surely give them some if he had a mind to.

"Property?" Wash asked.

The soldier gave a confident nod "That's right."

"That's right," Wash echoed with a slow sneer.

The soldier clearly recognized the gleam in Wash's eyes as a warning one, and Flynn looked on in something close to amusement as the two uniformed men shifted restlessly in front of his partner. Even with one good arm, Wash was capable of so many things most men could never manage.

Suddenly, Wash's gun was in his hand and he had shoved it in the soldier's face. Flynn tensed and just barely stopped himself from lunging to interfere. Beside him, Cage jumped at the sudden appearance of the gun.

"This was property of the Army too," Wash growled, cocking the Colt Old Model Army .44 and placing the barrel between the soldier's eyes. "I got it when I was younger'n you and fighting against my brothers in gray. I think I have the right to say *no* man is property."

Flynn took a slow step forward, watching warily. It was never easy to guess which way Wash would go when he was riled. They had known each other since they had fought together in the 19th Indiana, part of the infamous Iron Brigade, and they had been together ever since. Still, Wash was anything but predictable, even for Flynn. Usually he managed to keep his temper and he was cool and even-keeled. But the one time every blue moon that he went off, there wasn't much that could stop him.

"How's about we settle this without the iron, Wash?" Flynn said carefully. Behind him, he felt Cage shift, his hand irons clanging intrusively in the overwrought silence. Flynn didn't know which way Cage would go, either. If violence broke out now, would he try to get away, after nearly a fortnight of being the perfect prisoner? Flynn didn't suppose so, not when Rose was still safely in custody. Rose may have been ready to skip off into the sunset without Cage, but Flynn had a gut feeling that Cage wouldn't leave Rose behind.

Wash narrowed his eyes at the soldier and then lowered the gun. Both of the soldiers released pent-up breaths and looked from Wash to Flynn.

"Now," Wash said calmly. "Let's start over, why don't we? I am US Marshal William Henry Washington, and I am charging this man with aiding in the attempted escape of a prisoner. I *am* going to be taking him to New Orleans for a federal trial. Do we have a problem with that arrangement?"

"No, sir," the two soldiers grumbled in unison, their tone decidedly unfriendly and resentful.

"Good, then," Wash drawled with a congenial grin as he holstered his weapon. He ushered them away daintily with his fingers. "On with you."

The two men backed off and then turned and walked quickly to their waiting horses. Flynn watched them mount up with a growing sense of apprehension. It didn't do to embarrass men publicly, especially young men who still thought they had something to prove in life. He hoped the encounter didn't come back to haunt them.

Cage stepped forward to stand beside him. George Hudson sat astride a third Army horse, with his hands tied to the pommel of the saddle, glaring at them evilly. His escorts had just taken one hell of a pistol-whipping to their pride. They would probably take it out on their prisoner, if Flynn was to guess.

Cage raised his hands and waved at the man mockingly, smirking. Flynn fought hard not to laugh at the silent parting shot.

"Well. I feel like a man again," Wash joked as soon as the soldiers were out of earshot.

Flynn tried to be stern, but he just shook his head and smirked. "Was that something that really needed doing?"

"Probably not. But it amused me, nonetheless," Wash crooned. He glanced at Cage and looked him up and down. "Now, let's see to the rest of our problems. Seems like all of us is gonna be going downriver. I'll have to find the telegraph office and wire the change of plans so's they're not expecting me in Natchez."

Flynn sighed heavily. He was glad that Wash would be accompanying him downriver, though. That was the only good turn this trip had taken so far.

They secured two private cabins on the packet *James Howard*, a side-wheeler steamboat that was called Oil Cake Jim by the men who worked her, though Flynn had no idea as to why. He wasn't really interested in finding out, either. She was a large boat, not lavish like the newer ones, but with nicer accommodations than Flynn was used to.

The most prominent features of the steamer were not the two large paddle wheels inside their wheelhouses on either side of the ship, but rather the two thirty-foot-tall smokestacks near the bow of the vessel. A carved wooden anchor hung between them just over the pilot house, the trademark of an Anchor Line ship.

Flynn stamped his foot to bring some warmth into his toes. St. Louis was one of the few cities on the St. Louis to New Orleans trade route that had actual wooden docks by the river. Fancy. Flynn certainly appreciated the planks under his feet this morning. River mud was something that stuck with a man after slogging through it. The swinging landing stage at the bow had been fixed to the dock. It was wide enough for two people to walk up it side by side, and it had shaky rails. Flynn could almost see Rose trying to launch himself over the edge to escape.

When they set off, the landing stage would be swung back over the water, and it would stick straight out from the bow as the ship made its way downriver. It didn't always have a nice solid dock to moor to, though. Flynn had seen landing stages of these huge riverboats attached to trees, rocks, and even a pair of oxen one time at the smaller stops along the route.

The ship wasn't loading passengers just yet. The cargo took priority, and official business such as what Wash and Flynn were discussing with the ship's captain. Even so, many people had gathered at the waterfront already, and the calliope on the hurricane deck played a lively tune. The incredibly loud steam-powered organ gave the scene a circus-like feeling. Families with small children swarmed the landing and picnicked not far off, men led skittish horses away from the noise and commotion, and loved ones bid excited farewells as they prepared to board for a luxurious trip downriver.

As Flynn and Wash stood on the dock in front of the landing stage speaking with the captain, Flynn noticed that Cage had turned away from the chaos and was staring off down the bank. The marshal's attention was split between the conversation Wash and the captain were having, and watching Cage to make certain he didn't dive off the docks into the water. Rose had roused not long before, and he was tied securely to the end of the wagon, sitting with his dog and watching them blankly from the muddy area full of carriages, wagons, and horses. He hadn't said a word since waking back up. Flynn wondered if maybe he'd had his brain rattled just a bit too much.

"We're certainly no strangers to having lawmen aboard, Marshal Washington," the captain was saying to Wash with an amiable smile when Flynn turned his attention back to them. "As long as your prisoners are escorted at all times, we feel quite confident in your abilities to keep them under control." He cleared his throat and looked around the dock warily, then stepped closer to Wash and lowered his head. "All that we ask is that you remain discreet. We sometimes have rough types, but our passengers are generally of a . . . gentler breed. They like to feel safe. Seeing a man come to dinner in hand irons would cause a bit of a stir."

"Understood, Captain," Wash responded.

"That's good," the captain replied with a relieved nod. Then he scowled. "I'm sorry we couldn't locate two unoccupied cabins that were next to each other."

"As long as we have four beds, we'll make do," Wash assured the captain. Marshals escorted prisoners amidst the general public all the time; sometimes on boats, often on trains, and on the rare occasion, stagecoaches. They were used to it.

Flynn glanced over at Cage again and found the man frowning at him. As soon as Flynn met his eyes, Cage gestured for him to come closer and look.

Flynn took a wary step toward him. "What is it?"

Cage turned and pointed down the dock, past the huge paddle wheel to where several wagons of cargo had been delivered for loading onto the boat. Soldiers were wheeling crate upon crate of what appeared to be something very heavy toward the landing stage. Further down, a man in uniform sat astride a horse with a shotgun over his lap as he watched the proceedings, and several more armed, uniformed men stood along the loading gangplanks that led to the wooden dock. They scanned the rooftops of the buildings surrounding the waterfront, and their eyes peered into the darkness of the alleyways.

It was obvious to Flynn's well-trained eyes what they were doing. The soldiers weren't supervising the loading of the crates. They were keeping a lookout.

Flynn squinted and examined the crates curiously, trying to read what was written on them. All he could make out was that the words stenciled on the crates indicated the contents were property of the United States Government.

"What in the hell?" he murmured.

Cage tapped him tentatively on his elbow, and Flynn looked back at the silent man. He tensed as Cage reached out for his lapel pocket, but he allowed the movement. Cage's fingers gently plucked at the gold chain that held Flynn's pocket watch, and then pointed again at the crates.

Flynn watched Cage's fingers, then he scowled down at the crates in confusion. It dawned on him suddenly, and he glanced back at Cage.

"You think it's gold?"

Cage nodded.

Flynn examined the crates more closely. "Well," he finally said with a small huff. "Ain't none of our concern." He placed a hand on Cage's shoulder and urged him to turn away. If he knew anything about soldiers on guard duty, it was that they didn't like overly nosy onlookers. The milling crowd around the busy docks was enough to make those soldiers tense already.

They headed back over to the wagon as Wash continued to deal with their lodgings. Rose still sat on the end of the wagon, his coat held over his hand irons, swinging his legs freely. He either didn't know or didn't care that the right side of his head was covered in dried blood. Flynn suspected that he knew what a stir his appearance was causing and enjoyed the looks passersby were giving him.

Flynn pointed for Cage to go join him, and he watched as the big man shuffled over to the wagon obediently. Rose's eyes followed him, and as Cage sat beside him, their shoulders touched, and they both smiled

Flynn scowled at them. He couldn't help but get the feeling that he and Wash had been bamboozled somehow. Rose didn't seem at all put out over his escape attempt being foiled, nor did he seem upset that he had dragged Cage into deeper trouble. It made Flynn uneasy.

"Sourpuss."

Flynn actually jumped. He turned around and smacked Wash in the arm. "Don't sneak up on a man with a gun."

"Ow!" Wash cried, but he was laughing as he rubbed at his arm.

"Sorry!" Flynn winced and placed a hand on Wash's injured shoulder. "Sorry. I keep forgetting."

"Yeah, I barely know it's there," Wash said wryly. He looked back at Rose and Cage. "Getting irritated at Rose is like barking at a knot, friend. He don't care, and he likes it that way."

"Yeah, I know," Flynn said with another disgruntled glance at their prisoners. He kept his hand on Wash's shoulder as Wash rubbed it.

"They really bother you that much?" Wash asked. His fingers grazed over Flynn's.

Flynn yanked his hand away and rubbed his palm over his mouth and chin. "No."

Wash raised an eyebrow as he watched the movement of Flynn's hand. He shook his head. "Let's get them settled," he suggested softly as he brushed by Flynn and headed over to the wagon. "I want to get them in the cabins before the other passengers start boarding."

Flynn closed his eyes and jerked his head to the side irritably. When he opened his eyes again, he found Rose watching him with a small smirk as Wash unlocked his hands from the wagon. Flynn glared at Rose briefly before looking away. He pondered the soldiers laboring with their mysterious crates until he could wrangle in his temper.

He had gotten twitchy around Wash lately, and it was all Gabriel Rose's damn fault. Flynn didn't know why or how exactly, but he was sure it was.

"That dog ain't coming, Rose," Wash was saying sternly when Flynn finally looked back over at them.

"But he can't swim to New Orleans," Rose protested in all earnestness.

From what Flynn had seen of the dog's loyalty, Rose was probably legitimately worried that the mutt would try it.

"Tell him to stay here, then," Wash said.

Rose stared at Wash mutinously for a moment, then his shoulders slumped and he sighed. Flynn looked on with the barest hint of sympathy as Rose turned to the dog and pointed for him to go away.

"If you want to go downriver, you have to walk. No swimming, you understand? Now, go on." Koda sat and gazed up at him adoringly, completely ignoring the order. "Go on," Rose repeated. The dog lowered its head, looking up at Rose expectantly. Rose pointed again and the dog slowly turned away, slinking off and whining as he went.

Rose watched him go, then turned to Wash and raised his chin. For a man who had seemed to worry overly much about the dog, he didn't strike Flynn as being all too upset about finally sending him away. Flynn would have put up more of a fight for his horse, let alone a constant companion like that mutt. He was sure it wasn't a question of Rose's character, either. Rose obviously thought he would see the dog again soon enough. Wondering what Rose had planned for the trip downriver raised the hackles on the back of Flynn's neck.

He reminded himself to remain suspicious and wary of the Englishman until he was no longer Flynn's responsibility. It was too easy to be drawn into his charismatic personality and forget that he was a very capable shootist and a clever grifter. Wash had fallen for it at the hotel, being convinced to leave them alone.

It had surprised Flynn to discover during the fiasco that Wash was a bit of a romantic. He would never have guessed it before this morning.

Flynn watched his fellow marshal with what might have been longing as Wash rearranged Cage's chains and then gathered Rose's duffel bag. He unceremoniously dumped the heavy bag in Rose's hands. Flynn looked away again before Wash could catch him.

Wash gestured for Rose and Cage to head up the gangplank toward Flynn. Flynn cleared his throat and turned his head to watch them as they made their way to him.

"You ever play poker, Marshal Flynn?" Rose drawled as he neared where Flynn stood at the foot of the landing stage. "Your bluff is highly impressive."

Flynn glared after him as Rose and Wash passed by, but said nothing. He refused to let Rose draw him into any discussion even remotely related to his emotions.

Cage followed them and glanced at Flynn as he passed by, something close to pity as he made brief eye contact.

"Shut up," Flynn grumbled to him as he took the man's elbow and fell in beside him.

Cage bit his lip, presumably to keep from smiling.

Flynn shook his head and glanced down at the stained oilskin clothing Cage was wearing. He stopped short and tugged at Cage's elbow to stop him as they headed up the gangplanks of the landing stage to the steamer.

Cage furrowed his brow, as if expecting him to change their plans at the last minute, but he stood there obediently waiting for Flynn to speak.

"Hey, Wash," Flynn called.

Wash and Rose turned to look back down at them.

"We should get him some new duds if we're going for laying in the grass." Flynn waved his free hand at Cage. "He's going to stick out like a damn sore thumb in these."

Wash scowled and cocked his head critically. "You might just be right," he agreed. "But we used all our folding money on the passage. What do you want to do, commandeer trousers and boots for him?"

"I wouldn't be averse to bending an elbow in the saloon while you gents talk this over," Rose said. He squinted up at the sun, as if judging the time.

"Shut up," Wash and Flynn responded in unison without even looking at the man again.

"He's too big to borrow any of our duds," Flynn argued. It wasn't like they had an overabundance of spare clothing anyway.

"I ain't saying he don't need new clothes, Flynn, I'm just waiting to hear how you intend to get them," Wash said patiently.

"If I may," Rose interjected as he raised one slender finger to get their attention.

"Shut up!" Flynn turned his attention back to Wash. "Maybe we can open a line of credit at the Emporium. Let the government pick up the tab."

"St. Louis is a lot rougher than last time you was here." Wash shook his head. "They don't take credit from strangers no more, no matter if they're wearing badges."

"Marshals?" Rose said as he stepped forward. They both looked at him in irritation. "May I remind you that you have at your convenience a fairly adept player of cards? Perhaps we could take a short bypass to the saloon and I could acquire us additional funds?"

The two marshals stared at him expressionlessly for a moment before sharing a look. Wash finally raised an eyebrow and pursed his lips.

"No."

"But—"

"Wash, you can't really be considering—"

"I don't see the harm in it," Wash interrupted with a shrug. "He knows next time he tries to escape I plan to shoot him, so he won't try nothing."

"He's quite right," Rose muttered as he rubbed the side of his head. "Besides, Cage needs new clothing, and I'm wholly willing to assist."

Flynn glared at Rose, trying to see the truth in the words. He was leaning toward believing the man, just this once. Rose did seem to genuinely care about Cage, to the point that Flynn was now almost positive he had engineered his attempted escape with the express purpose of having Cage charged with helping him. It was entirely possible he'd known if they charged Cage with the crime he'd have to make the trip to New Orleans with them. It made Flynn nervous to think they'd given Rose what he'd wanted.

He shook his head as he met Wash's eyes, and Wash shrugged carelessly. "We'll see if maybe we can find a place that'll deal with us on good faith," Wash decided as he took Rose's arm and began walking back down the gangplank toward them. Flynn gestured for Cage to head back toward the dock.

Rose sighed heavily. "I suppose we could just use *my* line of credit," he said, as if that option had been an afterthought.

Flynn turned and glared at him over his shoulder.

Rose shrugged. "Perhaps I could even find a new hat."

"You're getting a new hat when you jump out that window after your old one," Wash snapped.

Flynn breathed deeply and turned away, resisting the urge to knock Rose into the river. He remembered hearing that Rose's family back East had been wealthy. What was the harm in letting him use his own money? It was no skin off their noses.

Flynn scrubbed at his face in irritation. "Let's get this over with, then," he muttered as he tugged at his silent prisoner's elbow. He suddenly grinned with relish as they headed back down the gangplank. "Come on, Cage. We'll find you something nice and expensive to put on Rose's tab."

Cage stood back with Flynn, watching with amusement as Gabriel dragged Wash all over the Emporium in search of proper clothing. Cage could appreciate a nice new set of clothes, but he wasn't what one would call fussy. As long as it fit, he didn't much care what it looked like. Hell, sometimes he didn't even care if it fit.

Gabriel, obviously, had a different view on the matter.

Flynn sighed and shifted his weight. Cage glanced over at him apologetically, his fingers finding the chain between his hand irons and playing with it, fighting down a flutter of nerves.

"Ain't your fault," Flynn muttered to him.

Cage snorted. They'd had him measured, an awkward process when the tailor was frightened of the two prisoners and trying to work around the chain that bound Cage's hands. Of course, they didn't have time to order clothes made for him, and parcels bought off the shelves weren't going to fit as well as something tailored. But Gabriel insisted it would make the marshal's lives easier if Cage looked respectable, and off he'd gone with Cage's measurements to find pieces he thought suitable.

Cage sought him out again, and found Gabriel with Wash at his side, arguing over something on the shelf in front of them. Cage couldn't tell what it was, but he almost hoped the sensible marshal would win the argument. There was no telling what Gabriel would dress him in if they allowed him to do as he pleased.

"You're going to end up in evening dress and ascot," Flynn said wryly under his breath.

Cage nodded, and he turned to point at Gabriel and Wash. Then he gestured to his neck. Neckwear was probably what they were arguing over. Gabriel probably would try to get an ascot for him, that was certainly his style, but they usually had to be worn with a stickpin. Cage was surprised that the marshals hadn't confiscated Gabriel's stickpin when they first picked him up.

"They're looking at choke straps, fighting over the stickpin," Flynn agreed as he offered Cage a small smile. "Let's go hurry this along."

Cage trailed after him, and was both amused and exasperated to find that they'd been right. Wash and Gabriel were discussing ties, and even as they approached, Wash reached to Gabriel's neck and pulled the stickpin out of his collar.

Gabriel huffed at him indignantly. "What damage could he possibly do with a stickpin?" he asked Wash as he reached up and yanked at the limp ascot around his neck. He waved it accusingly, as if Wash actually cared that he was less dapper without it.

"*He* might not do any damage with it, but I don't trust *you* any farther than I can throw you," Wash responded with an easy smile as he waved the stickpin and then slid it into the pocket of his vest. "Now pick out a four-in-hand or he'll go without."

Gabriel turned back to the shelf where a scant few ties were on display. He looked at the more ordinary ties for a moment, his fingers fidgeting with the ascot in his hands, before his eyes drifted over the display shelf and he inhaled sharply and ducked his head to hide behind the free-standing case.

"What in the Sam Hill are you doing?" Flynn demanded between gritted teeth. He calmly pushed his jacket back to make the butt of his gun easier to reach as Rose cowered at his feet. "Get up!"

Cage frowned down at Gabriel in confusion as the man shook his head, putting a finger to his lips to shush Flynn. Cage saw nothing to be alarmed at when he glanced over the display case; just a man in a gray suit, browsing through the rack of dime novels on the far wall. Cage met Wash's eyes and shrugged. The imperturbable marshal shrugged back.

"That man over there," Gabriel whispered to them, pointing over the display. "He tried to kill me once!"

"Shocking," Wash said wryly.

"He did!"

"Only once?" Flynn asked, his voice taking on the same tone Wash's had.

"This is not a joking matter," Gabriel said as he squatted on the floor at their feet. He put the ascot over his head, as if he could disguise himself with it. "Go over there and arrest him or . . . something. Oh! Let me shoot him!"

"No!" Flynn and Wash both replied in harsh whispers.

"His name is Baird. He works for the government in some fashion."

"Is he a lawman? Because technically we're hoping to kill you too," Flynn responded as he glanced over at the man Gabriel had identified as Baird.

"Decidedly not a lawman," Gabriel mumbled. He crawled a few feet, then craned his neck to peer around a large barrel full of peanuts. Cage watched him incredulously, wondering if this was another attempt at escape, or if Gabriel was sincere in his peculiar brand of caution. He looked positively ridiculous.

Cage bit his lip so he wouldn't start laughing.

"Would you get up off the blamed floor, please?" Wash muttered as he bent to take Gabriel's elbow.

"Marshal, what portion of 'he tried to kill me' was difficult for you to understand?" Gabriel whispered as he let Wash yank him to his feet.

He still hunched, ducking his head and keeping his face hidden behind Wash's shoulder and holding the ascot against his mouth and nose.

The effort was wasted, in Cage's opinion. Anyone who had looked into Gabriel Rose's black eyes would recognize them from a mile away.

Cage frowned again. He didn't think Gabriel was actually afraid of the government man—and he certainly was a government man, Cage could tell that much just by his appearance. Stiff shoulders, straight back, heavy walrus-style mustaches of an indistinct brown color drooping over his lip. He stood with one hand in a pocket of his gray frock coat, and in the other hand he held a dime novel he had picked from the rack.

Cage recognized the dime novel as the very same that related the misadventures of one Dusty Rose.

He carefully touched Marshal Flynn's elbow to get his attention. The marshal was already standing with his hand on the butt of his gun; Cage didn't want to give him reason to draw it. But Flynn merely glanced at him, his eyes following the finger Cage pointed at Baird. Flynn obviously noticed which dime novel Baird had picked up as well, and he took a step closer to Wash and Gabriel.

"Let's get him out of here," he murmured to Wash.

Wash had an expression of mixed amusement and vexation on his face, but he must have seen something in Flynn's eyes because he nodded almost instantly without saying a word. He took Gabriel's elbow and pointed him toward the door. Gabriel quickly handed off everything he'd been clutching to his chest, depositing it all unceremoniously into Cage's arms, then he ducked his head again and let Wash lead him from the Emporium.

Cage and Flynn stood together, nonplussed.

Finally, Flynn sighed and turned to look at Cage. "Man should pick out his own hat. Find you one and let's get before we meet anyone else who wants to kill him."

Cage glanced over to where Baird had been, but the man was gone. He scanned the Emporium quickly, searching for the dove-gray top hat Baird had been wearing. He shook his head and met Flynn's eyes worriedly.

"Faster we get to the river, the better off he'll be," Flynn said.

Cage nodded jerkily. Flynn took the clothing Gabriel had dumped into Cage's arms, and then Cage reached out with both cuffed hands to pluck the closest hat from a nearby shelf. It was a brown bowler with a square crown, made of fur felt with hand stitching. It was a fine, expensive hat, and when he put it on, it fit him reasonably well.

"Is it pricey?" Flynn asked as he adjusted the brim.

Cage nodded and winced. They were putting everything on Gabriel's tab by necessity.

Flynn actually grinned as he clapped Cage on the shoulder. "Good. Go ahead and get two," he suggested with childish delight, and he headed for the front counter to tally their purchases.

"You want Cage or Rose?" Wash asked Flynn quietly as soon as they'd reached the first of their cabins on the large paddle steamer. One was on the Cabin Deck, which was the second deck up. The other room, the room they were in now, was a floor higher on the Texas Deck and at the very end of the starboard side. The lower cabin was a larger suite, opening up into the main area of the Cabin Deck. The Texas Deck cabin was barely big enough for all of them to stand together, and the door opened up to the outer decks. It did have a small porthole window that looked out on the promenade deck, which didn't make Flynn feel one bit more comfortable about the tiny space.

Rose had already stretched out on the cot they had caused to be set up, and Cage sat gingerly on the edge at Rose's hip. Whether he was trying not to tip over the flimsy cot or was self-conscious of where he touched Rose, Flynn didn't know.

"I'll take Rose," Flynn answered grudgingly, looking over them. Flynn knew, on the surface, that it seemed Cage was the easier prisoner to control, and he knew that it would seem that Flynn was giving him to Wash to guard for that reason. But Flynn was afraid of what Rose would say to Wash, more than what he would do to him.

Even with just the one hand, Wash was no leisurely fight. But he was susceptible to a silver tongue and a sad story; he had already proved that in regard to Cage and Rose and their unlikely little burgeoning romance. Rose was a silver-tongued devil if Flynn had ever seen one. And while the silent scout may have had a tale sad enough to win over the hardest of hearts, he certainly wouldn't be telling it to anyone.

"You want to risk putting him in the dining salon for supper?" Wash asked with a frown.

Flynn shrugged. "I think we can handle anyone who recognizes him."

Seeing the man in the Emporium had spooked Rose, but the charismatic Englishman had recovered quickly from the incident. He didn't seem worried now, and so Flynn had brushed the incident aside entirely. Unless they tried it while Rose was in his custody, it was no business of Flynn's who wanted to kill him. Flynn narrowed his eyes at Rose. He wasn't worried about the other passengers. If trouble came, it would come from Rose himself.

"I'll mind my manners, marshals," Rose crooned, as if he knew what Flynn had been thinking. "We'll be on the river, after all. I can't exactly throw myself overboard and doggy paddle to safety."

"You may not be able to swim it, but just remember you can still be thrown overboard," Wash warned with a quirk to his lips.

Rose raised one eyebrow and gave Wash a slight bow of his head to acknowledge the threat, his mouth twitching with a smile. To Flynn's mounting unease, Rose seemed to be enjoying himself more and more as his situation became increasingly difficult to escape. At this rate, the man would be practically giddy once his neck was in a noose.

Cage glanced at Wash and cocked an eyebrow as soon as they shut the cabin door behind them.

"If that man don't beat the Dutch, huh?" Wash said. "Some men just got guts of iron, I reckon. I'm surprised Flynn ain't killed him yet."

Cage smiled. So was he, actually. Gabriel was pushing the already cranky marshal a little too much for Cage's comfort, but he supposed that was just the kind of man Gabriel was.

"Ain't ever seen someone poke Flynn like that," Wash mused. He put his hand gently on the back of Cage's elbow and led him discreetly down the outer deck toward the grand stairwell all the way near the bow of the boat.

Cage glanced sideways at Wash, inclining his head.

"It's just this side of amusing," Wash admitted. He looked at Cage and shook his head, a teasing light entering his eyes. "Don't you go telling Flynn I said so, though."

Cage raised his hands and nodded, smiling crookedly. His chains clanked when he lowered his hands again. Cage found himself hoping they didn't meet any of the other passengers as they made their way down the stairs. Their cabin was a deck below, right across a small corridor from the huge main cabin area and opposite the dining salon, where people would soon be gathered, socializing and playing cards and sipping genteelly at expensive liquors. The large room had struck Cage stupid when he'd first entered it, with its high sweeping ceiling, ornate chandeliers, shining tin tiles on the walls, and plush carpet.

He was wearing the new clothing they'd purchased, the highest quality the store had possessed, all at Gabriel's insistence. They'd also had time to visit the barber, and he was clean-shaven. His hair had been cut as well, a little too short probably. But at least it wasn't dirty anymore. He looked like a gentleman, save for the irons on his wrists. He tried to hide them, but it was nearly impossible, and he held his new hat between two fingers, trying to make it cover the chains.

"Found you a nice hat, I hope?" Wash asked as they strolled through the vacant cabin area of the Cabin Deck. "Nice beaver one, maybe?"

Cage smiled fondly at the marshal and nodded. He liked how the marshal always spoke to him as if he might one time respond with more than a nod or shake of his head. It spoke of the man's eternal optimism.

Cage had found, over the years, that you could hear a lot about a man if you stayed quiet long enough.

Flynn sat staring at Rose after Wash and Cage had left them. He was thinking of all the possible escape routes the dining salon would offer: the unguarded exit and the bank of stained glass windows at the bow. All the people milling about and all the weaponry the other passengers would be carrying. It was a horrifying thought, all of the ways in which Rose could cause trouble. Especially if they were going to have to keep him low-key and unrestrained like the captain had requested.

The captain might just have to be disappointed tonight. Flynn would put Rose in irons if he had to, even if it did cause trouble.

Maybe having food delivered to the room would be the better option, after all.

Rose grinned at him as if he knew what Flynn was thinking. "We could go to dinner early," he suggested helpfully.

"We'll go at the time we agreed on."

Rose merely shrugged and continued to smile. Several minutes later, he shifted and cleared his throat. "You know, if the goal is to draw little to no attention, you may want to go ahead and take these off." He raised his wrists and clanked his chains noisily.

"And why is that?"

"To give the marks on my wrists time to go away," Rose answered, as if that should be obvious.

Flynn frowned and leaned forward as Rose held out his hands. He was surprised to find the skin beneath the iron rubbed red and even bleeding in places. Flynn hadn't realized they were so tight. He opened his mouth to say something—an apology for not allowing him to pad the irons with anything—but he couldn't force the words out as he met Rose's eyes. He just couldn't make himself say sorry to the man.

"Give 'em here," he said gruffly instead, gesturing for Rose's hands as he extracted the keys from his pocket.

Rose shifted closer to the edge of his cot and draped his hands across the narrow space between them.

Flynn took the chain that attached the two cuffs and pulled it, glancing up at Rose as he placed the key against the first lock.

"One more blow to the head and you're likely to slobber the rest of your life."

"I'm well aware," Rose said wryly.

"I'd take your word for it if you said you won't try nothing else," Flynn offered. He may have been taking a foolhardy risk by doing it, but Rose seemed the type to honor his word when he gave it, as odd as that observation seemed to Flynn.

Rose pressed his lips together tightly, obviously mulling over the offer. "I am a man of my word, Marshal Flynn," he said in a low, smooth voice. Flynn waited with eyebrows raised, and Rose simply smirked at him. "I wouldn't feel right giving it, in that respect."

Flynn rolled his eyes and sighed, turning the key and releasing Rose's hand anyway. He unlocked the second cuff and watched warily as Rose rubbed at his sore wrists.

"I reckon I could allow you to change into something clean," Flynn mused as he scrutinized Rose. His clothes were still damp from his escapade in the bath, and he looked tattered.

"That would be quite human of you. If you'll just hand me my bag—"

"I'll hand you whatever you want out of your bag," Flynn interrupted sternly. "Your hands ain't going in that thing where I can't see 'em."

"Fair enough," Rose said with an elegant shrug.

Flynn got up slowly, his eyes never leaving Rose as he opened up the bag and extracted several items of clothing. It was all high-quality fabric, obviously stuffed haphazardly into the bag by someone who had not cared much for Rose or his belongings. The deputies in Junction City had made a quick job of gathering his things.

"If they left me any valuables, I'll be quite shocked," Rose murmured with a huff.

Flynn patted down a white linen shirt and then handed it to Rose. He inspected a pair of pinstriped trousers and a black silk vest as well, and finding nothing in the pockets or in the lining, he handed them over. There were no undergarments of any sort to be found.

"That's low," Rose grumbled to himself as he disrobed unselfconsciously. "Stealing my underthings. Those were from Paris."

"I'm sure they were something to write home about."

Rose snorted at him unhappily and went about putting on his clean clothing. Flynn had to admit the man cut a striking figure once he cleaned himself up, much like Cage. They might turn heads, but it wouldn't be because they were in irons.

Flynn handed Rose a wool frock coat to top off the attire and the man shrugged into it with a nod of thanks. He patted the lapel pocket and then winced. "My pocket watch is gone."

"Was it a good one?" Flynn asked, not particularly feeling sorry for the man.

"It was a Howard," Rose answered, patting the other pockets and frowning. "My grandfather's. It was . . . it was the only thing I had left of him."

Flynn was surprised that he looked genuinely upset. He hadn't thought the man capable of true, honest-to-God feelings.

"Will you check the bottom of the bag?" Rose requested as Flynn pondered him.

Flynn narrowed his eyes suspiciously, but he bent back over the bag to rummage around the loose things at the bottom. He shook his head when he found nothing that felt like a pocket watch.

Rose's shoulders slumped. Flynn again had the fleeting impression that he might actually harbor real emotions under all his charisma, that he just hid it all away under an infuriating smile.

"Well. Nothing to do about it now, I suppose," Rose murmured as he adjusted the jacket and smoothed it over.

Flynn slid into his own jacket and fixed his collar, then stared at Rose almost sympathetically for a moment. "Come here," he said as he stepped forward and took hold of Rose's necktie. He adjusted it and tied it tighter, straightening it and fixing it with just one glance up into Rose's eyes as he did it, trying to ignore the flush he could feel rising to his cheeks and the warmth in his belly. He moved back when he was done and nodded in approval.

"Thank you, Marshal," Rose said, sounding surprised. He stood with his hat in his hands, and he frowned down at it thoughtfully. After being crushed and thrown out the hotel window, then carried all around town in the dog's mouth, the battered bowler had definitely seen better days. The dog had brought it to him just before they had reached the gangplank to board the ship after their trip to the Emporium, and Flynn had thought both man and mutt were going to cry as they finally parted a second time.

Koda had struck Flynn like he was just doing what he had been told as he sat obediently in the mud, like he was grudgingly following some prearranged plan. The dog, Flynn had realized, bothered him even more than the man did.

"Perhaps I would do better to go without my hat tonight," Rose murmured as he finally looked up at Flynn and held the hat up for inspection.

Flynn examined the bowler hat, then Rose dubiously. "Good call," he agreed with a nod at the door. "You'll do fine. Let's go."

They walked side by side down the breezy outer deck toward the grand staircase, Flynn's hand discreetly resting on his gun the entire way. To his surprise, Rose in no way tried to draw attention to himself as they moved through the sparse crowd. The man kept his head down and kept touching his finger nervously to his hairline, as if wanting to find a hat there. It hit Flynn suddenly that Rose was used to hiding his face in crowds, and that he was probably afraid of being recognized. Perhaps leaving the hat behind hadn't been such a good idea after all.

"You're looking a might all-overish there, Rose," Flynn murmured to him as the brisk wind off the river caught at their clothing and tugged at the tails of their jackets. Flynn stopped and took in a deep breath of the river air. It wasn't exactly a pleasant smell.

"I don't like crowds, Marshal," Rose responded irritably. He sniffed at the air and winced. "Ah, the aroma of river mud."

Flynn nodded and smirked. They turned around the curved bow of the ship and headed down the grand staircase, which fed them right into the main cabin. It was a beautiful boat, with all the luxuries you could want while traveling down the river. Flynn wished they could take the riverboat back to St. Louis on the return trip, just him and Wash together. It would be quite a treat to experience all this with his friend instead of the annoying outlaw he was escorting.

They cut through small groups of milling, chatting people. The ladies and children, what few there were, were all impeccably dressed and done up, flounces and lace and umbrellas galore. Every one of them could have been going to the highest of society functions. The men were a different matter altogether. Some were dressed in fancy clothes, like Rose. Others wore a more traditional, less impressive suit, like Flynn. And some of the men were in working clothes, still dusty from the trails as they chatted politely with the womenfolk. It was a typical scene, one Flynn had heard many a tenderfoot remark on. Apparently, west of the Mississippi was the only place a man wasn't judged by his clothes alone.

Even knowing this, Flynn was glad they had thought to outfit Cage in more traditional clothing. The homemade oilskins would have looked too close to a savage's attire for the comfort of inexperienced or uninformed passengers. The days of the mountain men lumbering around in their oilskins were long gone. The oddity would have drawn far too much attention to their group for Flynn's peace of mind.

As Flynn observed their fellow passengers, a man passed by them and bumped hard into Rose's shoulder, sending him off-balance and falling into Flynn. Flynn's hand tightened on his gun, immediately thinking it a ploy of Rose's to try to escape again. But Rose merely righted himself with a hand on Flynn's shoulder and turned to the man who'd nearly knocked him over.

"Pardon me," Rose offered politely to the man, who went on his way with only a cursory glance at Rose. Rose faced Flynn and shrugged. "Ruffians," he said with sarcastic relish.

Flynn watched the stranger go, then shrugged as well when he met Rose's eyes. "Some of these folks been drinking since they boarded. Might do well to stay to the shadows, hmm?"

"For once we agree," Rose said, looking around uncomfortably.

Flynn caught sight of Wash and Cage waiting at the entrance to the dining salon behind the base of the grand stairs, and he discreetly took Rose's elbow and led him onward.

He smiled at Wash as they approached and received one of Wash's crooked grins in return. It wasn't the first time in his life he'd been struck by how well Wash cleaned up. Or by what a good-looking man Cage had turned out to be. He immediately pushed back the thoughts and cleared his throat as they drew closer.

The two marshals and their prisoners converged at the entrance to the salon, and Flynn could hear the laughter, chatter, and music playing from within.

"Shall we?" Wash asked cheerfully.

"I want it understood," Flynn said to the two prisoners sternly. "The first sign of trouble and you're being dragged out of there unconscious. Got it?"

Rose and Cage both nodded obediently. Cage was wearing one of the new hats he'd purchased in St. Louis, but he was holding the second one Flynn had told him to buy. He lifted it to show Flynn that the hat was the only thing in his hands, then he held it out to Rose carefully. Rose took it, and the two men shared a significant look and warm smiles as Rose slid the gray hat onto his head with a nod of thanks.

Flynn gave them both a last once-over and then gestured for them to head into the salon. If this went smoothly, Flynn would have to start attending church regularly again.

# CHAPTER 8

age and the others stepped into the dining salon, and Cage looked around uneasily. The place wasn't overly crowded, but it was busier than he'd expected it to be at such an early hour. There wasn't much else to keep passengers entertained on the steamer; of course the saloon would be crowded. He hesitated, slowing until Flynn was at his back. He didn't know if the marshals would decide to leave and come back later or go on with dinner now. Cage could feel how tense Flynn was in the chaotic atmosphere, and so he stuck close to him, hoping to reassure him that he didn't intend to try to escape. Edgy lawmen with loaded guns were just as dangerous as cornered outlaws.

Cage didn't plan on running. It was too hard on the nerves, for one. But he trusted in Gabriel to have a plan, and he was going to stick around to see how it turned out. If it worked and they somehow got out of this legal mess unscathed, then Cage thought maybe they had a chance at something worth risking it for. The few moments they'd been able to steal together had felt special. If Gabiel's plan didn't work, then the aftermath would at least be entertaining to watch.

The tables were lined up down the center of the room, with the ornate and polished stove off to the left and a bar lining the right wall. No one got to sit with their backs against the walls on a riverboat. Even with the gilded mirrors lining the salon, Cage shifted nervously in his seat, not liking the feeling of his back exposed to the large room and the crowd of strangers coming and going in it. Beside him, Gabriel seemed calm, but Cage could see his head turning every so often as his eyes darted to check behind him.

"This should prove to be charming," Gabriel murmured to him.

Cage smiled. They weren't restrained, at least. He held up his hands and laced his fingers together, setting his joined fists on the table in front of him.

Gabriel was watching him sideways. "I agree," he said with a smirk. "A shame we can't make better use of our newfound freedom."

Cage turned his head toward Gabriel carefully as a dull, slow heat bloomed inside him. Just the prospect of being alone with Gabriel was exciting.

"Enough of that," Flynn said sternly.

"He wasn't talking about escaping, Flynn," Wash said under his breath.

Cage tried not to smile at the scandalized expression on Flynn's face. Gabriel did laugh, and Cage could feel his face growing warmer as he glanced away. He took his hands from the table, placing them on his knees to keep from fidgeting.

While Gabriel lightly poked fun at Flynn, Cage used the opportunity to study him, to truly ponder him. He couldn't explain the almost instant feelings he'd developed for the man. He didn't really want to try because deep down he feared they might not be real. And Cage wanted them to be real, he knew that much, and he figured if he left them alone long enough, they'd be real eventually. If they had time before a hangman's noose caught one or both of them. And if they weren't real already.

Cage closed his eyes and cleared his throat, telling himself not to let his mind wander. He was surprised when Gabriel's hand found his under the table, his fingers sliding over Cage's and then closing around his palm. Cage's head jerked up, and he looked at Gabriel with wide eyes, taken aback by the warmth that continued to spread through him at the simple touch.

Gabriel was watching him, smiling almost serenely. He winked when Cage met his eyes. Cage wondered about the expression on his face. He frowned, but Gabriel just squeezed his hand and continued to hold it under the table. Cage got the message. Soon, Gabriel was saying.

Cage nodded and sat back in his seat. He'd never been an edgy person or a worrier, but if he chose to be any sort of companion to Gabriel Rose, he could see himself becoming a nervous wreck very quickly.

He met Gabriel's eyes again, and his lips twitched into a smile. It would probably be worth it.

Dinner was surprisingly civil, very nearly enjoyable. Flynn found himself distracted much of the meal by worrying about Rose's hands beneath the table, but he kept telling himself there was no way the man could have obtained a weapon, and if he had one, he would have used it by now.

It wasn't until the salon was beginning to fill up and they were leaving to get some fresh air before returning to their cabins that trouble presented itself. They had left the salon through one of the ornate doorways toward the bow that led out to the foredeck, enjoying the cool evening air that flowed over and around the deck.

Flynn had just taken hold of Rose's elbow to make certain he didn't lose him in the crowd when Wash stopped him, pulling them over to the side, out of the way of the diners coming and going. "What say we give them some more time to themselves?" he asked Flynn, his voice a bare whisper. Rose and Cage stood just steps away, both their heads bowed as they tried to appear like they weren't eavesdropping.

"Time alone?" Flynn asked incredulously. "You mean like before, when they tried to escape?"

"Where are they gonna go?" Wash posed, his voice even. "What's the harm in clearing one of the cabins and letting them have an hour or two?"

Flynn closed his eyes and shook his head, not even able to fathom what Wash was thinking.

"Put yourself in their shoes a minute," Wash urged, but Flynn continued to shake his head.

"Our responsibility is to get them to New Orleans for trial, not to make sure they're happy when they get there. You know what they'd do with those two hours, and I for one do not plan to sit in a hallway and guard a cabin while that goes on."

"Why not?"

"Wash, really!"

"Dusty Rose!" a voice shouted suddenly from behind them.

Flynn whirled and saw a man standing near the outer railing of the boat, the same man who had bumped into Rose before dinner. His coat was pushed back over his low-slung holster and his legs were spread slightly apart. There was no mistaking that stance, nor the challenge he had called. Every greenhorn and tin star in the country thought a gun battle went down like Hickok and Tutt in the town square in '65. But calling a man out like that was a good way to get killed, not famous. Flynn's heart skipped a beat and his breath caught as the world slowed around him.

Rose faced the man, his hand going to his hip instinctively. Flynn saw the color drain from Rose's face as he remembered too late that he was unarmed. The man who had addressed him smirked slowly, and drew his gun.

Flynn went for his own pistol even as Rose ducked and turned, reaching for the gun at Flynn's other hip. A shot sounded before Flynn could even clear his gun, and he watched in confused relief as the stranger staggered back and dropped his six-shooter to the planks of the deck. He hit his knees as he stared at Flynn and the others in disbelief, holding his ruined and bleeding right forearm to his chest.

Flynn realized that his heart was racing and he was gaping. He had never seen anyone that fast in his life. The fact that the shooter hadn't even been armed made the feat that much more impressive.

Rose stood just in front of him, looking at the bleeding man with much the same shock that Flynn felt. They both stared at Cage, who was calmly holding Wash's smoking gun in his hand.

Cage lowered the weapon, spinning it around his forefinger and thumb as if it were second nature. He then flipped it and slid it back into Wash's holster like he hoped no one would notice the action if it were done quickly enough.

The three of them gawked at him.

"I'll be damned," Wash finally breathed. He replaced the gun he had drawn from his other holster without taking his eyes off Cage.

Cage cleared his throat and looked at the man he had shot, seemingly without remorse, as the world returned to its rightful speed and women began swooning around them.

"That's got to be one of the fastest draws I've ever seen," Gabriel was saying as the marshals ushered them hastily back to their cabin. His eyes shone excitedly, and he sounded like a small child nagging his father for another piece of candy. "Marshal, give him your belt, let him do it again!"

Cage blushed deeply and ducked into their cabin with relief, going to the far wall and keeping his head bowed. He held his hands in front of him, waiting for the chains to be clapped back on. Now that the marshals knew he could handle iron, they'd be sure to restrain him heavily just like they were Gabriel.

Flynn shoved Gabriel into the room and slammed the door behind them. Cage glanced up, nerves jostling. Wash was staring at him with his mouth still ajar, and Gabriel was grinning delightedly. Flynn glared at Gabriel like he might hit him just to have something to do with himself.

"You saved my life," Gabriel said to Cage with a grin that seemed permanent now. He took a step closer, but Wash automatically reached out and halted his progress without taking his eyes off Cage. "I've only ever seen a few men who could handle a gun like that," Gabriel continued in a soft, rushed voice, almost eager as he edged closer despite Wash's hand across his chest. "Who are you, really? A man doesn't handle iron like that without being known."

Cage swallowed and shook his head. He pointed to his own chest and shrugged.

"You're just you," Gabriel murmured, sounding an odd mixture of amused, impressed, and worried now.

Cage nodded, his throat aching oddly as he met Gabriel's eyes. No matter what he tried to say, Gabriel always seemed to understand. It was just one more reason Gabriel was swiftly becoming important to him. Important enough to give away his own secrets for him—like the fact that he could handle a gun like few men could.

Gabriel moved as Wash's arm dropped away from his chest, and he stood in front of Cage, head tilted back as he searched Cage's eyes and grinned. His eyes glinted, like he knew what Cage was thinking

"All right, break it up," Flynn said, though he still sounded more shocked than anything else.

Gabriel's smile softened. "Thank you, Cage," he whispered.

Cage's lips parted in surprise, and Gabriel kissed him before he could react further.

Behind him, Wash cleared his throat and laughed. Cage saw the marshal glance away as Gabriel backed up. Flynn's jaw had dropped, and he looked slightly scandalized. He turned bright red and stepped forward to take Gabriel's arm and move him away.

"Enough of that."

"What's the harm in it?" Wash asked with a grin that matched Gabriel's. "That was some mighty fine shooting. Let him get his reward."

"I don't give a Continental what sorta shooting it was! Anyone can handle a gun like that ain't gonna be let loose to do as he pleases under my watch. That goes for you too!" Flynn snapped as he rounded on Gabriel and wagged a finger in his face before turning back to Wash. "We got to keep them separated."

"Flynn, he's not dangerous. He reacted, same as you and me. He just did it a heck of a lot faster," Wash said wryly as he winked at Cage.

Cage felt himself blush again and cleared his throat uncomfortably. He hadn't handled a gun in months. He was no longer accustomed to the attention the skill brought.

"You drew across your body," Gabriel said to him, seemingly ignoring the two marshals.

Cage met Gabriel's eyes and swallowed with difficulty.

"You wear your guns backward?" Gabriel asked him.

Cage gave a short, jerky nod in answer, though he didn't want to answer at all.

"Means you spent time around the border, yeah? Texas, maybe? New Mexico?" Gabriel guessed.

Cage blinked rapidly and looked away, unable to answer and unable to look into Gabriel's eyes and lie, even if the lie was only a shake of his head. His gaze darted back to Gabriel to find the man watching him. He was no longer smiling. His brow was furrowed as he stared at Cage. Cage could practically see his mental gears turning. He held his breath, waiting for Gabriel's sharp mind to make a decision with the new information he'd gleaned.

Then Gabriel winked at him suddenly, the corner of his mouth twitching into a brief smirk before he schooled his face into seriousness once more. Cage stared at him in confusion. He didn't understand the man at all. He seemed to jump from emotion to emotion like a tumbleweed in a dust storm, and Cage couldn't keep up. He was relieved by Gabriel's easy acceptance, all the same.

When he turned his attention back to the two marshals, it seemed that Wash had won a concession. Flynn was red-faced and clearly trying to keep his temper under control.

"I'm going to go and see what's what," Flynn told them all, obviously flustered and doubly embarrassed over the fact that he was.

He headed out of the cabin before Wash could comment. The marshal huffed and then turned to Cage as soon as the door was shut.

"Color me impressed, son," he said with a smile.

Cage's face flushed again but he nodded in acknowledgment. He glanced at Gabriel almost pleadingly.

The marshal looked between them and tried to hide his smirk. "I'm going to go . . . stand out in the hallway for a minute. Just to catch some air," he announced, then he slipped out of the cabin and left them alone.

Cage stared at the door in shock. After the morning's adventures with Gabriel's escape attempt, he couldn't imagine what Wash was thinking.

"A trusting soul, isn't he?" Gabriel murmured as he stood examining Cage. "Odd quality for a man in his line of work."

Cage nodded almost imperceptibly and shifted his weight from one foot to the other. Gabriel took a few steps closer until he was standing within reach once more. Cage raised his hand until his fingertips rested against Gabriel's cheekbone, and he slid them across it, tracing down Gabriel's jaw.

Gabriel grinned. Then he moved even closer. Cage's hair had come loose from its leather string as they'd been hustling to get back to the cabin, and Gabriel ran his hand through it. He pushed it back, off Cage's face, his fingers trailing down Cage's ear. His eyes didn't leave Cage's.

"Where'd you learn to shoot like that?" he asked in a whisper.

Cage pressed his lips tightly together. They both knew he couldn't truly answer, and they both knew deep down he didn't *want* to answer. He slid his hand around the back of Gabriel's neck and tugged him closer, his heart racing as he took liberties he had not dared take with someone in almost a year.

Their eyes still locked, Cage gave into the urge and kissed him. He pulled Gabriel to him and wrapped his other arm around his body, holding him and bending him backward with the force of the sudden motion. His hand tightened on the side of Gabriel's neck, his thumb digging under Gabriel's chin as he tilted his head up and kissed him hungrily.

Gabriel didn't struggle against the rough treatment, merely moved with it and moaned into Cage's mouth. He held Cage by his upper arms, fingers clutching at Cage's new jacket.

Cage turned him and pushed him against the wall, and Gabriel's hands dragged up into his hair again. The kiss was a tinge desperate, but Cage didn't care. Even as Gabriel tried to speak, Cage delved into more kisses. Harder kisses. Biting kisses that smothered the attempts.

For the second time since meeting him, Cage found that he wanted to say something to Gabriel. It was almost a physical need, one that mingled with the other physical needs Gabriel had stirred in him. He couldn't speak, though, and so he merely kissed Gabriel with all the pent-up sentiments he had been harboring. Oh, how he wished the marshals would really give them those few hours alone.

"It's okay," Gabriel finally managed to murmur into the kiss. He caressed Cage's neck and then wrapped him up in a hug.

Cage relaxed his grip and licked his own lips as he rested his forehead against Gabriel's temple. They stood together in the intimate embrace, Cage desperately wishing for more and trying to decide how he could let Gabriel know what he was thinking.

"It's okay," Gabriel repeated, his voice low and confident. He gave a little laugh. "I talk enough for the both of us."

Cage smiled and released a slow breath. He let his hand slide down the side of Gabriel's neck to his shoulder as they put some distance between their bodies. There was too much temptation here for them to remain as they'd been, and Cage knew Wash wouldn't give them long. He heard Flynn's voice outside the door, demanding to know what Wash was doing out in the hallway.

His heart was still racing as he looked into Gabriel's eyes.

Gabriel, too, seemed flustered. His cheeks were flushed and his dark eyes shone in the low light. He was grinning, obviously having fallen victim to the same physical desires Cage was now battling. Cage enjoyed the idea that he had done that to the normally imperturbable man. He enjoyed a lot of things about what he had just done. So he went ahead and did it again, grabbing Gabriel and pressing him into the wall to steal more kisses.

"I'm not going to have this fight again," Wash said as Flynn glowered at him.

Flynn recognized his tone of voice as one that meant the end of an argument. He took a step toward him anyway and pointed at the closed door to the cabin.

"They are dangerous men, Wash. You've been doing this long enough to know what a dangerous man who's cornered is capable of!"

"And you're well aware what *I'm* capable of," Wash snarled back at him, his green eyes flashing. "You want to keep treating me like a child, you can step off at the next stop and find your own damn way back to Lincoln. Hell, you can step off now, for all I care. I ain't yours to protect, understand?"

Flynn staggered back and stared at him as if he'd been slapped. The words cut deep, and Flynn didn't want to examine why. His jaw tightened, and he reached up and banged on the door without looking away from Wash. "Rose!"

Several tense seconds later, Rose came to the door and moved out into the narrow corridor, surprisingly obedient.

"Thank you, Marshal," Rose murmured to Wash as he moved past him.

Wash nodded, his hard eyes still on Flynn. "Everything okay with the shooter?" he asked Flynn coldly.

Flynn merely nodded and took hold of Rose's elbow. "Meet you in the morning," he huffed, and he led Rose away.

"Am I sensing some strain between the two of you?" Rose asked as they made their way down a small side hall and to a set of cramped stairs that would take them up to their deck. "I hope I've not been the cause of too much—"

"Shut up."

"If I may offer some advice—"

"I said shut up," Flynn gritted out.

"A man like Marshal Washington is not accustomed to being thought weak," Rose continued, heedless of Flynn's warnings. "Especially with the use of only one arm now, you might try showing you have more faith in him."

"You might try shutting your damn mouth," Flynn snapped as they mounted the wooden stairs. "And stop trying to escape!"

"I haven't! Not . . . recently."

Flynn practically growled at the man as they came to the door of their cabin, and he gestured for him to enter first.

"And you must admit you would have been disappointed had I not at least made one attempt."

"Shut up, Rose. Just get ready for bed. I'm chaining you to your damn cot tonight."

"That should be quite effective," Rose said with a nod as he shrugged out of his frock coat and tossed it onto the flimsy cot. "Or I'll just pick the cot up and take it with me when I decide to make my great escape. Perhaps it will even float."

Flynn fought back the urge to throttle him. He ripped his tie off and tossed it at Rose in frustration.

It fluttered between them, and they both watched it until it landed at Rose's feet. Rose looked up at Flynn, obviously struggling to repress a laugh as his lips twitched.

"Don't say a damn word," Flynn grumbled.

"I assure you, Marshal, I wouldn't dare."

Hours later, Flynn lay in the cabin's bunk, awake and thoughtful and restless. He wanted desperately to go knock on Wash's door and apologize. He had taken the time to cool down and really think about what Rose had said to him. It made a certain sort of sense, loath though he was to admit it.

He glanced over at the dark shape that was his prisoner. He appeared to be asleep, motionless and breathing evenly. But Flynn knew better. He cleared his throat.

"Is it true you're . . . What I mean to say is— Uhh . . ." Flynn closed his eyes and shook his head in the darkness.

"You don't strike me as the type to stutter, Marshal," Rose said in a muffled voice. He lay with his hat over his face and his hands neatly folded on his stomach. "Is it true I'm what?"

Flynn glared at the man, wishing he had never opened his mouth. Now, he would have to ask his question or think up something else on the fly. He could just tell the man to shut up and be done with it, but his curiosity was getting the better of him. Just because Rose had kissed a man who had saved his life didn't mean the gossip about Rose was true. He sighed and peered at the flickering hurricane lamp that was bolted to the wall of their cabin.

"Is it true you bed men instead of women?" he asked, his interest winning out over embarrassment. He blushed hotly in the dark of the cabin anyway.

"Why, Marshal, wherever did you hear such a thing?" Rose asked in feigned innocence, obviously aware of Flynn's discomfort and enjoying it a little too much. He raised his shackled hands and lifted the brim of his hat, peering sideways at Flynn with a smirk. Flynn was glad that the flickering light masked his blush as Rose examined him. "Yes, it is."

Flynn turned his head with a jerk and blinked at his prisoner in shock, more from the easy admission than the actual answer. "Why?" he blurted.

Rose rested his head back against his thin pillow and laughed. "Marshal, you are endearingly naïve sometimes," he gasped as he tried to contain his laughter. He snickered as he slid his hat back over his eyes.

Flynn stared at him. Whenever Rose spoke, it always seemed like some sort of mental trap, and Flynn again found himself regretting ever having opened his mouth and yet struggling against the urge to ask more.

"And you, Marshal Flynn? Do you prefer men as well when given the choice?" Rose asked, as if questioning whether the sky was blue.

"That's none of your goddamned business. Shut up. Go to sleep," Flynn ordered as he rolled onto his other side, thoroughly scandalized and done with the conversation.

Rose's soft laughter echoed behind him. "There is a certain amount of awkwardness to figuring it out, I admit. At first. But the way you touch yourself is the way you touch another man," the prisoner continued in that slow, lilting drawl that Flynn had long ago begun to hate. "It's not at all difficult to figure out for those who may be inclined."

"I said shut up," Flynn growled in annoyance. He didn't know whether the discussion was embarrassing him or causing too much interest, but either way he wanted it stopped. A brief thought of Wash lying in the cabin several decks down distracted him from growing even more outraged at the subject.

"You were the one who asked. Do you truly want a real answer as to why?"

Flynn swallowed hard, determined to remain silent.

"I never made a conscious decision about it," Rose said after a few moments. "I suppose I was just made that way. You won't hear me complaining. I find an emotional connection much easier to form with a gentleman. Physically, it's quite stimulating as well."

Flynn snorted loudly and shook his head. The answer struck too close to his own mind for his comfort. He'd always found himself admiring the physical features of gentlemen far more than those of ladies, seeking out the company of other men rather than women during social gatherings and pining for the easy camaraderie of another man rather than the awkward social intercourse of any woman he'd ever courted. He supposed Rose was right, mostly. That was just the way he'd been made.

"I think you're more than merely curious. There is purpose to your inquiries," Rose went on insightfully. Flynn heard his chains clank once more. "Who is the lucky gentleman who has earned himself the honor of your amorous affections?"

Flynn sat up so fast he nearly hit his head on the shelf above the cabin's berth. He flopped back down onto his other side and glared at Rose through the flickering light. Rose had rolled onto his side as well and was looking at Flynn with eyes that danced in the low light.

"I ain't got amorous affections for nobody."

"The lady doth protest too much."

"What?" Flynn demanded.

"It's Shakespeare, Marshal."

"Don't care what it is, you call me a lady again, you'll be swimming to New Orleans," Flynn promised. He stood and reached for the hurricane lamp, dousing the flame and throwing the cabin into darkness.

"Come now, Marshal, I'm dying of curiosity," Rose drawled. "Is it some poor stable boy in Lincoln?"

"No," Flynn grunted as he rolled onto his back and stared up into the darkness.

"Ranch hand? Mercantile man? Wandering gambler?" Rose prodded.

"I done told you—"

"Is it me?" Rose asked with a mischievous smirk.

Flynn shot him a dirty look. "Hell, no."

"It's the good Marshal Washington, isn't it?" Rose asked with an audible grin.

Flynn blinked and licked his lips nervously as he lay there, trying desperately to think of something to say and feeling cornered by Rose's unusual insight into his mind.

"All right, Marshal, if you want to stay quiet, that's your right. It's not as if you have yourself an opportunity to ask questions of a man who knows and doesn't mind to give you answers. I keep a secret quite well too."

"Shut up," Flynn ordered, but his voice had gone hoarse.

"I dare say he would be receptive to such a thing," Rose said before he rolled onto his back again and placed his hat over his face once more.

Flynn glanced over at him in surprise. "What do you mean?"

"Do sleep well, Marshal Flynn," Rose drawled quietly.

# CHAPTER 9

age lay awake in the cabin's berth, frowning up at the circle of waning moonlight that was the porthole in their large cabin. It had come equipped with a double bed, and Wash had insisted they share it rather than utilizing the cot, pointing out that the bed was larger and so was Cage. Cage told himself that it was because the berth was sturdier to chain him to than the cot would have been and that Wash was being smart rather than kind, but he sort of doubted it. Wash just struck him as that type of man. Cage hadn't known many truly good-hearted men in his life. He was having trouble reconciling it.

A thump on the main deck one level below them startled him out of his thoughts, and he raised his head, trying to hear.

"Something wrong?" Wash asked from his spot on the other side of the bed.

Cage glanced over at him in the darkness, scowling at him.

"Sorry," Wash said after a few seconds of silence. He rolled up onto his elbow and reached for the hurricane lamp. When he turned it on, the shadows in the room danced as the flame grew bigger, and Cage could see him better. Wash was smiling at him sleepily. "Keep forgetting you can't answer. You just got that quiet look about you, anyways."

Cage sat up in the bed and crossed his legs, ducking his head to listen. He pointed to his ear and then pointed again at the window.

"I know you can hear fine, Cage," Wash said as he sat up as well and rubbed at his eyes with the heel of his hand.

Cage shook his head in frustration and sighed.

"What?" Wash asked. At least he knew he had misunderstood. Most people didn't even grasp that much. Or care if they did realize it.

Cage made to stand but was stopped with a jerk when the chain that attached one hand to the wooden slats under the bed halted his progress. He sat back down on the bed with a thump and a grunt.

Wash leaned forward, frowning. Cage pointed again at the window, then to his ear once more.

"You heard something?"

Cage nodded.

"What was it?"

Cage winced and shook his head.

"Something out of place?"

Cage frowned and shrugged helplessly. It was hard to say with certainty because of the noise from the paddle wheel and the rushing water, and Cage wasn't exactly accustomed to life on the river in the first place. But he would bet his life on what he thought he'd heard: the heavy landing of someone boarding the steamer. He made a motion with his hands like a man climbing a ladder.

Wash watched him carefully. "I don't understand, son," he finally said apologetically.

Cage sighed and nodded, lowering his head.

Wash sat in bed for another moment. Suddenly, he stood and walked around the end of the bed to Cage's side, digging in his pocket. Cage watched in confusion as he came closer and leaned over him. He realized with a bit of shock that Wash was reaching for the chain that bound him to the bed.

He looked up at the marshal questioningly.

"I may not trust Rose as far as I can toss an ox," Wash murmured, "but you don't deserve to be chained to your damn bed like an outlaw."

Cage wet his lips and watched as Wash unlocked the cuff and removed it from his hand. He automatically rubbed his sore wrist, looking up at Wash again. He swallowed around an unfamiliar tightness in his throat and mouthed the words "thank you."

"You're welcome, son. Just don't go tellin' Flynn," Wash said with a smirk as he turned away.

Cage snorted at him and smiled.

Suddenly there was a ruckus from the lobby outside, banging and shouting up and down the corridor. When the pounding reached their door, Cage had already jumped to his feet. Marshal Washington whirled in alarm, his gun out of reach as the door was kicked open and a man stepped in, shotgun leveled at them.

"We're havin' a party down yonder," the stranger drawled from behind a dirty handkerchief tied over his nose and mouth. "Why don't y'all join us?"

"Marshall Flynn," Rose hissed in the darkness.

Flynn was immediately alert, blinking into the darkness as he tried to locate his prisoner.

"Marshal Flynn," Rose repeated, his voice an urgent, sharp whisper. "You've got trouble, Marshal."

Flynn's gun was in his hand as he peered at the dim circle of light cast by the porthole of the cabin. Rose's cot lay directly beneath it, and the moonlight filtering through the mist and clouds was blue on his dark hair as he sat peering at Flynn.

"What?" Flynn demanded hoarsely as he eased his thumb off the hammer of his gun.

"The boat just picked up a rowboat of men," Rose whispered.

Flynn blinked and rubbed at his eyes with his free hand as he lowered his gun. "It's a passenger boat, Rose, that's what the hell it does."

"They didn't use the landing stages. And I saw a lot of iron in the moonlight, Marshal. I'm telling you, you've got a storm coming."

As if to accentuate his words, a gunshot sounded suddenly from the main level of the boat, followed by a woman's high-pitched scream. Flynn bounded up and toward the door, but stopped at the last moment and turned to glare at his prisoner. "If this is somehow your doing—"

"I assure you, Marshal, I don't have the resources to storm a paddle steamer from my cot," Rose said, and the undertones of alarm and urgency in his voice made Flynn lean toward believing him.

He licked his lips and glanced around the cabin again indecisively as shouts and screams sounded from below.

"They're after the gold," Rose asserted, his voice soft but still somehow worrying. "The crates in the hold, that's why they're here."

"Shut up," Flynn said automatically.

He could hear the pounding of heavy footsteps in the corridors of the deck below them. He could hear ladies protesting loudly and gentlemen shouting in outrage over rough treatment.

Flynn decided the newcomers were herding all the passengers and crew into a central location, probably the dining salon since it was the largest enclosed area on the paddleboat: easy to defend, hard to escape from. He knew most of the passengers who'd be carrying weapons would congregate in the main cabin or the salon at this time of the evening anyway, drinking and playing cards to pass the time. Moving to pen all the passengers in there, where they could be used to keep the more dangerous men in check by simply being in the way, made sense from a tactical point of view.

"They must have a lot of men," Flynn realized in horror as he thought about the manpower and brashness it would take to round up an entire riverboat full of passengers and crew in the short amount of time that was required to maintain the element of surprise.

"Marshal, you've got to think." Rose yanked at his irons, and they clanked accusingly. "They'll be coming."

"Shut up." Flynn opened the door to their cabin and peered out. Had Wash's cabin had been reached yet? Had Wash identified himself as a US Marshal and been killed by the gunshot they had heard? Had Cage been telling them lies and really could speak after all, and had the man given Wash away? Irrational paranoia and fear assaulted him, and he worked hard to push it all away and think clearly.

"Flynn!" Rose whispered urgently, pulling at his chains again. "If you don't move, they'll have us both just like all the others! They'll kill me if they recognize me!" He was nearly pleading as Flynn turned and met his stare.

For perhaps the first time, he thought he saw true fear in the shootist's eyes. And Rose was right, if the shipment of gold was being taken, then the men doing it wouldn't hesitate to kill a famous gunman in their midst. Or the deputy US Marshal escorting him.

"Unlock me and give me a gun!"

"Hell, no," Flynn grunted as he closed the door again. He engaged the flimsy lock and then reached across the small cabin for the chair that sat at the writing desk. It was a sturdy piece of furniture, with the

Anchor Line's trademark anchor logo carved into the back of it. He jammed it under the doorknob and then grabbed his bag.

Rose watched him as he riffled through his things, searching for his backup shooters and ammunition.

"Do you plan to leave me here?" Rose asked him calmly. His voice was suddenly detached, as if he expected Flynn to abandon him to his fate and was already calculating his odds of survival and how to get away.

"No. Just be quiet." He pulled out his spare six-shooter and a belt of ammunition and slung it over his shoulder as he looked around the tiny cabin. He nodded at the tiny porthole. "Think you can get through that window?"

"Sure, have you got some butter and lard to grease me?" Rose asked sarcastically.

Flynn scowled down at him. A loud bang came from the cabin adjacent to theirs. Rose held up his chained hands without another word. After a brief moment to second-guess himself, Flynn extracted the keys from his pocket and unlocked the man, then stepped back warily as Rose stood.

"Any tomfoolery on your part and I'll kill you," Flynn warned in a low voice. "The rules just changed."

"I understand, Marshal," Rose whispered. "The man you love is out there."

Before Flynn even knew what he was doing, he'd hit his prisoner, sending him crashing back into the cot. "You watch your damn mouth," he snarled, then he yanked Rose back to his feet and shoved the cot out of the way and against the door.

Rose merely cleared his throat and nodded as he rubbed at his cheekbone, not even protesting the punch.

Flynn stepped up to the porthole and pushed the glass outward, judging the size and whether they could even attempt it.

"You won't make it with your holsters," Rose advised quietly as the doorknob to their cabin rattled.

Flynn hesitated. Rose was right; he had to remove his belt if he was going to fit. He could either toss his guns through ahead of him and risk being unarmed in the tiny room if he couldn't fit through the porthole, or hand them to Rose and risk being shot in the back by the outlaw as he tried to shimmy through the small opening.

Neither option was a particularly honorable end.

A shout sounded at the door and someone banged heavily, cursing. It was followed by the very distinct sound of a shotgun shell being chambered.

"Get the lead out, Flynn!" Rose said as he gestured for Flynn to give him the guns.

Flynn gave him a hard glare and then shoved his old slim jim holster and ammunition belt through the window. They landed with a thud on the outer deck. He'd be damned if he trusted Rose with those guns.

There was another shout, and Rose glanced back at the door, then knelt under the porthole and linked his fingers together. Flynn stepped his booted foot into the cup of Rose's hands and let the man lift him to the window. He squeezed his shoulders through one arm at a time, and then pushed on the outer shell of the ship, forcing himself through as Rose helped him from behind.

He hit the promenade deck with his shoulder first and grunted in pain as his body rolled gracelessly. He looked back up at the window as Rose peered through, then he scrambled to his feet to reach for the porthole and help him.

Just as Flynn got to his feet, a shotgun blasted from outside their door. He hit the deck again as Rose disappeared from view. Flynn pushed up and scrabbled for his guns, grabbing them and strapping them on as he ran for the side deck that encircled the upper levels and led to their cabin door. When he rounded the corner, he found that the door to their cabin had been blown open by the shotgun. Two men grappled on the floor in the ill-lit causeway, one straddling the other. The man on top held a double-barreled shotgun, pressing it down against the other man's throat, choking the life out of him.

The man on the floor wore a dirty handkerchief over the lower half of his face. He kicked and clawed at his attacker, slashing viciously at his side with a short-handled knife in a desperate attempt to dislodge him.

Rose lifted the shotgun and brought the butt of it down like a club against the stranger's face. Flynn heard the bone of the man's face crunch and blood splattered even through the kerchief. Rose brought the shotgun up again and jabbed it one last time for good measure.

Flynn winced at the sickening, wet sound of the impact.

Rose lurched to his feet and turned to face Flynn, chest heaving and his face and shoulders speckled with blood. He swung the shotgun around and leveled it at Flynn as soon as he saw his shadowed form. For the first time, Flynn really saw the killer all the stories talked about, his eyes black and lifeless and his handsome face marred by shadows and blood.

Flynn stopped and gasped, realizing that he might as well be a dead man as he met Rose's eyes. Even if Rose did recognize him in the darkness, that certainly didn't mean he wouldn't still pull the trigger.

To his eternal surprise, Rose blinked at him and lowered the shotgun. He stumbled closer, looking slightly dazed, his breathing coming in difficult gasps. His side was bleeding heavily where the man's short knife had ravaged his ribcage.

Flynn stared at him. He couldn't remember the last time he had witnessed such a brutal act that hadn't been personal or performed in battle. But then, he supposed this was a battle now.

A shout from below brought them both out of their stupor with a lurch. Rose glanced over his shoulder and then began to limp toward Flynn, who was hastily affixing his holster and gesturing for Rose to hurry. Rose threw his arm over Flynn's shoulders as soon as he was close enough.

"Are you okay?" Flynn asked as Rose leaned on him.

"Yes," Rose gasped unconvincingly. "We've got to hole up somewhere. They'll be hunting for us."

"What's the matter, boy, cat got your tongue?" one of the men taunted as he roughly shoved Cage and the marshal toward the elegant curving stairwell.

Cage was one of the only men not kicking up a row about being prodded like cattle, and his conspicuous silence had drawn the notice of their captors. He didn't even bother to shake his head in response.

"He's too good to talk to you," another man sneered as Cage felt a gun barrel jabbed at his lower back.

"Maybe we'll just have to teach him some manners," the first man threatened.

Neither Cage nor Wash looked at each other as the men herded them across the main cabin and toward the salon with several other passengers and officers of the ship's crew.

Cage pressed his lips tightly together and was careful not to react like he wanted to the baiting. He had counted at least four men just in passing while being led through the main cabin of the ship and toward the stairs. All of them were heavily armed, each with a piece of cloth covering his face. Any moves Cage or the marshal made could be misconstrued as putting up a fight and wind up getting one or both of them shot. And they hadn't even managed to bring a knife to this gunfight.

The man behind him jabbed Cage's back harder, and Cage stumbled. He balled his fists, telling himself again not to fight back.

"Leave him the hell alone," Wash finally growled to the man, who continued to jab Cage in the back even as he tried to right himself.

"Shut your mouth, mister," the man ordered. "Move it."

Cage wished he could point out that prodding one prisoner for not talking and then yelling at another to shut up gave a lot of insight into why he might not be the lead hoof on the horse. That meant that this particular man was probably going to be killed by his more intelligent colleagues when he finished whatever job they needed him to be doing. One always needed a few expendable men. Stupid ones, preferably. They never saw it coming.

The thought of that pending vengeance made Cage smile.

The man shoved Cage harder, and he staggered through the doors of the main salon. There were ten people crowded into the corner near the stove—all gamblers or hard men who had probably already been in the salon when the ship had been boarded. The little group of angry men were all being made to sit on the floor as two men with strips of linen over their faces stood guard over them with double-barreled shotguns. Across the room, along the long wooden bar that normally served the salon's guests their alcohol, sat an array of guns and knives and other weaponry that had obviously been taken from the gamblers.

Out on the foredeck, several bodies were being pushed overboard into the river.

Cage assumed they had been passengers or deckhands who had initially fought the boarding party, or possibly members of the boarding party itself, killed by resistance. He found himself worrying about Gabriel. If anyone was likely to put up a fight, that man would do it, if for no other reason than just because it was what no one else was doing.

As they were forced into the room, Cage and Wash were both searched for hidden weapons. Cage, of course, had none. He was thankful that the marshal had unlocked him, though. If these men had found him in hand irons, they would have either killed him or put him to work for them, and Cage really wasn't keen on either option. He was even more thankful that Wash didn't sleep with his badge on. The men had not searched their cabin. They didn't know Wash was a lawman, or Cage was certain they would have killed him on the spot.

A woman in a long white nightdress and green brocade dressing gown was shoved into the salon behind Cage and Wash. The man who'd rousted her from her sleep pushed her roughly past Cage's shoulder, and once she no longer had someone at her back to force her onward, she fainted dead away. Cage turned his head and watched her fall to the ground impassively. He didn't dare move quickly and try to catch her, not for any reason. She was better off down there, anyway.

The man behind Cage holding the gun in his back laughed heartily as the swooning woman was dragged to the corner and deposited none too gently on the ground. Several other passengers who were cowering and crying pulled her into their arms and watched the intruders with the odd sort of hopeful wariness Cage had seen on captives before. He had always wondered what they were thinking when they looked at you like that. Were they hoping that after all the planning and effort to capture and restrain them had been expended, their captors would have a change of heart and just let them go?

Cage supposed it wasn't normal to be calm and logical under stress. That was one thing the West did to men. Stress and danger were part of everyday life; if you weren't calm and logical, you were dead.

A trickling stream of passengers filtered into the salon under the watchful eyes of several armed men. Cage estimated there were fifty or so people present so far, and the number was growing as more groups were led in. The ship only held about one hundred and fifty. Cage couldn't understand why no one was fighting back. He knew why he and the marshal hadn't. Their cabin had been on the first passenger deck. They had been given almost no warning, were caught unaware and unarmed, and had been overtaken quite handily. If they'd fought, they would have died, and died needlessly at that. But Cage could not believe that the people in the higher decks didn't know what was going on by now. He wondered where Gabriel and Flynn were, whether they had managed to put up a fight or if they had gone docilely like the rest of the people being herded in.

Like cattle.

"What have you got there?" a man called from the other side of the room.

Cage halted at the sound of the voice, his entire body going just as cold as if he'd been thrown overboard into the rushing Mississippi. He knew that voice.

"Cleared out the first floor, Caporal," one of their captors answered with a gratuitous shove at Cage's back. They referred to the man in charge as if they were ranch hands speaking to the roundup boss. Cage knew they were anything but.

Cage stumbled forward, and Wash was jostled against him, yelping softly when his injured arm collided with Cage's elbow. Cage paid him no attention, eyes locked on the big, dark man who was strolling toward them. Cage straightened and raised his chin to meet the man's eyes. His lower face was covered, but Cage would know those eyes anywhere.

Bartholomew Stringer slowed when he caught sight of Cage, obviously surprised to see him there. But he recovered quickly and continued toward them in his usual, self-assured gait.

"Well, well, well," he murmured when he got close. He pulled down the faded kerchief that covered his face, and Cage's heartbeat sped up as he set eyes upon the man for the first time in almost a year. Stringer's lips twitched into an ominous smile. "Hello, Cage."

"You know this feller?" one of their captors asked incredulously.

The grandfather clock on the far wall of the salon began to chime the hour. Cage counted nine of the low, mournful tolls as he looked into Bat Stringer's familiar eyes. The man was taller than Cage by an inch or so, and his unshaven face and unruly hair made him look even larger and more dangerous than he really was. And Cage knew he was plenty dangerous.

Stringer grinned as his brown eyes raked over Cage. "He and I go a ways back," he said, just before rearing back and hitting Cage with all his immense strength.

# CHAPTER 10

Flynn had been on his share of boats, mostly as a soldier earlier in his life, being transported up and down the rivers, but he was quickly realizing that he had rarely paid attention to the way the damn things were laid out. He had no idea where anything was except for his cabin, the main cabin and dining salon. Rose kept saying words like prow and port and aft and starboard, and Flynn wanted to hit him and tell him to speak English.

Rose was guiding them, deciding whether to turn left or right when they came to a causeway and up or down when they found stairs and pulling Flynn into empty crevices to wait out ominous sounds. Flynn just hoped that he knew what he was doing. They couldn't afford to get lost or wander aimlessly. He at least *looked* like he knew what he was doing.

He also looked hurt, his hand holding his side as blood slowly soaked through his expensive shirt and vest. Flynn took care to make sure the blood didn't leave a trail, but that was as much thought as he gave to Rose's wounds. He knew they needed to find something to bind those ribs before Rose bled himself weak. But first, they had to make sure they were safe.

All of the action sounded as if it was coming from the lower decks. The screams and shouts were rising toward them as they topped the last stairwell and emerged on the Hurricane Deck. Flynn had not been up here before. The only thing he knew about it was that this was where the calliope, the huge steam-powered organ, was located. But it was obvious that there were no passenger cabins on this level. It appeared to consist mostly of an observation deck and several dark, quiet rooms used for storage. Across a vast open space, they could see the pilot house, unlit and silent. That didn't bode well.

Finally, they ducked into a closet full of mops and brooms and extra linens. Rose sank to the floor in front of the wooden shelves that lined one wall. He was gasping every few breaths and still holding his side. Flynn peered out the door to make certain they hadn't been seen or left a trail and then pushed it closed with a quiet click.

"You hit?" he asked Rose in a whisper.

"He found me with the knife a few times." Rose unbuttoned his ruined vest with shaking fingers.

Flynn knelt beside him. He pushed the shotgun Rose had been carrying aside and smacked Rose's hands away from his buttons. He helped him open the shirt beneath the vest, fighting against the rising discomfort the close contact caused him. If it had been anyone but Rose, he felt sure he would have been fine. Knowing what he did about Rose, though, and what was worse, Rose knowing about *him*, made it hard for Flynn to catch his breath as he tugged at Rose's clothing. He could feel Rose's eyes on him, but he refused to look up.

He told himself that it shouldn't make a difference, knowing that Rose liked men, or knowing that Rose suspected it of him. But it did make a difference, nonetheless.

Rose straightened with a wince and pulled the shirt aside as soon as Flynn had undone it, grunting in pain as he twisted. Flynn carefully lit a match, shielding it with his hand as he frowned and examined the series of shallow cuts the knife had made in Rose's side. None of them were very deep. They looked to be shallow slashing wounds. They were surely painful, but they weren't going to kill him.

"You'll live." He shook out the flame, then took his kerchief from his pocket and pressed it to Rose's side.

"Ow."

"You attacked a man with a shotgun already aimed at you," Flynn said harshly. "You're lucky all you got was cut up."

"At least I had the advantage of surprise," Rose said softly, voice amused but still strained and tight.

Flynn couldn't help but smile and huff a small laugh. He supposed that a man launching himself at you through a door while you held a shotgun to his face would indeed be a bit surprising. Rose was just lucky the man hadn't pulled the trigger.

"Thank you for coming back for me," Rose murmured as Flynn tried to staunch the bleeding.

"Wasn't 'cause I like you," Flynn said gruffly. He searched around the small closet, relieved to find several stacks of clean linens on the shelves. He got hem down, tearing them with his hands and teeth to make strips.

"All the same, Marshal," Rose whispered with an embarrassed nod as Flynn tended to him. "You didn't leave me there to die like a caged dog. I thank you for that."

Flynn looked up to meet the man's eyes briefly. He looked and sounded sincere. Flynn was certain Rose didn't have much need or inclination to thank people in his life.

He turned his head as he reached around Rose's body and tied one of several strips of linen around his ribcage.

"Yeah, well," Flynn muttered as he finished tying the last of the strips. "Don't mention it."

He took Rose's hand and slapped a hand iron on him.

Rose gave a stifled shout of surprise and jerked his arm away, but not quickly enough to prevent Flynn from hastily turning the key and attaching him to the wooden shelves behind him.

Flynn stood up and looked down at him, putting the key in his breast pocket pointedly. Rose stared up at him in silent disbelief, his mouth ajar and his eyes wide.

"Keep quiet, you won't get hurt," Flynn told him.

"You can't leave me here, Flynn."

"That's exactly what I'm going to do."

In the unearthly silence of the besieged ship, the grandfather clock in the salon began to ring out the hour. Flynn held his breath and listened to the mournful chimes until the echo faded away over the water. Nine o'clock.

"I'm going to go find Wash," he told Rose determinedly, and turned toward the door.

"Flynn, you can't just leave me here!" Rose hissed. "I can help you!"

Flynn closed the door on his protests and moved away carefully.

Cage was on his knees, head hanging and blood dripping down his cheek and off his nose as he tried to clear his head. Bat Stringer still hit like he was holding a hammer.

"I liked your other name better," Stringer mused, squatting next to Cage. "Had more of a ring to it."

Cage looked up at him as he turned his head. Stringer's brown eyes were glinting.

"Whistling Jack Kale," Stringer drawled ominously, low enough that only Cage could hear. "Strikes more fear into the heart, don't it, Cage? That what they call you now? Do you just go by Cage again? I reckon that has its own . . . charm."

Cage shivered violently as he looked up into Stringer's eyes. Memories, both good and bad, were flooding him. But he shook his head minutely in denial. He wasn't that man.

"Oh, but you are," Stringer whispered maliciously, understanding Cage's meaning perfectly. "Just 'cause you're back to your Christian name don't mean you ain't Jack Kale no more, Micajah," he went on in a voice meant only for Cage.

Cage glared back at him, trying not to let his upset show.

"Who's your new friend?" Stringer asked, and he eyeballed Wash critically.

Wash stared at him from several feet away as Cage glanced between them furtively.

"Oh, don't tell me he can't speak neither," Stringer drawled, obviously amusing himself as he stood, then bent over and hauled Cage to his feet. He reached up and took Cage's chin in his hand, glaring into his eyes with sadistic pleasure. His fingers dug into Cage's cheeks. The fourth finger on his right was missing, and Cage knew exactly how that had happened. Stringer didn't seem to be bothered by its loss now. Cage jerked away and huffed at him, jaw clenching angrily. The number of guns at his back helped him to keep his temper in check.

"Leave him be," Wash ordered in a low voice.

Cage was surprised at the marshal's continued attempts at protecting him, but he also knew that the man was asking for a beating if he said much more. He discreetly gestured for Wash to be calm and quiet.

"Leave him be?" Stringer repeated in a soft, taunting voice. He put his hand to his chest and offered Wash an apologetic pout. Then he lashed out, catching Wash under the chin with his closed fist.

Several feminine screams emitted from amongst the passengers, then dissolved into whimpers and sobs.

Cage reached for the marshal as he staggered backward, but missed him completely. To Cage's surprise, Wash kept his feet, only swaying before righting himself and turning to look back at Stringer with a glint in his green eyes as blood trailed down the side of his mouth. Cage had rarely seen Stringer hit someone who didn't end toe-up, just like he himself had done.

Cage stared at Stringer emotionlessly. He couldn't let Stringer think that he was upset over the attack, or Wash would take more beatings just so Stringer would have the pleasure of seeing Cage in distress.

Stringer was rubbing his knuckles absently and pondering Cage. "Why are you here, Cage?" he asked finally. "Are you here for the cargo as well?"

Cage was determined not to answer in any form.

Stringer stepped closer and narrowed his eyes. "Or is it merely Lady Luck that set you in my path? I know you can answer me," he murmured in a voice that was much too intimate for Cage's comfort.

Cage remained still and silent, looking back at Stringer blankly. Stringer moved quickly, backhanding Cage with all the force his large frame could deliver. Cage staggered sideways as several of the terrified women and children in the salon screamed again. Stringer kicked at the back of Cage's knee and it gave out on him. He fell to his knees hard, pain lancing through him as his kneecaps slammed into the Oriental rug that covered the wooden floor.

Stringer's hand clenched hard in Cage's hair, yanking his head back so he could tower over him. "Talk to me, my dear old friend," Stringer drawled out. The anger was beginning to show through his calm exterior. He wasn't accustomed to Cage being unresponsive and unreadable; Cage knew it was frustrating him. He murmured against Cage's ear. "You were always more expressive when you were on your knees."

Cage repressed another shiver and continued to stare into the distance silently, not making eye contact with anyone. Stringer always had liked it rough.

"Do we need to find somewhere private to discuss this? Or would you rather your friend answer for you?" Stringer asked in a whisper.

Cage jerked his head to look up at him, and Wash shifted defiantly between the other two men that held him. Cage shook his head in answer to Stringer, glaring up at him briefly before returning his gaze to the floor.

Stringer released him and straightened up, studying him for a long time before turning to give Wash the same unnerving once-over.

"You found these two together?" he finally asked one of the men who had dragged them out of their cabin.

The man nodded and shifted his weight from one foot to the other, scowling heavily at Cage.

"Show me," Stringer demanded as he smirked at Cage. "Let's see what they were up to in there."

Cage returned the look with barely concealed contempt. Stringer thought he and Wash were here as partners, working to steal the cargo themselves. Or as lovers, maybe.

Stringer merely grinned at him, obviously pleased to have finally elicited some sort of emotion. He ordered that Wash be kept in the salon, but separate from the other passengers, until they returned.

He spoke to his men, loud enough for all the captives to hear. "Don't harm none of 'em unless someone kicks up a row. He comes with us," he added with a crooked smile as he pointed for Cage to be hefted to his feet, and then gestured for his men to lead the way. Stringer took Cage's elbow and walked beside him, squeezing hard as he gripped him. "I'm happier seeing you again than I would have reckoned," he whispered to Cage, amusement and anticipation clear in his voice. "This thing just keeps getting better and better."

Cage tensed and shook his head as Stringer marched him toward the rear of the boat, past the graceful, curving stairwell in the main cabin. He jerked his arm away, only to have Stringer snatch it back, gripping it even harder.

"It's good to see you again, partner," Stringer said as he pulled him closer. "I'm gonna enjoy paying you back for what you done."

Flynn crept along the upper causeway of the steamer, stopping and flattening himself against the wooden siding of the ship whenever he heard a noise. There were no passenger cabins on the top level, and so apparently after their first sweep, no one from the boarding party had bothered to come up here.

He stopped next to the top of the large paddle wheel on the side of the ship, listening as it churned through the water and splashed back down rhythmically far below. He calmed himself and tried to reason through the situation. Rose had been right; they had to be after the gold. There were a lot of men involved with the hijacking and there was nothing else valuable enough—not that Flynn knew of anyway—that would split that many ways and be worth the trouble they were going to.

This was an operation led by someone with *cojones* the size of a bull's. Flynn knew that part of the appeal of robbing a riverboat was the notoriety it would gain the group of robbers. It certainly hadn't been done too many times. With this many men, they could have just boarded, overpowered the crew, taken the gold, and left without ever touching a passenger. Hell, Flynn thought maybe they could have done it without being detected by the majority of the people on board. It would have been a straightforward operation, he decided. Get on board, kill anyone guarding the cargo, and then get out fast. No one would be the wiser if it went smoothly.

But they were gathering up witnesses and making a big scene, moving everyone on the boat around and stirring up trouble. Trouble they may or may not have been able to handle. The plan was full of holes and things that could go wrong, which led Flynn to believe they weren't merely after the gold. They were after something else as well. The only other thing Flynn could think of was the notoriety that would accompany such a feat.

That meant two things to Flynn. One, they weren't likely to kill many of the passengers, if any of them at all, because they would want witnesses to spread the story about the robbery, and they would want to be heroes in the retelling, Robin Hoods not murderers. Or two, the scarier option was that anything they could do to further the brashness of their actions, they would do. Killing a US Marshal or two was one thing that could appeal to them. Killing a famous shootist and gambler was yet another.

Flynn thought of Gabriel Rose, aka Dusty Rose, the Desert Flower, famous gunman, gambler, and grifter, locked up in the broom closet, hurt and without a weapon if anyone found him. The chances of him being found were slim, but it could still happen. And they would kill him if someone recognized him. Rose's face was pretty well-known. People recognized him. People tried to kill him.

Flynn had seen it with his own eyes, and he was becoming more and more of the opinion that with all those charges he'd faced in the past, maybe Rose had only acted in self-defense after all.

He'd seen it plenty of times before: a young kid with stars in his eyes challenged someone with a name and a gun just to make his own name famous. It was possible that Rose was an innocent man. Did Flynn have the right to leave him defenseless like he had? Even if Rose was guilty of killing those two men in a showdown, did Flynn have the right to decide his fate like this? Because it was very nearly a death sentence if someone found him.

The law don't work like that, Wash had told him.

Flynn crouched down in the shadows and listened intently to the sounds of the riverboat, indecision flooding him. He'd killed men in battle. He'd escorted men to the gallows. But those were different, weren't they? It hadn't been his decision to fight that war. It was never his decision to sentence a man to death. His conscience had always been clear. Flynn had always seen the law in black and white. Guilty meant you paid for it. Wash, though, he saw the shadows amidst the rules, the ones that gave his conscience a hard row to hoe sometimes when he walked a man to the gallows. Flynn had never been concerned with those shadows, not until he'd met Rose and Cage. Damn it.

After a long moment of silence, he cursed under his breath in utter disgust over his indecisiveness and glanced back and forth down the causeway. He then began creeping back the way he had come. If they had as many men as Flynn thought, he would need help. It wasn't a matter of innocent or guilty, he reasoned with himself, it was simple numbers. He couldn't take them on alone, not if he planned to win the fight.

He reached the closet door and waited, listening. He could hear movement and shouting on the deck below, but there was no one close. Slowly, he pushed open the door. The hinges, constantly attacked by the elements, creaked under the pressure. Flynn stopped, his heart pounding as he listened to the shouts from the deck below getting louder. When they died down again, he shoved the door open and stepped inside, turning quickly to close the door behind him.

He was hit from behind with what he thought might have been a broom. The wooden handle snapped with a crack as it made contact with his head, but he was hit again in the lower back with what remained of the handle, and again in the ribs before he could even react. He turned and grabbed at it, trying to stop the next swing before it hit him in the head again.

Rose held the broom's handle with his one free hand, his grip shockingly strong as Flynn grappled with him in the confined space. Neither man made a sound above a grunt or huff as they struggled, until Flynn finally gasped, "Rose! It's me!"

Rose tugged on the broom handle one last time and then calmed in the darkness. Flynn warily let the broom handle go, and Rose raised it quickly and whacked him. "I know it's you! Bastard!"

"Son of a bitch!" Flynn snatched at the broom handle and tossed it against the wall with a muffled curse.

"Shh!" Rose hissed angrily.

"You shh."

"You left me!" Rose said, heedless of his own advice. He swung at Flynn again, hitting him with his bare hand this time. Flynn shielded himself and tried to take cover against the door as Rose swiped at him.

"Quit hittin'!" Flynn snapped. "I come back for you, didn't I? Calm yourself!"

"Calm myself? Go fuck yourself!" Rose practically shouted.

Flynn pounced on him and clapped his hand over his mouth. They tumbled to the ground awkwardly, since Rose's hand was still attached to the wooden shelves, and Flynn used his weight to restrain him after they landed.

"I'm sorry, all right?" he whispered as Rose struggled weakly beneath him. "I'm sorry I left you, but I seen I was wrong and I come back for you, see? I was wrong to do it."

Rose snorted against Flynn's hand and stopped struggling, his black eyes glittering up at Flynn in the near darkness. Flynn slowly removed his hand and Rose glared at him, remaining silent.

"Good," Flynn whispered as a loud bang sounded just below them. They both jumped, and Rose shifted, yanking against the irons restlessly. "Now," Flynn said in the eerie silence that settled after the loud sounds. "If we want to see sunrise, we're going to have to work together. Can I trust you?"

"Trust me?" Rose repeated, his voice incredulous. He yanked at the chain again and narrowed his eyes. "I think the question is: can I trust you? I've not been convicted yet, Marshal. You tie me up somewhere and leave me to be found, it's as good as a hangman's noose!"

"I know. I said I was sorry, all right? Now give me your word."

Rose glared stubbornly, jaw set. "Fine," he finally said. "You've got my word I won't handcuff you to a blasted piece of furniture and run off to frolic by myself. Now, let me loose."

"Rose," Flynn growled warningly.

"What do you think they're going to do, Marshal!" Rose asked urgently. "A US Deputy Marshal and a prisoner who refuses to speak when they question him? They won't believe Cage can't talk! They'll kill them both and be done with it! They may have done already, so let me loose and let me help you!"

Flynn stared at him for a long moment, the truth of his words sinking in with a sickening lurch. He nodded and retrieved the key, unlocking Rose carefully.

"What did you find?" Rose demanded as he shook off the irons and stood with difficulty. His side was caked in dried blood, but he didn't seem to be favoring it much any longer, even after their little tussle. He bent and picked the handcuffs up again, clutching them in his fist.

"There's a lot of action below us," Flynn said grimly. "I didn't get much farther 'fore my conscience caught up to me."

"All right, then. We need to reconnoiter," Rose said as he pointed to the door.

"We need to what?" Flynn asked flatly.

"We need to take a gander at the works, Marshal, have a look-see at the enemy," Rose said wryly, his accent flattening until it sounded almost like Flynn's. He shoved at him and reached for the door handle, the hand irons jangling in his fist.

"Well, why didn't you just say that, then?" Flynn whispered. They listened at the door and then carefully exited the closet.

"Americans," Rose grumbled.

Cage stood out in the hallway with Bat Stringer as their escorts pointed the big man to the cabin Cage and Wash had been sharing. Stringer shoved Cage into the cabin ahead of him. Cage stumbled, but caught himself before he could run into anything.

Stringer stalked in after him and looked around, frowning as he surveyed the cabin's interior. Cage could clearly see the chain still connected to one side of the cabin's berth and the marshal's badge sitting on the side of the water basin where Wash had set it after washing his face.

And so could Stringer.

Stringer stepped over to the basin and picked up the piece of round metal. Cage had never looked at one too closely, and they were all different depending on what town you were in and which territory had deputized the man wearing it. Most of them were carved out of coins because the government didn't actually issue them. This was one of those badges, made from a silver Morgan dollar. It was a simple circle, about one and a half inches wide, with a marshal's star cut out of the center, connecting the circle with its points.

Stringer palmed it and turned deliberately to look at Cage, shoving the badge into one of his pockets. "Did you go and turn marshal on me, Cage?" he asked quietly.

Cage stared at him and fought back the urge to make a rude gesture. Stringer had known him well enough to understand almost everything he tried to communicate; he would definitely understand those.

Stringer stepped closer to him and snagged his hand. Cage wrenched it away and shoved at him, but Stringer grabbed his wrist again and yanked him forward, then slammed him against the wall of the cabin. Cage was a big man, but Stringer was bigger, and his strength worked to his advantage. It always had. The gun at his hip didn't hurt either.

Stringer held Cage's forearm and looked at his wrist, which was bruised and chafed from the hand irons. Stringer's eyes moved up to meet Cage's, and he smirked. "Finally got yourself caught, did you?" he asked, taunting, flawlessly understanding the clues he'd gleaned.

Cage jerked away from him and pushed at him, snorting hard through his nose in anger. The men who'd accompanied them moved restlessly, hands on their guns. Stringer waved them off.

"Well, we'll take care of that," he said gleefully as he stepped right back up to Cage, crowding him against the wall. "One bullet to that marshal's head, and you're a free man again."

Cage shook his head furtively, hating himself for pleading with a man he had grown to despise. But he knew what Stringer was doing, and playing into it a little wouldn't hurt anything but Cage's pride.

"No?" Stringer asked mockingly. "Why not, Cage, you got a thing for the bull? You sure were sharing a bed with him."

Cage clenched his jaw and shook his head again.

"I didn't peg him as the type you liked," Stringer murmured, so low only the two of them could hear him. Stringer stepped closer, trapping Cage. Cage put a warning hand on his chest. Stringer ignored it and pressed in, placing his hand on the wall beside Cage's head. He tapped his fingers against the wall and Cage glanced over at his hand. He looked pointedly at the missing finger and then back to meet Stringer's eyes, letting the corner of his mouth curve into a smirk.

"I owe you for that," Stringer growled, reading even the smallest of Cage's gestures correctly. He continued in an oddly intimate voice. "Before the night's over, I promise you . . . you'll be missing a lot more than your fingers."

Cage snarled and shoved him, only to be backhanded again and pushed into the wall harder. He licked his bleeding lip and met Stringer's eyes with open hostility. Stringer stepped into him and kissed him roughly. Cage was still for a moment as memories of an old life assaulted him, but then he jerked his head to the side and shoved at Stringer again. His hand moved quickly at Stringer's belt, searching for a hidden knife or some other type of weapon he might be able to pocket.

Stringer merely laughed at him, pressing their bodies closer. "What's wrong, Cage? I don't hear you complainin'."

Cage gritted his teeth, ready to take more violent steps to stop Stringer before he went further.

"Caporal!" one of the men called breathlessly from outside the cabin.

Stringer met Cage's eyes for a long moment and then smirked as he stepped away from him. He moved well out of Cage's reach before glancing toward the door, obviously conscious of how dangerous Cage still was when cornered.

Cage took advantage of the distraction and slid the badge he'd lifted into the pocket of his new trousers. What good it would do him he didn't know, but it was something.

"What?" Stringer asked in exasperation when the man who had addressed him didn't continue.

"Ed run into some trouble upstairs," the man stuttered, panting as if he had sprinted to find his boss.

Cage's heart jumped into his throat as hope and dread assailed him all at once. Could Gabriel and Flynn be the trouble the man was talking about? Gabriel could certainly make enough of it if he wanted to.

"What kind of trouble?" Stringer asked. He was frowning heavily now, and he took a step toward the door.

"Someone got away," the man in the hallway answered with an almost audible cringe.

Stringer's brow furrowed more, and Cage could see the beginnings of a fit of temper forming. Stringer had good control of his temper, usually, but when he lost it, there was hell to pay. That had always been one of Cage's biggest issues with Stringer; he didn't like hiccups in a plan and could rarely deal with them effectively.

"Where's Ed?" Stringer asked through gritted teeth.

"Got his face smashed in."

Stringer stood stock still for a long moment, fuming. Cage watched him, back still pressed against the wall, wondering if Stringer would forget his presence altogether with this new problem arising. That, however, was too much to hope for. Stringer reached out and took him by his elbow, jerking him forward and shoving him out of the cabin ahead of him.

"Take me there," he demanded of his man, gripping Cage's elbow so tightly that Cage could practically feel his bones protesting.

They tramped up the stairs, stopping at the third deck. Cage's heart skipped another beat. They turned down the right corridor, heading toward Gabriel and Flynn's cabin. Cage could see two men crouching over a third who lay in the middle of the deck at the far end. Blood had pooled under his ruined head, and it was obvious that he would not be getting back up.

Stringer cursed under his breath and jerked Cage to a halt. Cage's heart was racing. That had been Gabriel's door. He knew it. He knew Gabriel would fight back. With a mix of pride and sheer terror, he wondered what had happened to his other two traveling companions.

"What happened?" The two men who had been crouched over the dead bandit both stood and gave identical shrugs. Stringer began to fume. "No one was with him?"

"We was hurrying. He was rousting 'em and we was herding. He said he could handle the last door hisself," one of the men answered defensively.

Stringer shoved Cage ahead of him, obviously not willing to let him slip through the cracks, and they entered the cabin through its busted door and looked around. The cot had been tossed at the door, as had the sturdy little chair that accompanied the tiny writing desk in the corner. It looked as if they had first tried to block the door when the man named Ed tried to get in. The porthole was open, and a cold wind whipped into the cabin off the river through the window and out the open door. Cage stood out of the way as Stringer took it all in.

When he began to talk, Cage snorted softly. Stringer had always been the type who needed to talk through his thoughts.

Cage didn't have that problem.

"Whoever was in this room went and attacked him *after* he shot open the door," Stringer murmured, talking to Cage and the other men as much as to himself. "Did he try to go through the window first? He might not've thought he'd fit, then decided he wanted to gamble with the buckshot instead."

Stringer took several slow steps to the berth, putting his hand to the thin mattress. It seemed that nothing was there. But to a man who could track, it may as well have been a body lying there still. Cage could clearly see the impression left by the man who had been resting in the crumpled bedcovers. And he knew Stringer could see it as well.

Stringer turned with a frown and looked at the window again, then back at the bunk as he judged the former occupant's size and weight. "He would have fit," he finally decided. He rested his hand on the gun at his hip, handle turned backward, border style, just like Cage wore his. Stringer continued as he worked it out. "He wouldn't a fit with his iron. But I don't see no irons laying around." He turned again and frowned at the ruined cot, lying crumpled on the ground near Cage's feet, and then slid his eyes to meet Cage's.

Cage's eyebrows rose as Stringer looked at him. If he expected help from Cage, he'd better have another think coming.

"There were two men in this here cabin," Stringer murmured. "I'm willing to bet one of 'em was restrained, same as in your'n. You know who this was, don't you?"

Cage stared back at him silently for a long, tense moment before slowly shaking his head in answer.

"You're lying to me, Cage," Stringer practically purred to him as he stalked closer. "Same as you always was."

He shoved Cage back into the bulkhead and backhanded him. It took everything in Cage's power not to fight back. If he fought back, he'd be killed. And for the first time in a long time, Cage had something he wanted to live for.

# CHAPTER 11

Rose crouched at the top of the stairs, listening intently as Flynn knelt beside him. "I need my bag," Rose whispered to him, his voice barely carrying above the wind and the rushing water of the Mississippi.

"What for?" Flynn asked in a harsh whisper. He was still wary of giving Rose any leeway.

"Weapons, Marshal. I would like to bring more than one shotgun to this particular fight."

"Right," Flynn muttered with a frown.

They had Flynn's two Colts and the stolen shotgun, plus Flynn's knife, which was still tucked into his boot. But Flynn understood the desire to have more, especially considering the daunting task at hand. The thought of Rose being heavily armed was not one that brought him much comfort. He knew that if they lived through the ordeal that was to come, Rose would turn on him in a heartbeat and try to escape. Flynn would have to be doubly vigilant if they further armed themselves.

"I like you, Marshal," Rose said in a voice that Flynn thought might be meant to be reassuring. He continued in a whisper that turned into a boyish snicker. "I'd be sure to only maim you."

Flynn glared at him.

"Joke," Rose said with an innocent shrug.

"Shut up."

A ruckus from below caused them both to flinch and scuttle backward, flattening themselves on the floor and peering through the ornate stairwell railing. Several men came stomping toward the stairs below them. Flynn watched them through the railings, confident that the darkness and the burgeoning fog would conceal them. He heard a sharp intake of breath from Rose beside him as they caught sight of Cage being dragged along by a large man with dark, curly hair spilling out from under his wide-brimmed black hat.

The man looked vaguely familiar, but Flynn didn't know why. "You're going to tell me what you know," the big man was saying to Cage as they approached the stairs. "Or your marshal friend is going to do it for you."

Cage stopped suddenly and jerked his arm away. The big man turned to face him and Cage made a series of angry hand movements that Flynn couldn't even begin to decipher. The big man seemed to understand them, and he lashed out and hit Cage so hard that he slammed against the bulkhead of the ship. His knees gave out and he began to slide down the wall, going limp from the ferocity of the blow.

Rose made to rise and interfere, but Flynn reached out and restrained him.

"Think." He pointed down at the group and then put his finger to his lips to keep Rose quiet.

One of the other men in the little group had Rose's bag over his shoulder. They had obviously been to their cabin. Flynn wondered if Cage had led them there, or if the man Rose killed set off the alarm when he didn't return. Flynn didn't think Cage was in league with these men, or even cooperating with them. They had to do something to help him, but Cage wasn't the only one they needed to think about.

"You kill them, it still leaves others with Wash and on the alert. He'll be dead before we can get to him."

Rose's jaw worked angrily, and he glared at Flynn, but he finally nodded and returned his hard eyes to the men below. He and Flynn lay there, perfectly still and silent, until the group had descended the stairs, dragging Cage along with them.

As soon as they were gone, Rose whispered, "We have to get to some iron."

"No," Flynn said calmly, even though his heart was hammering with fear for what would be done to Wash. "We got to get to the gold before they do."

"What? Why?" Rose asked incredulously. "Who gives a Boston dollar if they get the gold? Let them have it!"

"No. If we do that, then you'll go and save your man and absquatulate while the rest—"

"Ab—what now?" Rose asked.

"Run off! Disappear!" Flynn said in utter frustration.

"Well, if you mean run off, then say run off!" Rose whispered in the same tone.

"You'll save your man and run off, then!" Flynn shot back as he covered his head with his hands in aggravation.

"Are you more concerned about me escaping or about retrieving those men?" Rose asked heatedly.

"Both! I'm even more worried about *them* getting away!"

"Are you telling me you want to *prevent* this robbery? Just the two of us?"

"That's my job."

"Well, hang your job. It isn't *my* job! The only job *I've* got is making sure I don't get dead, and your job and my job don't seem to go well together!"

"I heard you were a smart man," Flynn said through gritted teeth. "Start proving the dime novels right and use your head. If we have the gold, then we can bargain with it 'til help gets here."

"What help?" Rose asked with a pointed gesture toward the river.

"When we miss our first scheduled stop, someone will figure it out," Flynn insisted, even though he knew riverboats rarely had schedules to begin with.

"You plan to steal the gold out from under their noses, and then bargain with those men for the life of a man you claim to love?"

"I never claimed nothing," Flynn snarled. "And I ain't thinking about love just now."

"Then you aren't human."

Flynn glared at him with something close to hatred.

"Why is it so hard to say, Marshal?" Rose asked him earnestly. "Just say you care about him. You don't even have to say you love him, just—"

Flynn lashed out and hit him. Rose's head jerked to the side with the impact, and he closed his eyes without moving as Flynn glared at him some more. After a moment with his eyes closed, as he appeared to try to gain control over his temper, Rose sighed, long and low. He then opened his eyes and looked back at the stairwell, which was lit with flickering oil lamps. The light reflected in his eyes, giving him an otherworldly appearance that made Flynn uneasy.

"What will you be more ashamed of, in the end?" he asked without looking at Flynn. "Will it be harder to tell your maker you loved another man, or that you never let yourself feel it?"

The logic tugged at Flynn's gut, and he shivered in the cool air. Rose turned his head to look at him solemnly as they both lay flat at the top of the stairwell. "You're not big enough to admit it. You're more scared of him than you are of those guns."

Flynn's jaw clenched, and he pulled himself closer to Rose as the low river fog began to settle around the boat. "I fought with the Iron Brigade. I walked through the cornfield at Antietam. I saw the dawn at Gettysburg. I was scared then, and not ashamed to admit it. But I ain't scared of Wash!"

"I'll believe it when I see it."

Flynn's nostrils flared angrily, but he was beginning to realize what Rose was doing. He was trying to force his emotions into making the decisions for him. He turned away from Rose's dark, knowing eyes before he could lose his temper again and tried to regain control of himself.

"I don't give a good goddamn about that gold," Rose told him in a low voice. "And I don't care if those men get away scot-free tonight. What I do care about is Cage and seeing that he lives through it. I got him onto this boat, and I plan to get him off it. You and Washington . . . How does it feel to know you might lose him tonight?"

"Shut up," Flynn snarled. "Just shut your damn mouth. I ain't losing him tonight, not by a damn sight!"

"Good," Rose said urgently. "So let's go get them."

"We're going to go find the damn gold," Flynn said, "and we're going to use it to pay those men to leave this boat and let these people alone."

Rose pressed his lips tightly together in disapproval.

"You told me I could trust you," Flynn murmured as he met the man's eyes. "But you got to trust me too."

Rose stared at him blankly for a long moment. The fog was beginning to climb over the surfaces of the paddle steamer, coiling toward them. Rose's eyes flickered rebelliously, but finally, he nodded grudgingly.

"All right, Marshal. We'll do this your way. But if Cage is hurt in any way, I will kill you," he promised seriously.

Flynn narrowed his eyes suspiciously, but he nodded in acceptance of the deal they were making. It was only fair, he supposed. Rose nodded in return. They got to their feet and began creeping down the stairs.

"Do you know how heavy that gold will be?" Rose asked in a low whisper as he led the way. "Where will we hide it? *How* will we hide it?"

"You just keep moving and let me do the thinking," Flynn muttered.

"I hope they make note of that on my headstone."

"Shut up."

Cage was on his knees again, hands tied in front of him. Bat Stringer's hand gripped his hair by his loose ponytail and used it to yank his head back.

"Are you here to protect the gold?" Stringer asked Wash loudly as he held a knife to Cage's throat from behind him.

"No," Wash insisted through gritted teeth. "I got nothing to do with that gold, and neither does he!"

"You were traveling with someone else," Stringer said in a low growl. "Who are they and where did they go?"

"I don't know where they are," Wash answered honestly. Wash had never tried to deny that he knew Flynn and his prisoner. Cage wondered if the marshal had a deceitful bone in his body.

The knife dug into Cage's throat, and he felt the warm lines of blood begin to trickle under his collar. He inhaled sharply and closed his eyes before blinking them back open and peering up at Wash.

Wash glanced down at him furtively. "I'm telling the truth, damn you!" he shouted as he struggled against the two men holding him back.

Stringer pulled the knife away and shoved at Cage's head angrily, then he put his boot in the center of Cage's back and pushed him all the way to the ground. Cage caught himself with his bound hands before his face could hit the carpeted floor of the salon. He looked up at the marshal, wondering why the man was trying to protect him or Gabriel. Most lawmen Cage knew would have just given them over and begged to be let go.

"Do you know who he is?" Stringer asked Wash with a sneer, pointing down at Cage as he pushed up from the floor. Stringer put his booted heel in the center of Cage's shoulders again and shoved him back to the ground. "Why are you protecting him when you could save the lives of everyone here by just answering the damn question?" he went on with a gesture at the passengers and ship's crew who were cowering around the walls of the salon, all under armed guard. Cage knew Stringer didn't care. He was just grandstanding, using the other hostages against Wash.

Wash glared at Stringer and then took in the people in the salon. The men were watching him guardedly, and the expressions on the faces of the ladies and the few children silently pleaded with him to do whatever Stringer wanted. Cage watched the stoic marshal struggle with his loyalties. If he could have shouted out the answers to keep Wash from having to do it, he would have just then.

With one last look around him, Wash returned his steady green eyes to Stringer and merely shook his head and set his jaw stubbornly.

Stringer gave Cage's ribs a kick in frustration and he turned to his second-in-command; a small, ferrety man with eyes that couldn't seem to look at just one thing at the same time. Cage recognized him, but couldn't remember his name. And he didn't much care to try.

"Take a few men and go to the hold," Stringer ordered in a harsh whisper he apparently didn't think Cage could hear. "We got to move before we lose control of this."

The man nodded and turned away. He beckoned three men to accompany him, and they fell in line with an almost military precision. Cage watched them go with a scowl. If this was just about the crates of gold he had watched being loaded back in St. Louis, then Stringer and his men would have come and gone already. They wouldn't have rounded up the people on the boat and made such a fuss in the first place. That wasn't how they operated. There was something Cage knew he was missing, and it scared him.

"Why are you doing this?" Wash questioned, obviously thinking along the same lines as Cage.

Stringer gave him an amused, somewhat frightening grin. "You know who I am?" he asked as he stepped closer to Wash.

Wash leaned back away from him and watched him warily, obviously trying to gauge the correct answer before he spoke.

Most men in the West didn't want to be known. Many had run from something back East, changed their name, created a new man who they could live out the rest of their lives as. It was considered bad manners to ask a man's name, much less *who* he was, or who he had been. Some men in the West would even draw down on you if you asked them who they were.

Cage and Gabriel Rose were two men who prayed not to be recognized. They were men it *paid* not to recognize. But some men, mostly foolhardy outlaws and young colts who were too stupid to know any better, wanted their names known. They wanted that dime novel title, that reward poster circulated, and they wanted people to call them out in the streets. Usually, they didn't live long enough to see it happen.

Wash knew all this, just like Cage did. He seemed to be trying to decide which type of man Bat Stringer was. Finally, he just shook his head in answer to the question.

"I know you don't," Stringer cooed to him. "You know why?"

Wash just stared at him, seeing that it was a rhetorical question this time around.

Stringer turned to the passengers and raised his hands. A frightened silence fell on the room. He was an impressive figure, standing tall and foreboding, seeming to loom over Wash and Cage with his hands spread wide.

"There are two known outlaws on this boat with you tonight!" he shouted in a booming voice. "I ain't one of 'em! One of 'em is right here at my feet, though. You might know him as Whistling Jack Kale!"

Several gasps sounded at the mention of the dreaded outlaw. A lot had been said about Whistling Jack Kale in recent years, but Cage had never paid much attention to the rumors. The man had disappeared nearly a year previous, but the name still stirred terror in the hearts of those who knew it. And a lot of people knew it.

Cage glanced around in alarm after Stringer's words, his stomach roiling in a slow panic. Eyes were on him, looking him over, trying to decide if they believed Stringer or not. Cage had never been more thankful for a new suit of clothes. At least he didn't look the part of an outlaw just now. He glanced at Wash to find the marshal staring at him in disbelief. Cage shook his head vehemently, denying the accusation.

"You folks going to let this marshal forfeit your lives for the sake of a no-good, murdering owl hoot?" Stringer continued loudly.

"What do you want us to do?" one terrified man called out. "We got womenfolk and children on board!"

"Tell me who the other prisoner is!" Stringer demanded in a voice that boomed through the large room.

Several of the passengers cowered and others shifted restlessly. Cage knew that most of them would have shouted out the answer in a heartbeat if only they had known it. They didn't understand that Gabriel and Flynn being free and, more importantly, being anonymous and underestimated, was probably their only hope of living through the night.

It wasn't Stringer's style to leave crowds of witnesses, no matter what he was telling these people. Usually he came and went and no one was the wiser until they discovered the bank empty or the cattle missing. No one could even draw a picture of him, until now. This endeavor was wholly unlike Stringer, from top to bottom. Cage just didn't know why. All he knew was that none of these people would make it to port alive if Stringer had his say.

"It's Dusty Rose," a man suddenly answered from the far corner of the large room.

Cage's chin jerked as he turned to look at the man. His hand was bandaged and he stared back at Cage hatefully. Cage recognized him as the man who had drawn down on Gabriel earlier, the man Cage had shot.

Wash lowered his head and shook it sadly. Cage's heart sank. Now Stringer and his men would know what they were up against and react accordingly. Gabriel and Flynn didn't have a chance.

Stringer stared at the man who had spoken and then returned his attention to Cage. "That true?" he asked in a deceptively neutral voice.

Cage glared back at him, trying desperately not to give anything away.

"That who you've been partnerin' with these days?" Stringer asked with something close to jealousy. Stringer had always been possessive; Cage knew that all too well. Gabriel was a dead man if he showed his face now, regardless of how false the assumption was that he'd left the Scouts to ride with Dusty Rose. This farce had gone far enough that Cage knew Stringer wouldn't believe him even if he did answer now.

He shook his head in answer anyway.

Stringer viciously backhanded him. "Liar!"

Cage didn't move. He remained on his knees, twisted to the side, with his head hanging and his lower lip welling with blood yet again. He stared at the floor as a cold calm flooded through him. The next time Stringer raised his hand, he'd find himself missing another finger.

Stringer stepped closer and bent toward him, whispering in his ear so only Cage and the marshal could hear him. "You left us. You left me. High and dry, claiming you was tired of the life. You left me. And here I find you runnin' with Dusty Rose and a marshal's escort. You think he's better'n me? Hmm?"

Cage's gaze rose until he met Wash's eyes. The man was looking at him with a new glint in his eyes, obviously having decided that Stringer was telling the truth about Cage's identity, and probably wondering what Cage had really been up to all this time. He had no way of knowing that Cage wasn't that man anymore. Cage closed his eyes and lowered his head. And who would believe him now anyway?

Stringer straightened up and glanced around. "Spread out," he ordered several of his men. "Bring Rose here. Alive. I've got business with him."

"The gold's in the cargo hold," Flynn told Rose.

The shootist nodded as they stopped at the end of the deserted corridor on the third deck, and he peered around the corner. He motioned for Flynn to move and they continued until they were certain no one was patrolling the upper levels. It was odd that a search party hadn't yet formed. Surely, other passengers had been able to escape.

It was an intelligent preemptive move on the part of the hijackers, Flynn was beginning to realize, to put all the passengers and crew in one place. On a riverboat there was no need to set a lookout, and with everyone in one central location they could be guarded with a minimum of men while the bulk of the boarding party did the work of hauling the loot. That didn't explain why they hadn't just snuck down and offloaded the gold in the middle of the night with nobody the wiser. Flynn was past trying to decide why these men were doing what they were doing.

But it was strange that no one was out searching for errant passengers. It made Flynn's teeth itch. He and Rose knew one thing for certain: the intruders were now aware of their escape, and even though they weren't searching yet for whatever reason, Flynn knew they could soon be swarming the ship looking for them. He and Rose had to move quickly while they still could and be thankful of the reprieve.

It still made his teeth itch.

Rose stopped in a dark corner and knelt, holding his side and breathing hard.

"You okay?" Flynn whispered as he knelt beside him. The ruined material of Rose's fine vest shone dully in the light. He was bleeding again.

But Rose nodded, and he winced as he peered out at the approaching fog bank. It seemed their luck had turned. The fog would be to their advantage for now.

"Where is the cargo hold?" Rose asked as he watched the rolling mist.

"What? It's below." Flynn made an ineffectual gesture toward the bottom of the boat. "Below . . . decks."

"Yes, Marshal, thank you. But how do we get there?"

"I don't know," Flynn answered with a shrug.

Rose stared at him blankly.

"Don't you?" Flynn asked him in growing alarm.

"Have you seen me being shown the way to the cargo hold at any point in this prisoner escort? I don't know where I'm going!"

"But you said you knew ships!" Flynn hissed angrily.

"I know the *top* parts of ships! As a passenger!" Rose told him, practically spitting out the words as he tried to keep his voice down. "I don't know what's on the main deck any more than I know how to play a fiddle!"

Flynn fought hard not to reach out and throttle the man. He closed his eyes to calm himself and breathed deeply. "Just . . . head down," he said finally with another point at the floor. "Down."

Rose rolled his eyes and pushed away from the wall, continuing slowly toward a junction in the corridors and what Flynn hoped were the bowels of the ship.

Voices echoing through the soupy mist stopped them short, and Rose flattened his body against the side of the causeway. Flynn followed suit silently.

"Give me a knife," Rose said urgently.

"What? No!"

"Knife!" Rose demanded, and he held out his hand.

Flynn grumbled under his breath and slipped him the Arkansas toothpick he kept in his boot.

He watched with a growing dread as Rose handled the knife. The man took it and expertly twirled the long blade over his fingers, then gripped the handle upside down, holding it backward with the flat of the blade resting against his forearm. Flynn had seen some of the Rebel soldiers fight like that during skirmishes, the ones who came from the hills or the bayous, and later the Indians had shown him just how deadly a knife could be, holding their blades upside down in one hand and a tomahawk in the other, twisting round in circles as they slashed at their opponents. It had always struck Flynn as an oddly pretty sort of thing to be so destructive.

The voices began to materialize into shapes as they waited at a corner, and Flynn pulled his head back as Rose remained. There were two men, obviously on some type of patrol or finally performing the search Flynn had been expecting. They moved slowly, speaking in whispers as they approached the corner where Flynn and Rose were hidden on the other side. Flynn moved next to Rose to peek around the corner again, confident the fog would hide them.

"Got a bee in his bonnet 'bout something," one of the men was saying, sounding disgruntled.

"Something about that quiet feller he don't like," his taller companion said. "Steve says the boss knew him back when."

"That quiet feller is Whistling Jack Kale. Used to run tight with Stringer. Taught the auger everything he knows."

"Think he taught him to be fast enough to take Dusty Rose?"

"I don't know. But I'm sure looking forward to seeing that showdown."

"Sorry to disappoint." Rose lunged out into their path and turned in a graceful half circle, sliding the knife through the air and slicing through the first man's throat. Flynn winced back from the spray of blood. With a complete turn of his body and another arcing swing of his arm as he turned the knife outward, Rose took the second man down without so much as a shout being uttered by either of them.

Flynn carefully moved out onto the causeway, looking left and right, and then took a step toward Rose and the spreading pools of blood that were soaking the deck. Rose was watching him expectantly.

"Where'd you learn to do that?" Flynn asked softly.

"Their language wasn't the only thing I learned from the Santee, Marshal."

Flynn stared at him warily for a long moment and then merely nodded in acceptance.

"Should we hide 'em?" he asked with a gesture toward the two victims.

"Let them be." Rose bent and wiped the knife on one of the dead men's legs. He began a grim search for all their weapons, patting them down. "They'll serve as warning to anyone who finds them."

"Do we want them having warning?" Flynn asked as he watched Rose's movements warily. He was sorely tempted to ask for the knife back, but Rose was otherwise armed now, anyway. There wasn't any point in making an issue of it. Yet. He scowled at the bodies. "Seems to me we want surprise on our side."

Rose gazed up at him thoughtfully and then down at the bodies of the two men. "We can't hide the blood no matter what we do with the bodies. We'll just be wasting our time and vigor. Besides. They know we're here. We won't be surprising anyone, no matter."

"Right."

Rose continued to methodically relieve the dead men of their weaponry. To Flynn's surprise, he didn't go through their pockets looking for loot. Flynn was beginning to come to terms with that fact that Gabriel Rose was the real deal. The amusing nicknames and the self-deprecating jokes were just a façade. He wasn't some two-bit horse thief or common grifter looking to make a name for himself. He wasn't some dandy who'd ridden the rails out west and merely enjoyed the fame his luck had brought him. He was a deadly man, one who'd been taught and respected the hows and whys and rights and wrongs of killing. He was a man Flynn was sort of glad to have on his side tonight, a man he'd hate to have to go up against in a fight.

After stripping the two men of all their iron, Rose stood again and handed Flynn one of the spare guns, then after making sure it was clean, he returned Flynn's knife. Flynn took it wordlessly, and Rose nodded toward the rear stairwell.

Cage was still on his knees, head lowered, his eyes closed as he prayed. He had never been a praying man, and he had always scoffed at the people who had prayed at the end, just before their lives had been taken. Most had been wretched men living wretched lives, never having believed in God and with no hope of redemption in their last violent seconds. Sort of like Cage.

He didn't pray for himself now, though. He didn't know how or when it had occurred, but he cared about what happened to the two marshals. His conscience couldn't handle any more deaths, but especially not the death of someone he respected, like Marshal Washington. Marshal Flynn had his good points too. He was a decent, honest man, and he didn't deserve to die at the hands of Bat Stringer for trying to uphold the law and save lives.

Cage couldn't even think of Gabriel Rose without a violent shudder running through him. He thought maybe he could have loved the man, given the chance. Maybe he already did. The thought of finding that and then having it yanked away so suddenly was both terrifying and heartbreaking. He was desperately trying to think of some way to stop all this from happening, but he was no longer in a position of power or influence. He didn't even know what was going on, much less how to stop it.

Cage opened his eyes and jerked instinctively when he heard the sound of running feet on the wooden deck outside the salon. Stringer had been observing him, apparently, watching him for cues like he'd always done. Cage's hearing was excellent, perhaps a bit of compensation from his maker for not being able to speak.

Stringer turned away from him when Cage moved, aiming his gun at the open doorway.

"Cap," someone called from without before they ever came into the line of fire. The Border Scouts were still well-trained, Cage thought with a hint of pride. He was mostly responsible for that, even if these boys were all new. While Stringer had been the figurehead of the group, they had led it together, teaching their men to ride and shoot and fight and *think*. After the moment of self-congratulation passed, Cage cursed himself for having done any of it.

Stringer lowered his gun and two men stepped into the circle of light thrown by the gaslights in the salon. Cage blinked at the unnatural darkness outside the stained glass windows. There was no moonlight. He hadn't realized the fog had enveloped the boat so completely. It made it feel even more isolated on board the riverboat. There was no chance of outside help, no chance of anyone discovering their plight until it was far too late and the steamer had run aground full of dead passengers.

Suddenly, Cage wondered who was steering the riverboat. The captain and pilot sat trussed up with yards of flounces in the corner, just like the rest of the crew. Surely Stringer had thought of bringing someone to take the helm. But would that person know how to navigate the tricky Mississippi?

"Did you find them?" Stringer asked the new arrivals.

The brawnier of the two men shook his head in answer. The thinner man was breathing hard, as if they had run to get there. "We got two men dead up top," he said, panting as he held his hand to his hat.

"What?" Stringer asked in a flat, stunned voice.

"Logan and that new man, Harris," the man said with a nod. "There's blood ever'where. He butchered 'em."

Cage saw Stringer go pale. One thing Stringer had never been good at was dealing with the unexpected. That had been Cage's specialty, and that was something you couldn't teach.

As if he were thinking the same thing, Stringer glanced down at Cage and frowned. Again, Cage felt the brief pang of familiarity—memories of thinking their way out from between a rock and a hard place while looking into Stringer's eyes—and again, he missed the life and the people he had left. For a moment.

It passed quickly, however, when the two men began to tell what they had seen in more detail. Someone had attacked the two hijackers with nothing more than a blade, and quite handily at that. One of the men compared it to the aftermath of Apache attacks he had seen, their throats slit open and blood so thick the victims were barely recognizable.

"Rose." Stringer spat the name as if it left a foul taste behind. "That low-dealin' piece of horseshit. Get back out there and find him. And watch your damn backs!" he shouted after the two men as they hustled off to do his bidding.

With those men gone, just five men and Stringer were left to guard all the prisoners. Stringer didn't seem bothered by the numbers. Cage slowly began to work at the cloth that bound his wrists.

"Whistling Jack Kale," Stringer said, as if turning over the name and testing how it sounded aloud. He began walking toward Cage with his hands behind his back. "Know why he whistled?" He was asking no one in particular. The passengers were all too scared or distressed to respond in any way.

Cage swallowed heavily and tensed.

"Whistling Jack Kale couldn't talk," Stringer informed his rapt and terrified audience. "But he could whistle. Couldn't you Cage?"

Cage glared at him hatefully for a moment, then closed his eyes and lowered his head again. He wished he could speak and refute it, but the fact that he couldn't just lent more credence to what Stringer was saying.

There was a heavy silence that followed the words. Cage opened his eyes when he felt Stringer moving. The big man was kneeling in front of him, meeting his eyes. His lips curled into a smirk. "Let's you and me go have a little *quiet* time."

Another pang traveled through Cage's body like lightning. "Quiet time" had been Stringer's wry euphemism for the times they'd enjoyed each other's company.

Cage felt nothing of the old attraction he'd once harbored. Stringer had changed. While he was still a handsome man to gaze upon, there was no hiding the hardness in his eyes. His opinion must have shone through, because Stringer narrowed his eyes and inclined his head. He glanced over a shoulder to one of the other bandits.

"Harland. Keep an eye out. Me and my *compadre* here got some things to settle." He pulled Cage to his feet by the strip of cloth around his wrists.

Cage glanced to Wash, who was watching mutinously, looking as if he might try to intervene. Cage shook his head minutely. This was the chance he'd been hoping for. He'd see how Stringer handled himself without someone standing behind him with a gun.

Flynn and Rose made their way down silently, searching for the route to the cargo hold and hoping the back stairwell they were using would lead all the way to the depths of the boat. It had the advantage of being far enough away from all the action that they'd managed to slip past the cabin deck and the salon without being detected.

Flynn found himself twitchy and nervous, knowing that Rose was armed. He didn't trust the Englishman one bit, but he was the lesser of two evils right now. He also seemed genuinely set on rescuing Cage, if not the other passengers held with him. As they moved, Flynn quietly popped the leather straps off both his guns to allow himself a faster draw. Just in case Rose turned on him.

As they reached the main deck and neared what they hoped was the cargo hold, Rose stopped suddenly, holding his hand out to halt Flynn beside him. Flynn glanced around warily, but he neither saw nor heard anything. Rose turned in the dark corridor, and Flynn stepped closer to him.

"What?" Flynn asked in a voice that was barely a breath of air.

"The government would have men guarding that bullion," Rose said quietly, as if the thought had just struck him.

Flynn blinked in response. "You're right," he said. With all those soldiers who'd been loading those crates, some were probably down here with them.

He peered down the hall in the direction of the cargo hold. Down here, there were no Oriental rugs covering the floors and no brocade wallpaper on the rough walls. Passengers weren't meant to see these corridors. The lack of covering made sounds echo through the passageways. But for all the noise down here, they couldn't hear anything from topside.

"Makes you wonder if they even know anything's gone wrong," Flynn said with a furrowed brow. "There's probably a lot of guns in that hold."

"We could use their help. We just have to convince them not to shoot us first." Rose jerked his head that way, and they continued on. Flynn felt himself growing more confident in their position. If they could reach that detail of soldiers guarding the gold, they'd have plenty of men to take on the hijackers.

Just as they turned down the final corridor, there was a commotion ahead of them. Rose ducked behind the corner again, yanking Flynn out of sight by his shirtfront just as four men emerged from another stairwell. Flynn held his breath as they listened to the heavy footfalls of the newcomers. Rose slowly drew a knife he'd taken off one of the three men he'd killed tonight and held it out, squinting at the reflection on the scuffed blade. They could just barely make out the shadows of the men as they headed directly for the door to what Flynn assumed must be the cargo hold.

Rose cursed under his breath and lowered the knife, turning his head around the corner. Flynn peered around him, itching to move. He leaned on Rose, and Rose jabbed him in the ribs with an elbow. Flynn jabbed him back and they grumbled at each other quietly as they spied on the corridor.

He could feel Rose practically vibrating with the desire to attack, but both of them stayed hidden in the darkness of the corridor. It eased Flynn's mind to know the Englishman was cautious enough not to charge into the fray, no matter how badly he wanted to do so.

The man in the lead, a small, nervous-looking fellow with thin blond hair, walked up to the door of the cargo hold and banged on it. "Hey!" he yelled, sounding close to panicked as he continued to hammer his fist on the door. "We been hijacked, let us in! They're coming, let us in!"

Had other passengers escaped? These men did not look panicked despite sounding like it. Flynn shook his head in confusion as Rose cursed again with feeling.

The door swung open and a man stepped out holding a shotgun. The blond man raised his gun and fired, hitting the guard right between the eyes and sending him sprawling back into the cargo compartment. A gunfight commenced within the cargo hold as the man and his companions stormed inside.

Rose cursed colorfully. Before he or Flynn could do anything to help the guards within the cargo hold, the fight was over. One of the four hijackers had been hit in the arm, another in the thigh. But they had fared far better than the men who'd been bottled up inside the hold.

The massacre was too much for Flynn to take sitting down. Anger brimmed over into rage, and he stepped out into the hallway. "US Marshal!" he shouted. "Hold it right there!"

Rose reached out and jerked him back into the cover of the corridor as the four men turned and simultaneously fired in his direction. "What are you doing!?" Rose cried as bullets splintered the wall around them.

"I was arresting them!" Flynn shouted over the blasts of the guns.

"Are you insane?" Rose asked incredulously, covering his head as another hail of gunfire shredded the walls around them. "Have you never heard of sneaking? Just shoot them from behind, don't give them warning!"

"That ain't honorable," Flynn said as the shots began to taper off. At least one of the men was reloading, and Flynn ducked around the corner and fired off three quick rounds.

"Honorable," Rose repeated in dazed frustration.

Flynn fired a few more shots to keep the four men on their toes. Rose remained crouched with his hands over his head, muttering to himself.

Flynn ducked back behind the corner as the men returned fire once more, and he began to hastily reload. "This ain't working," he muttered.

"Tell me something my grandmother wouldn't know, Marshal. It's time to do this my way," Rose said as soon they were granted another lull in the return fire.

"What's your way?"

Rose thumbed two shells into the shotgun and then held it up and cocked both barrels pointedly. Flynn opened his mouth to protest, but Rose lunged to his feet and stepped around the corner, shotgun slung low on his hip. He fired two resounding blasts as he stood in the middle of the corridor, and Flynn covered his head and winced away in expectation of the return fire. He didn't want to see Rose blown away, no matter how much he still hated the man.

No return fire came, however. Flynn glanced up and looked at Rose, who still stood in the middle of the hallway. He peered around the corner cautiously and saw that three of the men lay on the ground, torn apart by the widespread buckshot that had ricocheted in the enclosed area where they'd been bunched together and helpless. The fourth man, the small man who had been nearest the steps, was disappearing into the stairwell. Rose dropped the shotgun and drew one of his six-shooters to fire at him as he fled, but the man was gone.

The last shot left a reverberating echo in the small corridor, and Flynn's ears rang from all the gunfire. "I'll be damned."

"Not just yet," Rose drawled with a wicked grin.

One of the three men was dead, another was well on his way, moaning and bleeding profusely from the wounds to his belly. The third was on the ground, badly wounded but frantically trying to reload his pistol and pull himself behind the heavy wooden door to the hold. Rose strolled toward them, calmly thumbing cartridges into his borrowed weapon. He sent two bullets into the head of the dying man, effectively putting him out of his misery. Flynn hung back, covering Rose and somewhat stunned by the cavalier attitude.

He heard the cylinder of the wounded man's revolver slam home. Rose turned to look down at the man, aiming his gun and firing two shots in quick succession.

The smoke hung heavy in the corridor, cloaking Rose and the men he'd killed. Flynn stepped forward despite the shiver that ran down his spine. Flynn was certain he'd never underestimate Rose again.

He surveyed the carnage somewhat indifferently. After what they'd done to the men inside that cargo hold, they'd deserved this as far as he was concerned. He nudged one of their hands and then bent down to take the gun clutched in it. Rose peered into the cargo hold and then stepped inside, disappearing for a long moment as Flynn disarmed the three dead men and collected the precious ammunition they carried. He shoved their six-shooters into his belt and vest and anywhere else he could conceivably carry them.

Rose came back several moments later, grim-faced and heavily armed. His expression told Flynn that no one inside had lived through the firefight.

"Still want to give them their gold and let them slide away into the night?" Rose asked him softly.

Flynn stared at him and then looked down at the blood on the floor. They hadn't even given those soldiers a chance to surrender peacefully. They had no intention of leaving anyone alive.

He shook his head solemnly. "Let's do this your way."

Bat Stringer picked one of the luxury cabins at random and shoved Cage in ahead of him. He slammed the door closed behind him and stood with one hand on the butt of his gun as Cage drew up his shoulders and turned to face him.

Stringer's mind raced, dozens of things he wanted to say bouncing around, but none of them seemed strong enough now that he had Cage here in front of him.

And damn the man, he still looked good. That fire in his eyes was something Stringer had sorely missed. He knew it was dangerous to be alone with him, but he didn't care. He could handle whatever his old friend chose to throw at him.

They stood staring at each other as the grand clock out in the salon began to chime the hour. The mournful tolling seemed appropriate to the mood in the elegantly appointed cabin.

"Only way both of us is leaving this ship alive tonight is if you tell me what I want to hear," Stringer told Cage after several long, tense moments. His words were soft and heavy with their shared past.

Cage snorted at him and shook his head.

"You used to think it was funny," Stringer murmured as he unbuckled his holsters and slid them off his hips. He couldn't risk Cage getting a hand on one of those guns.

Cage raised his chin, defiant and stoic. Stringer stepped toward him with the same care one would approach a wild horse, reaching for Cage's hands as his eyes stayed on Cage's. Cage didn't move. He didn't even blink as his eyes followed Stringer's every move. Stringer took the cloth at Cage's wrists, noting that it was loose. A few more minutes of working at it and Cage would have been free. Stringer smirked at him.

"I'm tempted to leave this on," he said as he yanked Cage's hands. Cage was forced to take a tiny step forward to keep from losing his balance, and Stringer pulled at him again to bring him closer. They stood almost nose to nose, Cage's measured puffs of breath ghosting against Stringer's lips as they eyed each other warily.

Cage's entire body was taut, like a coiled snake waiting to strike. Having him this close, looking into his angry eyes, Stringer could barely keep himself under control. He pushed his face closer, their noses touching and their eyes still open and locked on each other. Neither man was willing to blink.

Stringer smiled slowly, enjoying the tension in the air and the rigidity in his companion. Anticipation for the sort of violent encounter this hostility might produce began to swirl through him. He jutted his chin forward and kissed Cage, enjoying Cage's harsh intake of breath as their lips met. Cage didn't react otherwise, his eyes still locked on Stringer's.

Stringer smiled into the kiss and licked at Cage's lips. He pressed himself against Cage, at the same time pulling Cage's body flush against him. Cage finally gave in, parting his lips and dragging his teeth along Stringer's tongue. Stringer grinned wider with the small victory. He grabbed at the front of Cage's shirt and allowed his eyes to drift closed, letting himself sink into all the familiarities of the man.

It was his first mistake. He never saw the strike coming. Cage yanked away from the kiss and pain exploded just above Stringer's left eye as Cage ducked his chin and then rammed him with his head.

Stringer staggered back and shook his head as blood streamed down into his eye. He swiped at it with one hand just before Cage came at him again. They hit the wall of the cabin with all the force that Cage could put into it, and the air left Stringer's lungs in a rush. He managed a few weak jabs to Cage's ribs, but Cage had his shoulder jammed into the soft part of Stringer's belly and was pushing him up against the wall, stealing his leverage, pinning him there. He was trying for the knife in Stringer's boot, his fingers grazing the handle as he attempted to keep Stringer immobile with his shoulder. Realizing he was a dead man if Cage's hands found a weapon, Stringer shook off the surprise and kneed him in the gut.

Cage pushed away from him, then came at him again with both fists balled into one like a sledgehammer. He had no choice with his hands tied together, but it made an effective battering ram. Stringer just barely ducked the blow, and Cage's fists punched a hole through the wall where Stringer's head had been. Stringer dove sideways for the gun belt he'd discarded, and Cage kicked out at him.

He went sprawling, his hand finding the edge of the leather belt when he landed. He fumbled with the stiff leather, dragging it closer, but he had to roll onto his back and kick at Cage as the man attacked again. He found himself under Cage, a position he'd never minded on past occasions, but this time it had a decidedly different purpose. His saving grace was that Cage was still fighting the cloth tied around his wrists, and Stringer managed to wrap him up and flip them. Cage slammed into the heavy desk chair near the wall and Stringer followed him, straddling him and grabbing Cage's tied hands to hold them to the ground far above his head.

Cage's chest heaved and his eyes flashed. Stringer's entire being ached with the desire to have him again, for Cage to want that too.

"You couldn't have done that after we had us a little fun?" Stringer gasped as he blinked away the blood still oozing into his eye. "Damn, Boss, you used to have sense."

Cage shook his head and gritted his teeth.

"Get up," Stringer growled, and he clambered to his feet, pulling Cage with him. He made certain he had a good grip on Cage as he snatched up his guns, then turned Cage and shoved him at the berth, stepping up to crowd him against the edge of the thin mattress. Desire still raced through his body, but it was tempered now. He wouldn't force the man any more than he'd force anyone.

He didn't know if Cage was the better man in a fair fight. They'd come out pretty even the last time. But he didn't want to find out. Or lose another finger. Cage didn't try yanking away from him, even as Stringer forced him to bend over against the mattress. He knew to conserve his energy for his next attack. Stringer had to make certain there wouldn't be another one.

Despite how much he might still want the man, he had to make the smart choice here. Cage had taught him that.

He brought the holster up and pulled his revolver out. He was ashamed to see his hand was unsteady as he aimed the gun. But it had to be done. Cage was too much of a handful if he didn't plan on playing nicely.

First Cage, and then that bastard Rose.

Cage heard iron sliding on leather, and he tensed as Stringer drew his gun and placed the cold barrel against the back of his neck. He'd been expecting Stringer to try to cajole him into fucking him, but he hadn't actually prepared himself for this possibility.

"You got any last words?" Stringer asked grimly before pulling back on the hammer.

Cage turned his head and tried to look back into Stringer's eyes, determined not to flinch when the gun went off. It was a small victory to see Stringer waver almost imperceptibly as he held the gun to Cage's cheek and met his eyes.

They had been good friends. Trusted partners. Occasional lovers. Cage was morbidly curious to know if Stringer really had it in him to pull the trigger.

Fortunately, he didn't get the chance to find out. The sound of gunfire coming from the decks below them drew Stringer's attention, and he tilted his head, not daring to look away. He eased off the hammer as he stepped back, listening. There was a short pause in the firefight, then there was more gunfire. Finally, two shotgun blasts sounded, followed shortly by another round of measured shots. After the echoes had died away, all was silent aboard the riverboat.

Stringer sighed. "Your Desert Flower might be buying you a reprieve," he said in a low, almost relieved voice. He accompanied the words with a twist of his six-shooter. "Get up, let's move."

Cage obeyed warily, keeping his eyes on Stringer as they exited the cabin and headed back into the salon. Cage didn't have another chance to make a move. Stringer stayed too far to grab at him, and his gun was forever on that hair trigger. Even the passengers being held in the large salon were quiet after the gunfire, the group seemingly holding its collective breath as they waited for something to happen.

The first thing Cage noticed was the look of intense relief on Wash's face when he saw him.

"On your knees by your marshal friend over there," Stringer ordered, his voice harsh and strained.

Cage briefly entertained the thought of another attempt now, while there were others in the room to distract Stringer, but the first one hadn't ended well and he didn't want to risk anyone else being hurt. He did as he'd been told, aided by a gun at his back.

Stringer glanced around at his men and frowned. "Any of them fellers have a shotgun with 'em?" he asked, though the tone of his voice made it seem like he already knew the answer. His men shrugged or shook their heads in answer. Stringer looked back down at Cage and narrowed his eyes. "Your Desert Flower is puttin' up a fight."

Cage licked his lips cautiously and then nodded. Whether it was said out of jealousy or spite, Cage liked the sound of it. Of course, they had no idea whether it was Gabriel down there or not. More likely was the possibility that it was the soldiers guarding all that gold bullion. But the thought that it was Gabriel made Cage feel better, and apparently Stringer was just riled enough to blame every twist in the wind on the English gunman now.

Stringer growled at him and strapped his holster back on with jerky, frustrated movements. "At least he's proving himself worthy of you."

The words settled low in Cage's chest, and he very nearly smiled. He had to fight hard not to. If Gabriel really was free, he could easily escape the boat and be on his way now that Flynn had bigger things to worry about. If he was still on board, Cage knew it was because of him. The thought buoyed him, making him feel that if he could just live through the night, it might all work out.

Stringer turned to his remaining men and then looked at the passengers. "Start tying them up."

"We ain't got enough rope," one of the men said.

"You ever seen a lady's undergarments?" Stringer asked in frustration.

The man blinked at him in confusion. From the looks of him, he probably hadn't.

"Tear 'em up and use those! Make 'em tie each other up, and make sure it's done right!" Stringer shouted. His calm façade was beginning to crack as he hit more snags in his plan. Cage also knew some of it was physical frustration now. Stringer was a lot of things, but he enjoyed his partners only when they had a say in the proceedings. Stringer must have anticipated Cage cooperating, at least to some degree. Cage almost winced at the display. Stringer was mean enough when he wasn't all fired up with nowhere to take it.

The men scurried to obey the shouted orders. Cage remembered giving similar orders several years ago while they had been surrounded in a tiny bank in El Paso. He'd done so through gestures, of course, but Stringer had always understood him. They had stripped a woman of her petticoats and torn the yards and yards of flounces from them to use them to blindfold the people inside the bank. In the ensuing confusion and terror, they'd then hidden the linen masks they wore and blindfolded themselves as well, tying themselves up and making it appear as if the "bandits" had absconded under the very noses of the law, leaving behind a room full of people who were unable to even describe the men who'd robbed them. Cage and his men had then walked away from the bank after being rescued with the rest of the victims, leaving the money behind where they'd found it.

Despite the disappointment of not getting away with any loot, it had been a success. That had been the robbery that had given the Border Scouts such notoriety; the inexplicable escape that hadn't really been an escape at all.

Cage lowered his head as regret coursed through him. He had thought he could leave his misspent youth behind, toss off the wild ways that had driven him to become one of the more infamous men in the West and simply fade into the vastness of the country. He was still a relatively young man, not yet thirty years old, and he had thought he'd run far enough to escape himself. But he was beginning to realize that he would never be able to escape what he had done or who he had been. Even if he could make amends for all the harm he had caused, he could never stop the men he had left behind. Men like Bat Stringer.

Cage glanced over at Wash and found the man watching him intently.

"Jack Kale?" the marshal whispered. His voice was tentative; as if he wasn't sure he wanted to know the answer. But it was the first opportunity they'd had to speak, and Cage knew the earnest marshal just had to ask.

Cage swallowed hard and then shook his head vehemently in answer. Wash continued to stare at him uncertainly, but he soon nodded and clenched his jaw. Cage had the feeling that the man knew he was lying, but something in the way Wash looked at him told him that the marshal didn't care who or what he had been, so long as he did the right thing now.

That was the way of the West.

He was even more determined to do his part to stop what he knew Stringer was going to do, just like Flynn and Gabriel were off doing. He glanced over at Stringer and wondered whether he could take him now, while his back was turned and his other five men were busy scaring the passengers into tying each other up. If he waited until they were all tied, there'd be no chance of help. It was now or never.

Cage began working at the tie around his wrists again. If he'd had both hands before, he might have been more successful. In his haste, Stringer had never tightened the cloth, and it didn't take much to pull one hand free. Cage glanced up to meet Wash's eyes. The marshal looked torn, but he nodded furtively. Cage knew it might get them both killed, but it could be their last chance.

Cage pushed himself up into a crouch, eyes on Stringer's back. He waited a breath to settle his nerves and then launched himself at the man. Stringer moved when Cage did, drawing his gun and firing with lightning speed as Cage lunged at him.

The bullet passed through Cage's brand-new shirt, just under his arm. It seared his skin as he hit Stringer and sent them both crashing down to the Oriental rug.

The gun skittered across the floor and several people let out ear-piercing, terrified screams as Cage and Stringer grappled. Cage straddled him and managed a punch that he thought might knock the other man unconscious, but the larger man wavered only for a moment before he shook it off and retaliated with a jab to Cage's side, just above the bloody tear in his shirt. The fresh furrow caused by the bullet burned as if Stringer had set a match to it. Cage growled low and hit him twice more in rapid succession, then wrapped both hands around Stringer's neck, putting the weight of his body behind it. Stringer bucked and clawed at him, but Cage held fast, intending to choke the life out of him.

A shot was fired into the air.

Cage flinched and ducked, glancing over to see one of Stringer's men with an arm wrapped around a small boy who kicked and struggled in the man's arms. He put a gun to the boy's head.

Cage loosened his grip and raised both hands. Another man came up behind him and swung down with the butt of his shotgun. Cage tumbled off Stringer and sprawled on the floor, the world wavering precariously around him.

When he tried to push himself up, the toe of Stringer's boot caught Cage in the side of his head and sent him sprawling again.

This time, Cage didn't get up. He stayed spread-eagled on the floor and watched the ornate ceiling of the paddle steamer's salon spin above him as his head throbbed. He feared for a moment that he might lose consciousness. There was no telling what Stringer would do to him if he was incapacitated, so he took a few deep breaths, willing the dizziness to go away.

Stringer knelt beside him and grabbed his chin. Cage inhaled sharply as the warm barrel of Stringer's gun pressed to his temple. They locked eyes, and Cage could feel each beat of his heart thrumming through his body. Stringer bent over him, studying his eyes with a sneer before standing back up again and giving his ribs another wicked kick.

Cage tried to roll with the impact, but it still hurt like blue blazes, and he curled on the floor, holding his injured side.

"Anyone else want to be a hero?" Stringer bellowed to the cowering passengers.

The gamblers and shootists in the corner rumbled rebelliously, spurred on by Cage's actions, but they had been the first ones tied up. They couldn't attempt to help if they had wanted to now.

Cage coughed, pain lancing through him as he moved. He planted a hand flat on the floor and tried to gather himself in order to stand.

Stringer heard the movement and turned his head, looking down at Cage over his shoulder. His words of warning were soft and almost sad. "Stay down, Boss."

Cage shivered at the familiarity of the murmur. Stringer had never called him Jack Kale. It had always been just an affectionate "Boss." A part of Cage, a part he thought he had killed and buried, ached for the way they had been. The term was "thick as thieves" for good reason. Part of Cage longed to return to what he had given up. The rest of him wanted to cut the rest of Stringer's fingers off and toss them in the river.

He stayed down despite all that. He knew when he was outmatched.

As Cage floundered on the floor, the ferrety man Stringer had sent to the cargo hold came running back into the salon, bloodied and panting.

"Frank," Stringer said in surprise as the man stumbled in. Cage distantly realized he remembered the man. Frank Alvarado stammered the story of what had gone on below, recounting how they had been attacked by a man claiming to be a US Marshal. Cage's heart thumped with both renewed hope and with terror. One man. Could Gabriel be gone? Had he seized the opportunity to escape rather than sticking it out?

He rolled onto his hands and knees and gasped involuntarily as pain lanced through his newly cracked rib. It began to throb as he moved.

Stringer was listening to the tale with a deepening scowl, his upper lip curling into an angry snarl as Alvarado finished his story. "You sure it was just one?"

Alvarado shook his head. "Could've been more, I guess. I didn't catch sight of him at first, when he yelled at us. Only saw a dandy with a shotgun and then all hell broke loose."

Cage closed his eyes and his lips twitched in a relieved smile. "Dandy" certainly didn't describe Marshal Flynn. It didn't describe many marshals at all.

"So, they're on the loose," Stringer muttered, obviously coming to the same conclusion Cage had. He narrowed his eyes at Cage. "How much does he love you, Cage?"

Cage looked up at him and shook his head.

Wash had made an attempt at taking a gun from one of their captors as Cage had grappled with Stringer, but his too had been ill-fated. He was on his knees once more, a gun held to the back of his head. It didn't stop him from interjecting, once again standing up for Cage when he didn't need to. "They ain't known each other but a fortnight."

Stringer glanced at the marshal and then down at Cage in surprise. "A fortnight?" he asked. He knelt in front of Cage and peered at him incredulously. He began to laugh. "He don't even know what you are, does he? He's gonna get himself killed for you, and he don't even know who you are."

Cage met his eyes and then looked away as anger and guilt flooded through him. He hated that Stringer's words might have the ring of truth to them, and he despised even more that he couldn't quite find it in himself to hope Stringer would end up dead before morning.

# CHAPTER 13

F lynn and Rose waited in the cargo hold, anticipating that others would come running to try to pen them in after the firefight. They were confident enough in their position and their vast amount of ammunition to lie in wait like rattlesnakes in a pit. But no one came. Flynn didn't know whether that was a good thing or a bad thing. He had tried to think like the man running this show, but at every turn he had found himself guessing wrong. It was time for a new tactic, one he hated to resort to.

"What would you do?" he asked Rose begrudgingly as they sat in the cargo hold on two of the crates with the stenciled US government letters on them.

"What would I do when?" Rose was heavily armed now, having stripped the dead guards of their weapons. He looked like an armored porcupine, with knives and gun barrels sticking out of every strap and pocket in his clothing. He had "borrowed" one of the dead men's hats and now sat with a lit cigarette between his lips as he played with the felt hat, trying to mold it into a shape he liked.

"If you was the man in charge," Flynn said in a disturbed voice. He couldn't believe he was stooping so low as to ask an outlaw for advice. But it seemed logical. If you wanted to think like an outlaw, you had to *be* an outlaw. Right? "What would you do if you was running this show?"

"I'd take out a bar of gold and lick it," Rose said with a slightly far-off look in his eyes and a smirk.

"After that," Flynn asked, completely unfazed by the answer.

"I don't know, Marshal, I'm no paddleboat gold-thief," Rose said in annoyance. He glanced over at Flynn and twisted the felt hat. "And I know what you're thinking. I'm no outlaw, either."

"I didn't say you was," Flynn replied with forced patience and only a hint of dishonesty. He hadn't said it, he had merely thought it. "But you're supposed to have such a damn brilliant mind. And I know you been thinking 'bout how to get off this boat ever since I told you we was going downriver. This man don't go according to Hoyle, and neither do you, so out with it."

Rose glared at him for a moment and then sighed as he looked away. He stood up and paced a few steps, then shook his head and looked back at Flynn from under lowered brows. He watched Flynn carefully as he spoke. "If it were me. *If*, mind you," he emphasized with a point of his new hat in Flynn's face.

Flynn nodded impatiently and gestured for him to answer.

Rose sighed and slapped his hat against his thigh. He shrugged. "I'd blow the boiler."

"What?" Flynn asked in alarm.

Rose placed his hand-rolled cigarette between his lips and inhaled deeply, nodding. "It's quite common on these riverboats," he said as he exhaled, the fragrant smoke roiling toward Flynn with his words. "I'd round up all the passengers, just like they've done, into a big open space. Then I'd send men I trusted to load the gold onto a small boat."

It seemed to Flynn that he was making it all up even as he spoke. Flynn didn't know whether to be impressed or horrified.

Rose gazed at the stenciled crates of gold, his brow furrowed. "After making sure it was loaded, I'd set some dynamite on the boiler and run like hell."

"Leaving all the passengers to die?" Flynn asked incredulously.

"No," Rose said patiently as he walked farther away and began poking around at a stack of luggage piled beside the crates of gold. "They'd be left awake and aware of danger in an open space from which it would be easy to escape. Rather than asleep and unawares in their beds, left to burn and drown."

Flynn frowned and glanced up as if he could see through the ceiling and into the salon above them. "You think that's what they're doing?" he asked hopefully.

"No, I think he plans to kill them all," Rose answered distractedly as he fiddled with the edge of a canvas tarp. "They're probably tied up even as we speak, and think if they behave, they'll live through the night."

Flynn glared at the man.

Rose glanced over his shoulder, probably feeling Flynn's eyes on him. "What? You asked." He poked at a small box.

"Shut up," Flynn said with a tired huff as he stood restlessly and walked toward the door.

"What do you suppose this is, Marshal?"

Flynn turned to study the wooden box under Rose's hand. It was roughly the size of a bread box, and it was attached by thick leather straps to a pallet with handles on either side, made for two men to carry it.

"It's a box."

Rose glared at him testily. He slid his long fingers across the leather of one of the straps. "What do you suppose is in it? I don't recall ever seeing something shipped quite like this."

"Been holed up in a lot of cargo holds, have you?"

"More than you'd imagine," Rose said wryly under his breath. He knocked on the wooden box and cocked his head, as if waiting to hear a response from the contents. He gripped one of the wooden handles and hefted it. "It's quite heavy. If I'm not mistaken, I'd say it's lined with lead."

Flynn shrugged and looked away, examining the darkness of the corridor beyond the doorway. His concern didn't lie with the odds and ends of the cargo. "Open it up and see what it is," he suggested negligently.

"It's padlocked," Rose told him in annoyance.

Flynn turned and frowned at him. His eyes drifted over the boxes of gold bullion, and he scowled harder. The gold crates weren't even padlocked. He stepped closer. "You sure?"

"Why do you keep asking me that?" Rose snapped. "Yes, I'm sure."

Flynn found himself smirking as he met Rose's eyes. He cleared his throat and shook his head to dispel the urge to make another comment. It was almost a relief to see the man perturbed, and Flynn had to work hard not to poke at him a little more. He moved closer and peered at the padlock on the small box.

"Think it belongs to a passenger?" he asked as he knelt beside Rose.

Rose shook his head and leaned over it, reaching for the tarp that half-covered the box. Flynn found himself tilting away as Rose's hair brushed against his cheek. The man made him uncomfortable, and Flynn just couldn't get around that. How did he have any hope of ever telling Wash how he felt if he couldn't even let Rose innocently touch him by mistake?

Rose pushed the tarp away to reveal another government brand on the top of the box. "It does not belong to a passenger," Rose muttered as he tugged at the edge of the box experimentally. The box rocked, but the lid didn't budge. It was nailed down.

"Nailed down and padlocked," Flynn said. He checked quickly over his shoulder to make certain no one was out in the corridor, then he shifted, moving away from Rose and kneeling at an angle where he could watch the door as he examined the box.

"It's quite heavy too. I'm positive it's lined. I heard stories once of boxes that were moved like this," Rose said idly as he brushed his palm over the stencils. "Off a ship in New Orleans to a monastery. I forget the name. Holy relics, nailed shut and protected by boxes lined with lead."

Flynn shook his head distractedly as he looked around the cargo hold for something to pry the lid off the box. He knew they had more important matters to be tending to, but Rose's scrutiny and the odd security measures taken with the little box had piqued his interest. It might be what these hijackers were here for.

"What could be more important than gold?" Rose posed. The tone of his voice made it sound as if he had suspicions of what was in the box.

Flynn looked up at him critically. Rose was frowning down at the box, his brow furrowed and his lips pursed. He didn't appear to be playing games. "Any ideas?"

Rose's eyes shifted to meet his. He worked his jaw back and forth and shrugged. "I might have one or two."

"Care to share?"

Rose studied him for a time, then sighed and nodded. "Several months back I met with a man in Denver. The government man we saw in St. Louis, in fact. Baird. He wanted someone to steal something for him, an Indian artifact the Army was trying to recover from a burial."

"Did you steal it?"

"No, Marshal Flynn, I refused and the man tried to kill me, just like I told you," Rose said heatedly. "I am not a thief, and I am not a hired gun, no matter the low opinions you may have of me."

Flynn held up his hand to soothe him. "Okay, okay. How'd you get away?"

"An earthquake."

Flynn narrowed his eyes and peered at Rose. "An earthquake?" he finally repeated dubiously. "What, you just keep those lying around 'til you need one?"

"Don't be glib, Marshal Flynn. It doesn't suit you."

Flynn snorted and waved his hand through the air. "So you used a handily timed earthquake to escape from this government man who tried to kill you. Go on."

Rose glared at him. "You remember what I said out on the plains? About the Santee searching for something they called the 'terrible stone'? I believe Baird was looking for the same thing. He told me I had knowledge of the object he was seeking." He frowned at the box.

"What could possibly make you think this is the same thing?"

"That man we saw with Cage, the big man. His name is Bat Stringer. He was at that same meeting. If he's here, it has to do with what Baird was after. And it wasn't gold," Rose said pointedly. "And to be honest, that's the only object I can think of that I have special knowledge of."

Flynn pondered the lead lining the box and the nails and the heavy-duty padlock.

"The Santee spoke of it with something like fear. At first I thought it some sort of religious trinket, something spiritual to lift and unite their tribes. But now, I believe I was wrong. I believe they viewed it as a weapon," Rose said in a hushed voice. "And whatever power they believed it had, someone else obviously believed it too or they wouldn't be after it."

Flynn looked back up at him and nodded in understanding. Whatever was in that box was probably either very valuable or dangerous. Or both. Regardless, it didn't need to fall into the hands of the wrong people.

"Search those soldiers, see if one of 'em has a key," he told Rose as he stood and went to hunt through the darker corners of the big room.

Stringer sat at one of the dining tables in the large salon, scowling at the doorway. Finding Cage here had been a stroke of pure luck, an opportunity Stringer didn't intend to overlook. But his good mood had swiftly gone downhill with the discovery that Dusty Rose was on this boat as well. Of all the people in all the wide world to step into his path, he'd stumbled over the one person who might be able to figure out what he was doing.

The idea that Rose had teamed up with Cage made his blood boil. It was even worse when he considered that Cage may well have been in Denver with Rose when they'd had the meeting with Baird, despite what the marshal had said about how long they'd known each other.

Stringer gritted his teeth.

"Cap?"

"What?" Stringer snapped as Alvarado approached.

"Things still running to plan?" Alvarado asked as he knelt at Stringer's side.

Stringer glared at him.

Alvarado cleared his throat. "If Rose is down there with that—"

"I'm well aware," Stringer snapped. "We'll just have to make certain he doesn't leave this river alive."

Alvarado nodded and moved away, obviously sensing Stringer's mood and knowing not to cross him.

Stringer's eyes strayed to Cage, who lay on the floor where Stringer had left him. He was torn over what to do with his old companion. On one hand, he wanted to tear him limb from limb and drag him across the bottom of the river. But on the other, Stringer admitted to himself that he was still just happy to see him.

Cage must have felt his eyes on him, because he turned his head just slightly and cut his gaze at him. They locked eyes unflinchingly, and Stringer sat wondering what he would do with him when the time came.

If only Cage would come back to him, it would save him the trouble of having to kill him. Stringer didn't know if he could forgive him, but he was more likely to do that than pull the trigger.

A quick search produced no key to the padlock, but Rose and Flynn had managed to open several of the large crates of gold to investigate their contents. They'd been slightly nonplussed to find nothing but rocks and debris inside.

"We have ten crates of rock and one box of mystery content," Rose surmised. He stood with his hands on his hips and looked down at the rocks within one of the crates. "I think I've lost the thread, Marshal Flynn."

"You and me both," Flynn muttered. He was still staring at the little box, confounded by the way it was secured.

"Marshal."

"What?"

"We have no gold," Rose pointed out.

Flynn nodded, frowning as he stood. They had no gold to exchange. They could try to pass off a crate as their ransom, but Flynn wasn't fooling himself into thinking that would work. Not anymore.

"Are you done pondering this over now? There is no other choice. I'm tired of being on the defensive," Rose said in frustration as Flynn distractedly tried to listen for any sounds of approach. "We need to move, Flynn."

Flynn gazed at him dubiously. "You plan to pick them off one by one? Without warning? You want to sneak around and kill them all?"

"It's called guerilla warfare, Marshal." Rose put out his cigarette on the wood of the crate under him and slid the remainder into his pocket. "You Americans should know something about it."

"Hmm."

"During the Napoleonic Wars the Spanish knew they were outgunned, so they took to going about in small bands and undermining the larger French forces by attacking strategically and without warning. I believe we should learn from their ingenuity."

"Why the hell can't you speak plain English?" Flynn asked in frustration. He stared at Rose and scowled mightily.

"What I'm saying, Marshal Flynn, is they've obviously split up searching for us," Rose explained patiently. "They'll be easy to take by surprise if they're in smaller groups and isolated, and since they're men like you, they won't be expecting us to attack."

"Men like me?" Flynn bristled and turned to square up against Rose.

"I mean, they're Americans," Rose said without responding to Flynn's obvious ire. "Westerners. They expect us to stand up and wave our hands and say 'Here we are, please shoot us so we can die honorably!' You said we were doing this my way, remember? And my way is to go about this in as dastardly and underhanded a manner as possible."

Flynn stared at him, wondering if he was trying to be funny, or if he just didn't see the irony in that statement. Flynn didn't think Rose was joking, though. "I don't like it."

"I understand, Marshal. It's a wild and wooly western thing, right? Cowboy honor? The Rattlesnake Code? Always warn before you strike?"

Flynn nodded and shifted from foot to foot, scowling heavily. There was a difference between the rules of war and the rules of upholding the law.

"Believe me, I do understand that," Rose said grimly. "I live by it. The people who come after me looking to make a name for themselves? They don't. I always have to be aware of an ambush, and in learning how others would do them, I myself have learned a great deal about ambushing. And I would like to remind you of the exception to that little unspoken rule of the plains. They're here to kill *us*. They're out there hunting us as we speak, with every intention of gunning us down, with or without warning. If they don't expect us to be firing back, then that isn't our concern. The code doesn't account for stupid."

Flynn frowned and pursed his lips. There was a certain seductive logic to that. He wondered if that was how Rose's mind worked all the time. With cold, twisting logic, absent of morals or emotions.

He wondered if that was how he lived with the things he did, by convincing himself it was right.

"I'm not going to lie and say it's the easy way. What I don't like the thought of is Cage and Marshal Washington lying dead because we were too honorable to do anything about it." Rose stood and slid his new hat onto his head. It was a dark-brown felt with a wide, low brim. Rose had curled it until the sides had rolled up and the front hung low over his eyes. The effect was impressive, with the shadow always covering his already black eyes. It suited him quite well, much better than the bowler had.

"Ain't supposed to wear another man's hat. Don't you know that?"

"I don't think he'll come looking for it," Rose drawled with a nod of his head at the dead man he had taken the hat from. They'd left the hijackers where they'd fallen, lying dead in their own blood. The soldiers who'd been guarding the cargo, they had covered with empty burlap sacks. They lay lined up in a row that reminded Flynn far too much of his time in the wars. He looked over at them and grimaced, turning his head away again.

"You can stay here," Rose offered. "But I'm more likely to succeed if you're with me."

Flynn stared at the hat on top of Rose's head, then down to meet the man's eyes.

"No one would think less of you for protecting the government's hard-earned rocks. Marshal Washington certainly wouldn't."

Flynn gritted his teeth, his temper surging. "I'm going after Wash," he whispered.

"Good," Rose said happily. He picked up his shotgun and loaded three more shells into it. He closed it, the sound reverberating ominously throughout the large room. He took several long strides toward the door and brushed past Flynn as he stepped out into the hall. "Let's burn the breeze, Marshal!"

Cage lay on the floor and peered at the few men left guarding the passengers. Where were the rest of Stringer's boys? If they were out looking for Gabriel and Flynn, then when the shooting had started down below, they should have heard it and returned to investigate. That was, of course, unless Stringer's plans called for there to be shooting down below and none of the other men searching the boat thought it odd.

Cage decided with a sickening, sinking feeling that the reason no one had returned from the search was because they had all known to expect the gunfire. Those guards down in that hold with the gold had been slaughtered, and that had been the plan all along. The passengers, Cage knew, would be next.

"I swear, Cage, I think you were put on this ship just to vex me," Stringer uttered.

Cage craned his head to watch him warily. It was odd to hear Stringer call him by the name few men had known him by in that life. Stringer had known it, but he'd preferred to merely call him Boss. Cage couldn't help but think to himself that he had done very little to vex anyone on this ship. He hadn't really done much of anything but bleed, in fact.

Stringer stalked over to the bar where all the weapons from the passengers had been placed, and he picked up two Colts. He emptied one cylinder in each piece. Stringer had always sawed off the trigger guards of his guns to make his draw faster, but any man with a lick of sense knew that made your guns just that much more likely to shoot off your own toes. To guard against that, like so many men did, Stringer never loaded the cylinder that would be fired first. Even with the borrowed guns and their intact trigger guards, he didn't seem willing to go around half-cocked.

Cage didn't think it was the best idea to remove rounds, but he certainly wasn't going to point out that Stringer might want all the ammunition he could get his hands on going up against Gabriel. Stringer stuffed the guns into his belt and turned around. He met Cage's eyes from under the brim of his hat, and Cage caught his breath. Stringer had always been impressive to look at, to say the least, especially when he was riled.

Stringer stalked over to him, and Cage instinctively shied away when he got closer, expecting another blow. It didn't come, though. Instead Stringer knelt near him. Not close enough for Cage to reach him or do any damage to him, but close enough to speak in a voice that couldn't be overheard. "Pick your side now, Boss," he said, hoarse and grave. "You can still come back to us."

Cage's heart was hammering in his chest as he maintained eye contact with a man he had once cared for. He breathed out slowly, trying to calm himself, and his eyes flickered uncertainly. Stringer nodded at him eagerly, seeing the indecision and trying to urge him into his choice.

Cage met his eyes for a long, tense moment of fighting within himself. He knew, deep down, that he could never go back. And he knew that he didn't truly want to go back. The cold hard truth of the matter was that he'd risked his life to leave a year ago, and he'd forfeit his life tonight if he needed to. He wouldn't go back. Stringer knew that too, whether he wanted to admit it or not. Cage stared at him with a hint of pity, and then he very deliberately looked away.

# CHAPTER 14

lynn was trusting Rose's instincts more than he wanted to as they crept through the lower levels of the ship. Rose was certain there would be men in the boiler room, stationed to set dynamite and then wait for the word from their boss to light it. He insisted they needed to be rid of them first to ensure that the boat didn't catch fire.

Flynn wasn't entirely convinced that there even was any dynamite, but he was smart enough to know when he was out of his element. He was a straight shooter; confronting trouble and standing it down, that was how he worked. This kind of thing, this guerilla warfare Rose had spoken of, was not something he knew how to do.

"How many men you think they got?" Flynn whispered as they moved.

"We've killed six already. We've seen five more. Taking into account that we may have seen one or two of them twice, that's still probably eight to ten they brought with them. An operation like this, with prisoners to keep in control and crates of fake gold to heft? I'd say they have twice that."

"Twenty men?" Flynn murmured in disbelief.

"You know your maths, Marshal, consider me impressed," Rose said in a sarcastic, flat tone.

Flynn ignored it. "How did they expect to split that little box twenty ways?"

"They didn't," Rose said grimly. "If the expendable men didn't get themselves killed in the act, then Stringer probably planned to kill them and dump them in the river in the end, anyway."

"That's cold."

"That's smart."

Flynn glanced at the man warily and then returned his attention to the corridor they were following.

They came to a door with a wooden sign over it indicating the boiler room, and Rose pointed to it and then put his finger to his lips. Flynn nodded and removed one of his guns slowly, making no noise. They could clearly hear two voices coming from within the room. Flynn took a moment to wonder if these were innocent ship's crew they were about to attack, but the conversation soon answered his question for him.

"Would you put out your damn cigarette! Gonna blow us sky-high, you idiot."

Flynn met Rose's eyes and saw the shootist point at the door and roll his eyes. "Expendable," Rose mouthed.

Flynn pursed his lips. These men had obviously been sent to replace the engineer and his crew to keep the steamer moving.

Rose held up his hand and got Flynn's attention. "Ready?" he whispered as he held a large hunting knife up.

Flynn nodded.

"Quiet first. Then the guns if they're necessary. We don't want anyone alerted to the fact we've taken this room."

"Or blowing up the coal with gun powder?"

"That too."

Flynn nodded again and licked his lips, holstering his gun and drawing his hunting knife from its sheath. He was decent at a knife toss. Dusty Rose, he had heard, was better. After what he'd seen up above, Flynn was willing to believe it. But he had never seen anyone throw a knife as large as the one Rose had lifted from one of the dead guards, not with any accuracy or effectiveness anyway. It would just become a large, ungainly projectile as soon as it left his hand, akin to throwing a boot at someone and hoping the hard edge hit them.

Throwing knives were usually small, and the balance had to be perfect. Flynn knew how to throw his own knife because he'd handled it for years and knew it as well as he did his guns. He knew how far away he had to be and how he had to grip it in order to keep it from rotating more than twice before it hit its target. He wouldn't know how to begin with the pig sticker Rose now clutched by the handle like a spear.

Rose moved to the half-open door and kicked it open. From behind him, Flynn saw two men within the room, bent near the opening to the coal bunker, working to spread coal through the chute. They both lunged to their feet, coal and powder scattering on the ground in front of them, and reached for their guns as Rose entered the room. Rose tossed the large knife as he moved, throwing it underhanded with a flick of his wrist.

The knife sailed through the air with just a single spin and sank into the chest of one of the men. The other man drew his gun as Rose ducked. Flynn followed directly behind him, tossing his own knife over Rose's shoulder. The knife gave four smooth whooshing sounds and then hit home, striking the man in the shoulder before he could get off a shot. He dropped his gun and clutched at the knife sticking out of his arm, looking at Flynn and Rose in a mixture of horror and anger.

Flynn drew his gun, but Rose stood again before he could fire. He tackled the injured man and sent them both sprawling into the stack of loose coal spilling out of the chute to the coal bunker next door. Flynn kept his gun trained on them, just in case, but Rose seemed to know how to handle himself just fine without Flynn's help. He yanked the knife from the man's shoulder, slapping his free hand over the unfortunate's mouth so he couldn't scream. He then jammed the knife under the sternum, twisted it, and drove it deeper as the man bucked and writhed beneath him.

Flynn watched in stunned horror as blood gurgled up under the hand Rose kept clasped over the dying man's mouth. He found his boots rooted to the floor, his voice gone from his throat. It wasn't just that Rose knew *how* to kill people. It seemed to Flynn that he almost enjoyed it. During the act, anyway.

The struggling slowed as Rose held the man down, and finally ceased altogether. Rose waited several more long, tortuous moments before he pushed himself up and off the dead man. He wiped his hand gingerly on the man's shoulder and then sniffed daintily in distaste as he looked down at the body.

"Nice toss, Marshal," he said calmly. He stepped over to peer at the other man he had killed.

Flynn blinked at him several times, wondering if he would ever get the scene he had just witnessed out of his mind's eye. He'd seen a lot of violence and brutality in his life, and he hoped this would just fade in with all the rest of it. He told himself it had been necessary.

"Nice toss yourself," he finally replied in a slightly shocked, grudging voice for lack of anything else to say.

Rose bent and yanked the large knife out of the first man's chest after making certain both of them were dead. He wiped the knife on the dead man's pants leg and stood, glancing around.

"Never seen something like that," Flynn admitted hoarsely, pointing at the large knife. "That toss."

"Not as accurate," Rose said thoughtfully. He shrugged as he lifted the knife and turned it over, examining it with a frown. "But it does the trick in a pinch."

Flynn frowned at him, trying to figure the man out. He was deadly, that much was obvious, but so were many men in this country. Rose didn't flaunt his abilities until he was required to use them, but that wasn't anything special either. What was unusual about Rose was that he didn't seem to want anyone to know what sorts of things he was capable of, but he took pride in them, all the same. He was an odd duck.

Flynn was beginning to piece together bits and pieces of him. He was well-bred, and he had to have been naturally inclined toward handling a gun to be as good as he reportedly was. But he had obviously been taught by the Santee and probably others to perform a variety of violent actions on top of the gun fighting. He had sought out the know-how in addition to being to the manner born, and Flynn found himself, against his will, wondering why.

Why would a well-bred Englishman turn to a life of gambling and gun fighting? Why would he want to know how to kill with his hands? He didn't revel in the fame like some did. He didn't flaunt his prowess. Flynn simply couldn't figure him out. He was forming a grudging respect for the man, and not just for his abilities.

"What do you make of this?" Rose asked him, disturbing his thoughts.

Flynn cleared his throat self-consciously and stepped closer. He looked down at the black object Rose was gently nudging out of the dead man's hand with the toe of his boot.

"Looks like a lump of coal," Flynn answered drolly.

"Thank you, Marshal, again your powers of observation astound me."

Flynn smirked at him, enjoying the fact that he wasn't the only one who could be annoyed so easily. He then knelt and carefully picked up the piece of coal. It was heavier than a it should have been. He put it to his nose and inhaled deeply.

"It ain't coal," he declared with a sigh. He knew what it was, though. He was all too familiar with it. "You ever heard of the *Sultana*?"

Rose frowned and shook his head uncertainly. "I don't believe so. Should I have?"

"Might be before your time," Flynn said as he looked Rose over. The man probably wasn't even thirty yet, and the *Sultana* had met her end nearly twenty years ago. "She was a riverboat, 'bout like this one. Bigger, though. She was built to carry near to three hundred and fifty people." He stood again and absently stepped away from the spreading pool of blood on the floor. "Towards the end of the war, the *Sultana* left Memphis carrying about twenty-two hundred women, children, and released Union prisoners of war back North. There was an explosion in the boiler as she sailed upriver. About seventeen hundred people died when she went up in flames, burned to death or drowned in the river 'cause they was too injured to swim."

"I believe I have heard of her," Rose said softly, still frowning in confusion. "A tragic story, to be sure, but what's that got to do with us?"

"Well. I lost my only brother to her that night," he told the other man grimly. He turned the false piece of coal over in his hand. "I spent a lot of time dwelling on it, until Wash finally pulled me back to my senses. Before that, I heard tell in the saloons of St. Louis of a man who would get drunk and claim he had been responsible for the explosion. Said there was a captain in the Rebel Secret Service who had invented something called a coal shell. I started looking into it, and I found the northern papers had called these coal torpedoes when they reported about them. Seems the Rebs used them a lot there, near the end."

"Desperate measures." Rose stepped closer and plucked the bomb from Flynn's hand, examining it dubiously. "A coal torpedo."

"It was made kind of like an artillery shell, with a mold made of beeswax from a real piece of coal. The outside of it looked just like coal," Flynn explained as he pointed to the bomb as evidence. "Then, it was filled with black powder and all they had to do was go to the docks and set it in with the pile of coal being loaded onto a ship. As soon as it was shoveled in the fire, it'd catch and blow the boiler."

Rose chewed on his lip thoughtfully and weighed the bomb in his hand. "Doesn't sound easy for your average man to make," he finally murmured doubtfully. "Means they went to a lot of trouble to procure this thing."

"Makes me think your government man theory is getting more likely."

"Why not just use dynamite?" Rose asked.

"They meant for this to be slipped into the coal and have it take down the ship after they'd hightailed it out of here, after the crew thought it was safe. They get the loot with nobody the wiser; people'd just think it went down with the rest of the ship in a plain ol' boiler explosion."

"A fair plan," Rose said with what may have been admiration. "But if that's the case, then why have all the passengers been rounded up?"

"Plan changed?" Flynn suggested.

"Yes. I wonder what made them change it?"

"Well, we know it weren't us," Flynn said with a shrug. "We weren't even supposed to be on this boat, remember?"

Rose looked up and met his eyes, nodding almost imperceptibly as he bounced the coal torpedo in his hand. Flynn could practically see his mind working behind his dark eyes, and he found himself oddly eager to hear what Rose was thinking.

"I don't see a way around a showdown at high noon, do you?" Rose finally said in a troubled voice.

Flynn shook his head solemnly. "I don't like being in the dark when I'm up against something. And so far dark's all we've got."

Rose nodded. "Our only advantage is that they know that."

"How's that?"

"Whoever's in charge is smart," Rose explained, holding up the coal torpedo as evidence. "Whether it's Stringer or someone else, we have to assume he's already trying to decide what *our* next move will be. He knows we can try to sabotage their route of escape, but that still leaves us outgunned with a boat full of hijackers and hostages."

"All right, I follow."

"They know we have no other options but to confront them, in the end," Rose said regretfully. "We just need to figure out how to use that against them."

Flynn nodded but remained silent.

"Any ideas?" Rose asked hopefully.

Flynn stared at him, his mind churning with suggestions that would get them badly maimed or killed in a hail of gunfire. After a moment, he pursed his lips and shook his head. "Nope."

"Yeah, me either," Rose muttered as he looked back down at the coal torpedo in consternation.

"Got any more earthquakes up your sleeve?" Flynn asked wryly.

Rose shook his head dejectedly. "But New Madrid is said to sit on a fault line."

"A what now?"

"A fault line, Marshal. Where the earth clashes like Titans under the ground and causes such upheavals," Rose explained. He was smiling sadly as he said it, but as Flynn watched him the smile fell and his eyes lit up. "We need an earthquake."

"Thought you said you didn't carry those around in your pocket."

Rose pushed the coal torpedo against Flynn's chest and patted his shoulder. "I do now."

Cage sat bolt upright as the night was rent by a small explosion somewhere near the prow of the ship. Before he could move to stand, Stringer was beside him with a gun in his ear, telling him to get back down on his belly.

Cage did so slowly, putting both hands out in front of him and sliding them across the soft Oriental rug as he laid out. For the first time, Stringer appeared truly concerned. He either hadn't expected the explosion, or it wasn't supposed to have happened yet.

Stringer and several of his men held their breath, waiting and listening, all of them tense like they were ready to flee. When nothing more came of the explosion, they relaxed, shoulders slumping. Whatever they had been expecting to happen obviously hadn't. That meant whatever was coming was big.

Cage searched out Wash to find the man watching him, a frown set on his handsome face and his green eyes deeply troubled. Cage just shook his head helplessly. He had no idea what was going on.

"Go find out what it was," Stringer told one of his men. The man hesitated. Stringer narrowed his eyes. "You ain't gonna tell me you're afraid of him, are you?"

The unfortunate lackey swallowed hard. "Ain't many come back after checking. Maybe we should—"

Stringer raised his gun and fired before the man could finish. There were muffled screams and whimpers from the onlookers as the man's body hit the deck.

Stringer swung his gun around to aim at one of the others in the salon. "Go check on it."

The man scurried off obediently.

"Dusty Rose," Stringer murmured through gritted teeth. He turned to stare at Cage, who met his eyes from where he still lay on the ground. Stringer sneered at him, and Cage let himself smile slowly.

"What the hell are you doing?" Flynn shouted as they stood at the railing, both of them drenched from the spout of water the exploding coal bomb had produced when Rose had thrown it overboard into the hijacker's dinghy.

"You said we needed to hobble their other boat."

"I didn't mean blow it up!"

"You should be more clear," Rose said before he took off his hat and waved it around, throwing droplets of water.

Flynn swatted at the water and then reached out to grab Rose by his lapels, pulling him until they were nose to nose. He grumbled unintelligibly for a moment before taking a deep breath to regain control over his temper, then slowly released Rose without yelling or throttling him like he wanted to.

"Nicely done, Marshal," Rose said tightly. He smoothed out his shirt and drew one of his guns, checking it to make certain it was fully loaded. Then he gave Flynn a cheerful smile. "Let's see who comes to investigate, shall we?"

"If you live through this whole thing, I'm gonna kill you myself," Flynn grumbled.

"I look forward to the attempt." Rose plopped his hat back on his head. They could hear footsteps coming closer, booted feet on the deck trying to be quiet. Rose inclined his head, pushed the hat forward, and gave Flynn a rakish grin. "Let's dance," he said with relish as he drew the other gun and cocked them both.

More shouts sounded from outside the salon as Stringer yanked Cage to his feet. Cage doubled over and held his hand to his cracked ribs with a pained groan, playing it up a little in hopes that Stringer would drop his guard.

A man jogged into the room and waved a hand wildly behind him. "He got to the boiler room too," he gasped. "Blowed up one of our boats! What do we do now, Cap?"

Stringer placed the barrel of his gun against Cage's temple and pulled the hammer back with a growl.

"Let's go talk to the man," he said in a low, dangerous voice as he dragged Cage toward the doors to the salon.

All of the passengers were tied up, and Stringer's men stood by, restless and anxious. The thought of Dusty Rose and a US Marshal out there playing Indian in the Grass was making them all very nervous. It was a perfect disaster waiting to happen, and they all knew it.

Cage glanced over at Stringer as the man hauled him toward the door, his head turning against the cold barrel of the gun. He met Stringer's eyes warningly, and Stringer growled.

"I know they're tetchy," he snarled to Cage in response. "You just settle this feller of yours down and no one'll get hurt."

Stringer pulled Cage by his elbow, holding the cocked gun to his head, and they stepped out of the main cabin, into the soupy fog together. Two of Stringer's men dragged Wash behind them.

"Rose!" Stringer bellowed into the chilly night. The sound didn't seem to carry very far, smothered by the fog and muffled by the lapping of the water and the giant paddle wheel. Stringer eyed all the possible angles of approach, but Cage knew he was missing some. Gabriel would find the holes.

They were under the cover of the upper observation deck, and therefore it would have been nearly impossible to ambush them from above. Gabriel would have to hang upside down from his toes to fire at them from up there, and Cage just didn't think the man had that in him. Although, Cage wasn't going to underestimate Gabriel's penchant for the dramatic. He wouldn't put it past him to hang from the ceiling or ride the paddle wheel up from the water to get a shot off, no matter how difficult the feat might be.

The thick fog, on the other hand, made sneaking up on them from the main level all the easier.

Stringer shouted again, trying to make himself heard. "Dusty Rose! I got your man down here!"

Cage glanced around the ship's deck and swallowed heavily. Despite the muffling fog, he could hear the creak of the wooden ship in the moisture of the night; it sounded like soft footsteps. He could also hear the water rushing past the riverboat and the heavy turn of the paddle wheels as they churned ever on, like the paddles of a skiff sneaking up on them. The noises played tricks in the night. It was making *him* tense and he wasn't even the one being stalked. He knew Stringer was on a hair trigger, and that trigger was aimed at his head.

All else was silent as Stringer and his men waited for some sort of response. They would get more and more on edge, until someone finally went off half-cocked and started shooting shadows. Someone was going to die out here tonight, of that much Cage was certain. Maybe a lot of someones.

Even as Cage's mind raced to think of how Gabriel and Flynn might approach them, he was fighting the instinctive urge to give orders to intercept their attack. He'd never been able to speak, but natural born leaders didn't have to speak to have their orders followed. Someone should be watching the stairs, and someone should be watching the sides of the ship where it would be possible to climb or jump. He tried to tell himself it was because he didn't want Gabriel walking into this minefield for him, but he couldn't fool himself. Cage had helped to lead a band of outlaws for too long. He would never outrun the habits.

Would it spare all these lives if he just gave in and went back with Stringer and the Scouts? Cage closed his eyes in determination. No, it wouldn't. All that left him was being a man with the pedigree of an outlaw and not a single way left to redeem himself.

He had to dig his fingernails into the palms of his hands to keep himself from motioning Stringer to send men to the stairs.

"Come on down here, Rose!" Stringer shouted after long moments of tense silence. "I'll cut you a deal for him!"

Cage shook his head minutely and rolled his eyes back and forth, trying to see the periphery of the deck as Stringer's grip around his neck tightened and immobilized him. He was starting to get light-headed. His fingers dug into Stringer's arm.

"You even know who he is, Rose?" Stringer shouted as he pulled Cage farther out from under the cover of the awnings, and peered up at the upper decks of the ship.

There was a scuff, like a boot heel on wood, from above.

Stringer tensed and then laughed breathily. "We are the Border Scouts! I know you done heard of us!" he shouted at the landing above. "And this is Whistling Jack Kale!"

Cage struggled with him and shook his head desperately, hoping Gabriel was watching them from somewhere above.

"Don't let him lie to you, boy!" Stringer continued as he held Cage tighter and laughed. He pressed the gun harder against Cage's temple. "Those eyes of his don't lie! He's a killer! If you ever looked at him too close for too long, I know you saw it!"

Cage held his breath, listening. Stringer was right. Gabriel had looked into his eyes after he'd shot that man and had seen something there. Cage had wondered, at the time, what it was. Now he knew; Gabriel had recognized him for what he was in that moment, he was sure of it. But then he had kissed him. Cage hoped what he was didn't matter to Gabriel. The man wasn't exactly a saint.

After a moment of silence, there was another scuffling sound from above and then far down the upper deck, the sound of light steps running on the deck reached them through the fog. Stringer raised his gun and followed the sound, but was unable to see anything worth firing at. Cage briefly entertained the idea of trying to get free, but Stringer put the barrel of the gun back to his temple before he could follow through.

They heard a banging sound from the side of the ship, then all fell silent once more. Cage found himself holding his breath again and straining to see into the heavy fog as his heart sank. It seemed as if someone had just retreated.

"I think your Desert Flower just blew away, Boss," Stringer murmured into Cage's ear.

Cage closed his eyes and tried not to react outwardly, but he knew Stringer could feel his heart hammering in his chest.

"I couldn't get a clear shot," Rose told Flynn breathlessly. "Did you hear him?"

"Yeah," Flynn answered quietly. "Jack Kale."

Rose nodded, his frown deepening in concentration. "I don't know what . . . I don't know."

Flynn was surprised to see the indecision. Rose was clearly struggling with the disclosure, trying to decide how to handle it. Flynn didn't understand why. Even if Cage was the man known as Jack Kale, what did an outlaw like Rose care? Birds of a feather flocked together, after all. Now their almost instant attraction to each other even made sense to Flynn.

Flynn reached over and gave Rose's shoulder a gentle shove. "You're thinking about skinnin' out on him, ain't you?" he asked, appalled. "After all this time preaching to me about love and saving them and you're just going to abandon him now?"

Rose shot him a scowl. "Certainly not." A light entered his dark eyes and he smiled slowly. "But now that you mention it, that is a very good idea."

"How 'bout you, Mister US Marshal?" Stringer shouted after another long stretch of silence. "You going to come fetch your partner 'fore we toss him overboard? Going to be hard for him to stay afloat with just the one arm!"

Two of Stringer's men began forcing Marshal Washington over to the railing of the boat. Cage jerked instinctively, but Stringer held him tighter. Wash didn't struggle at all, something Cage thought was either very brave or very stupid.

"Flynn, you don't show yourself, you hear me?" Wash shouted into the night as they shoved him against the railing. "You kill 'em all!"

"Do it!" Stringer barked before Wash could say any more.

Cage struggled against him, trying to pry himself from Stringer's grip and help the marshal. Wash kicked at one of the men holding him and rammed himself into the other, fighting to keep from being heaved over backward. The man shoved back and Wash wrapped his one good arm around his neck, clearly intending to take him overboard with him if he went.

"Stop!" someone called from the cover of the enveloping fog.

Stringer whirled, putting Cage between himself and the voice. The men stopped struggling with Wash and drew their guns, inching away from the railing and pointing their firearms erratically at the thick fog, trying to see the man who had spoken.

"Let him go," Marshal Flynn ordered, materializing out of the enveloping fog, revealing himself to them as he stepped into the weak, flickering light of an oil lamp attached to the side of the ship. He had two guns drawn, one aimed in Wash's direction at the two men who'd been about to shove him overboard, and the other pointed at Cage and Stringer.

"We got the drop on you, mister," Stringer said to him. Cage could feel how tense the man was as he used him as a shield. Flynn was one twitch of Stringer's finger away from being dead.

There was the last resort of going completely limp. It would distract Stringer long enough for Flynn to shoot him. But Cage didn't know if the marshal would do it, and he certainly didn't want to be lying on the ground playing possum when Stringer decided to put one between his eyes. He decided to see how Flynn would play it.

"I don't want your gold, and I don't want you," Flynn told Stringer. "I just want them," he demanded with a nod of his head at Wash and Cage.

"Where's Rose?" Stringer asked.

"Gone," Flynn answered with a disdainful sneer. "When you started yelling, he said it wasn't worth it to get himself shot for Whistling Jack Kale, and he skinned out."

Stringer barked a laugh.

The marshal fixed his eyes on Cage and he narrowed them. "You really Jack Kale?"

Cage shook his head vehemently, and Stringer gripped his chin hard to stop the movement.

When Stringer spoke, his breath gusted across Cage's neck and caused him to shiver violently. "He is that." He put his lips against Cage's ear, and Cage could feel him smirking. "Whistle for him, Cage."

Cage snarled at him, shaking his head again at Flynn desperately. At the mere thought that Gabriel might have run when he learned who Cage was, the pain in his chest was worse than any punch to the gut. But he wasn't Jack Kale anymore. Nothing would change that.

"I'm not too sure I believe you," Flynn said to Stringer thoughtfully. "But Rose did. He took your little rowboat. We found your coal shell down in the boiler room," he went on in obvious disgust. "Put it in your skiff with a short fuse. I'm sure you heard the result. Now, I'll tell you which one of the lifeboats we didn't put holes in if you hand those men over right now. You can be on your way without any more blood."

"You saying Rose really hightailed it?" Stringer asked suspiciously.

Flynn nodded grimly and sneered again. "Didn't even leave me his guns."

Cage distantly acknowledged the odd sinking feeling in his chest as he stared at the marshal. He didn't know if he should believe it or not, but something deep down told him that Gabriel wasn't really gone. Would Flynn have truly let Gabriel out of his sight, knowing he might lose his prisoner in the ensuing melee?

Stringer snorted and looked around at his men, who were growing even more jittery as the talking continued.

"He was your prisoner," Stringer said to Flynn shrewdly. Flynn stared back at him, unwavering. "You let your prisoner escape? Just let him sail off in our boat and leave you here to deal with us? Didn't even try to shoot at him as he rowed off? I don't believe you. Your sleeve's out of aces, Marshal."

"I'd rather live to track him down again later than get shot now," Marshal Flynn answered coldly. "Now, I'll make you a deal. Last offer. I'll take my marshal and my prisoner with me, and we'll leave you the rest of the boat to do with as you please."

Stringer's grip around Cage's throat loosened slightly, but he was still tense and coiled like a snake. "You can take your marshal. Prisoner stays with me."

"No deal," Flynn said firmly.

Cage stared at the marshal, both impressed and exasperated by his fortitude. He was practically a dead man standing, of course, but he was a brave dead man nonetheless.

Stringer pointed his gun at Flynn. Several of his men cocked their weapons as well. "You can live to track him down later," Stringer murmured in a low, dangerous voice, "or you can get shot now."

Flynn wavered, glancing from Wash to Cage as Cage held his breath. Finally, the marshal nodded in agreement. Apparently, he was willing to sacrifice Cage in order to save Wash. Cage couldn't find it in himself to blame the man for his decision.

As they stood on the outer deck, tense and wary amidst the soupy fog, the very distinct sound of a shotgun's hammer being pulled behind them echoed across the water.

Flynn was careful not to look in the direction he knew Rose was lurking. There were too many guns to deal with for him to give away even the slightest advantage—like where his partner was positioned. He mentally winced away from the thought of Rose being his partner, and he narrowed his eyes at the scene.

The action of the shotgun was still echoing through the dense fog as Flynn watched the ripple of panic spread through the exposed hijackers. He smiled crookedly, more as a show of confidence than any real emotion of the sort. He was anything but confident or cocky. He was, in fact, terrified of what was about to happen. Any sane man would be. Suddenly, there was a flurry of frantic activity, but to Flynn's experienced eye, everything seemed to happen in slow motion.

Cage jerked his body in the big man's grasp, jamming his shoulder into Stringer and sending him off-balance. His captor's gun went off, sending a harmless round into the air as both men toppled over. Cage curled and held his side as if he was hurt as soon as he hit the deck, but then he scrambled up and tackled Stringer to the ground as the man tried to rise.

The shotgun blasted from Rose's hidden position, and one of the hijackers went flying backward and sliding across the damp wooden deck, leaving a smear of blood behind him as he did so. Another man fell as the buckshot struck him, tumbling and rolling. He got to his knees in a panic and tried to crawl toward the relative safety of the salon. Two others began firing haphazardly into the darkness as they retreated toward cover.

Flynn fired two quick shots, nicking one man and missing the other completely as he moved for the cover of a low wall that surrounded a service stairwell. His eyes immediately searched for Wash, fear coiling in his chest as the gunfight bloomed into a bloody, chaotic mess.

He saw Wash elbow one of his captors in the nose and send him falling backward over the railing, and then a burst of fire exploded from Wash's linen sling. Flynn was certain the man had been shot. He watched in terrified confusion as the outlaw standing beside Wash fell to his knees and then pitched forward onto the deck. Wash didn't go down, but instead bent and took the man's gun amidst the fire from the retreating outlaws. He then ran for the cover of the very wall Flynn had ducked behind.

Wash slid into the darkness beside him, panting and, to Flynn's eternal exasperation, laughing breathlessly as he met Flynn's eyes.

"Sling gun," Wash gasped gleefully. He wiggled his fingers and began trying to remove the sling from around his neck.

Flynn rolled his eyes and didn't even try to repress his relieved grin as wood splintered above their heads. They both flinched and ducked, covering their heads as slivers rained down on them. As soon as the firing had ceased, Wash rose to his knees and glanced over the railing. He nodded to Flynn and they began returning fire in a measured sequence. The few glimpses Flynn managed to steal told him that Rose had run out of shotgun shells and was now using two of his stolen six-shooters from his hidden perch—with slightly lessened effect—as they chased the outlaws back into the salon. Cage had lost his fight with Stringer and was once again being used as a shield as they retreated toward the doorway.

Flynn and Wash trailed after the others toward the main cabin, taking cover behind the ornate furniture that was peppered throughout the large room. There were doors on the other side of the salon that led to the foredeck, but there was no way off the deck. Flynn and Wash had the only exit covered from this spot.

Flynn cursed feelingly as the last of the men disappeared into the salon and safety. They had them sort of penned in, but all those passengers were in there with them and in serious danger. He and Wash may have the better position strategically, but the hijackers still had the upper hand. He felt Wash moving beside him, and he glanced over at his partner as they both knelt behind a table they had turned over. Wash was peering at the salon doors intently and gritting his teeth, his previous delight over finally being able to use his sling contraption forgotten.

"Goddamn it."

"You hurt?" Flynn asked in a hoarse voice.

"Just my damn pride," Wash said without facing him.

Relief flooded Flynn's body as he examined Wash with new eyes. His small amount of time with Gabriel Rose had caused him to reconsider his priorities quite a bit.

He knelt down again so he was facing Wash behind the overturned table. Without further thought to the consequences of his actions, he grabbed the man's shirt and tugged him close enough to kiss him.

# CHAPTER 15

age was half-dragged into the salon by his shirt collar, Stringer's hands digging into his neck as he struggled with the bigger man. He couldn't remember the last time he had been bested repeatedly in a fight like this. Either his year in anonymity had weakened him, or Bat Stringer had grown more adept at manhandling. It could possibly have been a little of both.

Then again, Cage couldn't remember ever having fought Stringer before, save for their last encounter when Cage had cut off the man's finger. Cage's no-nonsense demeanor, when he had been known as Jack Kale, had kept him safe from challenges, both physically and mentally. Stringer had loved him, and even *he* had been marginally afraid of him.

Cage had been lucky in that respect, he realized. If Stringer had ever gotten it in his head to hurt him, he could have done so just like he was doing tonight. He may have had Cage bested with his strength and possibly his ability with a gun, though he didn't think even Stringer knew that. Cage's bruised ribs didn't help any, but that wasn't really here or there now. Stringer had all the advantages, even with Gabriel outside trying to get to him.

Stringer released his collar, and Cage hit the floor hard. He snarled at the Oriental rug, growing angrier as the feeling of helplessness swamped him. He couldn't even remember his reasons for leaving, now. He couldn't remember why he had abandoned the men who were loyal to him, or the man who would have given his life for him. He reminded himself that his reasons had been good, and that even through the weakness brought on by pain and exhaustion, he still wanted to cut off the rest of Stringer's fingers. Gabriel was out there fighting for him. He hadn't left him here to die. Cage had to believe that Gabriel knew who he really was now and didn't care.

"What in the blue blazing hell is he doing?" Stringer bellowed. He kicked out at Cage again in frustration.

Cage curled up, trying to protect his vulnerable parts from more abuse.

"Who attacks twenty men with just two, huh? Who?" Stringer asked no one in particular as Cage fought not to gasp aloud. Stringer continued to rage. "This ain't the damn Alamo! Custer's fucking Last Stand! They all died in the end!"

Two of Stringer's men began blockading the salon doors as most of the passengers whimpered and tittered from the far end of the room. The rough and readies who'd all been tied up and gagged struggled against their bonds. Cage could see the fire in their eyes. If just one of those men got loose, Stringer and his men were as good as dead.

"What do we do, Cap?" one of Stringer's men asked breathlessly.

Cage raised his head, recognizing the signs of panic burgeoning in the ranks. Again, his first instinct was to calm them and give orders. He fought it back and closed his eyes.

Stringer didn't answer. He stood staring at the door, breathing hard.

"That goddamn trinket ain't worth dying for!" another of the men snarled when Stringer remained silent.

"You shut your mouth," Stringer snapped. He began to pace back and forth restlessly.

Cage followed his movements warily, covering his ribs with his arms as he remained curled on his side. If he didn't move, Stringer might just lower his guard again. Cage wasn't about to give up this fight yet.

"He said he'd leave if we give him his prisoner; I say we do it," Alvarado said. He was reloading his guns calmly. Stringer had picked a good man for his second-in-command. He didn't seem to be bothered by the situation or by the blood spreading on his shoulder. A right-hand man had to be unflappable and steady. Alvarado was, but he was only any good to Stringer if Stringer listened to him.

Another of Stringer's men cursed at Alvarado. "Well, that was before his other prisoner started shooting at us! That marshal weren't planning to leave any which way we went. I say we kill him." He pointed his pistol at Cage. "And then hightail it out of here."

"How?" Stringer asked, his voice calm once more. "You can't run out there with nothing but a lick and a promise, and plan to make it past that shotgun."

"Rose can't be as good as they say," the man argued. "And he's out of buckshot; all he's got is his irons."

"I seen Dusty Rose in action. He's as fast as they say he is, you better believe it," Stringer said as he stared off at the frightened passengers with a distant, thoughtful look. He seemed to be formulating.

Cage looked up in shock at what he'd said, as did all his men. He and Stringer had ridden together since they were both between hay and grass, and Cage knew neither of them had ever seen Gabriel before. Stringer was either lying to his men, or he had seen Gabriel in action some time in the past twelve months. Gabriel had told Cage he'd been laying low in Colorado and Missouri, trying to run from his reputation.

Again, Cage felt like he was missing something. Why would Stringer have been in either territory without at least a few of his men with him? Why would he go anywhere alone? And what had Gabriel been doing that Stringer had seen him?

Cage was still peering at him when Stringer turned. Their eyes met and Cage found himself foundering in a confused mix of the intimacy of their old connection and the unfamiliarity of the man Stringer had become in the last few years. This new Stringer was both attractive in his confidence and frightening in his anger. But most of all, Cage wanted him dead. He swallowed heavily as he recognized the light of an idea in Stringer's eyes.

"Gather up all the womenfolk," Stringer ordered quietly, his gaze unwavering. His men looked at him in confusion for a moment before turning to do as he had asked without question.

Stringer knelt in front of Cage and cocked his head. He reached out, and Cage flinched away from what he thought would be another swing of Stringer's fist. Instead, Stringer's fingers just barely brushed his cheek. Cage jerked his head away and tried to sit up. His pride smarted over the fact that he had to face Stringer from his back and couldn't do it eye to eye, toe to toe. He winced and curled back on his side as his ribcage screamed in protest, but he gritted his teeth and pushed up to his knees.

Stringer watched him with an impassive frown. "You love him?"

Cage stared at him, his breaths coming with greater difficulty as his ribs burned and throbbed. He met Stringer's eyes, searching for a trap in the question. He was surprised to find nothing there but sincerity. His eyes flickered away from Stringer's piercing gaze, and he gave a confused shrug and a minute shake of his head. A few more questions like this, with Stringer's mind full of his jealousy, Cage might be able to launch another attack. But the questions were troubling Cage too.

"Never known you to be indecisive."

Cage just licked his lips and looked back at him warily. Stringer was right. Cage had rarely been indecisive. He had always known exactly what he wanted and he had taken it. He knew he wanted Gabriel. There was something there, and he wanted to have more of it. He hadn't expected to run into his past here in the midst of it all and have the waters muddied.

It wasn't complicated, in the end. There came times in a man's life when a side had to be chosen. This was one of those times, and Cage had chosen his side. He didn't regret his choice, either.

He met Stringer's eyes again and nodded his head.

"That's what I thought," Stringer whispered as his knuckles trailed down the side of Cage's jaw in an uncomfortably intimate gesture. "Well, I'm willing to bet anyone you've gone and fallen in love with won't go shooting a lady."

Cage gritted his teeth and struck out. His fist caught Stringer on the chin, but the man had foreseen the attack and was leaning away. It was a glancing blow, worth nothing more than the satisfaction of making contact.

"Don't get your back up, Boss," Stringer said, infuriatingly calm. "If he is who you think he is, there's no reason to worry."

Cage balled his fist. The truth was that he had no idea what kind of man Gabriel Rose was. He didn't know if Gabriel would shoot through a woman to get to his intended target. And what was worse, he didn't know if he was more concerned about the womenfolk

Stringer planned to use, or for Gabriel. What would happen if Bat Stringer and Gabriel Rose went face-to-face in a gunfight? Would either of them live through it? Would *anyone*?

Stringer read his reaction just as clearly as he had always done. "You worried about him or me?" he asked almost sadly as he looked over Cage's face.

Cage stared at him, determined to let him know the answer wasn't him.

Stringer smiled grimly. "I guess we're about to find out."

Wash flailed in Flynn's grasp, but to Flynn's surprise, he didn't pull away. Flynn kissed him with everything he had as the smoke from the gun battle and the wispy fog from outside surrounded them, knowing that this was the last kiss he would ever take from someone. Either he would be killed in the ensuing gunfight or Wash would finish him off after for the unwanted advance. If, by some miracle, neither of those things came to pass, Flynn knew he would have no interest in ever kissing anyone besides Wash again.

Finally, Flynn pulled away from him. He moved slowly, hating to end it but knowing that it would have to end sooner rather than later. There were some things you just didn't hold off, and gunfights were usually one of them. When he leaned far enough away to force himself to look at Wash with a deep blush, Wash was staring at him with wide green eyes.

"Sorry," Flynn whispered, his voice betraying the surprise he felt over his own actions. Wash continued to stare at him in shock. Flynn blushed even deeper, unable to look away. "Always wanted to do that."

Wash blinked rapidly and then licked his lips. Flynn waited apprehensively as the sound of furniture scraping along the floor came from within the salon. He didn't pay it much attention. He was concentrating solely on Wash and his expressive eyes.

"What took you so long?" Wash finally asked, voice gone hoarse.

The knot of tension in Flynn's stomach snapped as if Wash's words had cut through it. His lips parted in surprise and relief, and Wash slowly grinned.

"That's real sweet," Rose said, voice absent of any inflection in the cover of the darkened room.

Wash and Flynn both jumped at the unexpected sound of his voice. Wash glanced over his shoulder and grunted in annoyance. He finally managed to shrug his sling off completely and tossed it onto the ground with a huff. Rose knelt down behind them without another word.

Flynn glanced from one man to the other, completely at a loss for what to do next. He was blushing furiously but elated, all the same, still trying to process what Wash had said and done. He hadn't just accepted the kiss. He'd welcomed it, returned it. Even enjoyed it.

"Well, go on," Rose huffed with a gesture between Flynn and Wash, "kiss him again. I'll wait."

Flynn and Wash shared a look that was an odd mixture of joy and guilt. But Rose seemed to actually be waiting for them to do it, because he hadn't yet pointed out that they were in the midst of a gunfight or that the man Rose had been so keen to rescue all night was being held captive and in very real danger. Flynn let the guilt pass by, reached out, and pulled Wash to him again.

The moment was marred by the sound of Rose calmly reloading his pistols, but Flynn enjoyed it all the same. Wash smelled like worn leather and fresh grass after it rained. His good hand slid into Flynn's hair and he pressed into Flynn until they lost their balance and toppled over backward.

"Greenhorns," Rose muttered. He spun the cylinder of his pistol home and then slid it into his belt.

Flynn tried hard not to laugh, but Wash snickered against his lips. They were going giddy, Flynn knew. And this was no time for that.

Wash pushed himself off Flynn clumsily with his one good hand, and he smirked as he helped him up. "Later," he promised, and Flynn nodded.

Rose was watching them impassively, much as Flynn had seen small Indian children watch him as he rode through their camp. Like someone who understood what was going on but either didn't really care or knew they had no part in it. Flynn glanced at him apologetically.

"They got two choices," Rose told them quietly, apparently choosing to forego any jibes he might make about them.

Flynn found himself grateful. It seemed the man wasn't *all* bad.

"And what are those?" Wash inquired as he wiped at his mouth.

"Either they wait 'til dawn and try to slip past us while we're nodding off, or they use those passengers in there as cover," Rose put forth, nodding at the door as he spoke.

"Dawn's a long way off," Wash said doubtfully.

Flynn glanced out at the sky through the open doors, trying to gauge just how far off dawn might be. But the fog was all-encompassing, and he couldn't remember the last time he'd heard the clock strike an hour. He had no idea what time it was.

"Not as long as you think," Rose said. "It's coming up on five now."

"You think they'll wait that long?" Flynn asked.

Rose peered at him and then lowered his head, his brow furrowing and his lips pursing in thought.

"If it was you," Flynn prodded. "What would you do?"

"Why am I always the one who has to think like the outlaw, huh?" Rose asked.

"Because you're the one who boarded in irons," Flynn said, though he was smiling as he said it.

"Point well made," Rose said, albeit grudgingly. He peered out at the darkness, his sharp eyes darting this way and that as he looked for something Flynn couldn't fathom. Finally, he shook his head slowly and sighed, as if he didn't like the answer he had come up with. "I'd gather those passengers, and I'd march them out in front of me."

"Hide behind innocent people?" Wash asked incredulously.

Rose nodded unapologetically. "Hide behind them, and dare you to shoot at them as I get away."

Flynn and Wash were both silent. Just the thought of watching helplessly as those men escaped behind the cover of some innocent civilian was appalling.

"So we got to get to them before they can move," Wash finally said determinedly.

"How?" Rose asked, voice going flat again. "There is one door into that room, and you can bet the farm they've got it covered."

"But the entire opposite wall is lined with windows and doors," Wash said. "We could—"

"That's wonderful," Rose said sarcastically. "But to what point? You can't get to them. Not unless you go in from the deck above, which is damn near impossible unless you did a stint with Barnum and Bailey when you were younger. And even if you could find your way through the windows from twelve feet above them, how long do you suppose you'd last after crashing through the glass panes and falling on your face amidst a battalion of unfriendly guns?"

"I see your point," Wash said dejectedly.

"There's nothing to do but wait them out."

"And what about Cage?" Flynn asked before he could think better of it.

"What about him?" Rose asked coldly.

"Not two hours ago, you were preaching to me about attacking and saving someone you loved. Now, you're playing it safe?"

"That was before we knew who he really is," Rose snapped. The pain in his voice was all too obvious. "For all we know, Cage is in league with them and he used me to get himself on this boat. In case you haven't noticed, I'm not one for self-sacrifice."

"He's here because *you* tried to escape. *You* pulled *him* along, not the other way around."

"I don't think he's in cahoots with those boys," Wash said immediately. "They ain't been kind to him. Got a few bruised ribs, I'm sure of that."

Rose looked at him almost angrily for a moment, and Flynn recognized the emotion in Rose's eyes as frustration. He didn't truly believe what he'd said, he was just trying to deal with the feeling of helplessness.

"What do you care if he's really Jack Kale?" Flynn asked, understanding what he might be dealing with.

Rose glanced at him warily.

"You might love him, right? You certainly care about him. Don't make the same mistake you kept me from making. Save him now. Question yourself later."

Rose stared uncertainly for another long moment before shifting where he knelt. "Why do you care?"

"I don't. I just need your guns," Flynn said, shuffling his weight from one knee to the other, hoping the observant shootist didn't see through the lie. He didn't know why he cared, but he did. He didn't want to have to try to explain why he gave a hoot about the lives of two outlaws, much less hoped that they were happy.

Rose snorted and shook his head. "I do love your honesty, Marshal Flynn," he grumbled as he began loading his other gun. "Okay. We're going after them before they can move. So what's the plan, marshals?"

Flynn and Wash looked at one another, mutually stumped by the predicament.

Rose glanced back up at them and sighed impatiently. "Have either of you stopped to wonder who's steering this blasted thing?" he asked as he spun the cylinder and flicked it back into place.

Flynn blinked at him and shook his head. He hadn't given it much thought. But someone had to be guiding the cumbersome paddle steamer through the treacherous waters of the Mississippi. If not, they would have long ago run aground.

Rose slid his last two rounds of buckshot into his shotgun. "You two cover those doors. I'll go see if I can't shake loose some varmints," he practically growled before slinking away into the fog.

Flynn watched the eddying mist open up to admit him and then swirl closed to cover his tracks. He shivered violently, then licked his lips and met Wash's eyes. They stared at one another, at a loss after essentially giving up their authority to their own prisoner, until Wash edged closer and kissed Flynn again gently.

"We better hope he don't get himself killed," Wash finally said, his breath gusting over Flynn's lips enticingly.

"Why? 'Cause he's the only one knows what the hell's going on?" Flynn asked dazedly, distracted by Wash's body so close to his.

"Well, there's that," Wash said. Then he gestured between them and smirked. He practically snickered into one last kiss. "But mostly 'cause he's the only one can tell us how to go about doing this sort of thing."

"Get up," Stringer murmured as he tugged at Cage's arm.

Cage managed not to groan in pain. Stringer slid his arm under Cage's chin, choking him as he tightened his grip. He lifted him to his feet, then wrapped one arm around Cage's chest to hold him securely from behind.

Cage hung his head and inhaled deeply, his breath hitching with the pain as his body was forced to stretch out. He fought not to lean his weight against Stringer. He didn't have much strength left, but he was determined not to lean on the very man who was probably going to kill him.

He looked up to see what was left of Stringer's boarding party gathering the women up and tying their hands behind their backs, then looping them together like a line of prisoners going to the hangman's noose. Cage craned his neck, trying to meet Stringer's eyes, shaking his head and opening his mouth, begging Stringer to reconsider.

"I ain't dying here," Stringer whispered to him. "I don't give a lick if they do."

Cage's brow furrowed, and he started to shake his head again, but Stringer wrenched him around and pressed their lips together violently. Cage didn't struggle this time, even though he told himself to. All the activity in the large room seemed to fall away. The pain in Cage's ribs faded to a dull throb. Nothing mattered but the kiss he was sharing with a man he had once cared for. It mattered because he realized in that moment that it meant absolutely nothing to him. The memory of what they had been was no longer strong enough to make up for what Bat Stringer had become.

Cage gasped against Stringer's mouth, trying to wrench away. Stringer kissed him hard one last time and then turned him around to hold him once more, Cage's back pressed to Stringer's chest and facing away from him. The barrel of Stringer's gun came to rest against Cage's jaw.

"Let's go," Stringer whispered into his ear.

Cage closed his eyes as he saw the men lining the women up in front of the door, guns to their backs and forcing them forward. They were crying and pleading with their captors, begging them to find some other way even as two men moved aside the things they had piled against the door.

Cage turned his head into the gun, brushing the side of his face over Stringer's nose and mouth. It was his silent way of pleading, and Stringer knew it well enough. He felt Stringer's breath catch and hope swelled briefly within him.

The boat lurched under their feet, making them both stagger. The echo of a shotgun blast sounded in the distance. Cage and Stringer both froze, apparently the only ones who had heard it. Seconds later, they both jerked and went tumbling to the deck as the ship beneath them made a radical change of direction.

Several guns went off as men lost their balance. Cage's ribs sent blinding pain through his entire body as he landed, making it impossible to breathe for a few crucial moments, and he didn't have the presence of mind to even think about what had happened, much less try to escape. He only had time to be thankful that Stringer had merely released the gun he'd been holding to Cage's head rather than squeezing the trigger. He foundered on the deck. The muscles between his ribs wracked with spasms, paralyzing him as Stringer rolled away. Stringer was back to his knees, looking around in confused alarm as Cage tried desperately to get up.

Stringer and several others had just regained their footing when the paddle steamer came to a jarring stop and sent everyone to the ground again with shouts and screams of alarm.

Around the room, no one had managed to keep his or her feet. People were piled on the floor near the door and cautiously struggling to gain their balance once more. Several of the women got to their feet faster than Cage would have thought possible and raced for the unchained door. They threw it open even with their tied hands and ran, leaving behind their husbands and fathers and brothers and sons, dragging the ladies who were still tied to them and not able to keep up. Some of the prisoners crowded against the far wall were fighting with their bonds, taking advantage of the sudden chaos and attempting to free themselves.

Cage struggled to his knees and then shakily to his feet as he observed the disarray.

Something had stopped the riverboat.

Flynn and Wash both lurched forward, unable to keep their balance even though they had braced themselves after hearing the shotgun. Wash grunted in pain as he landed on his bad arm, and he rolled onto his back, holding his arm and wincing. Flynn's gun skittered out of his hand and across the floor.

"Son of a bitch!" Wash shouted as he tried to get to his feet.

The deck was tilted, and Flynn ended up sliding even after he found his footing. He bent and helped Wash up, still blinking around in confusion. Rose must have fought with the man in the wheelhouse before he fired the shotgun or the crash would have been delayed much longer. Flynn glanced to the wheelhouse worriedly, wondering if Rose had even been the one to fire the gun.

How many people had been inside the wheelhouse? How many people could Rose take on before he lost a fight?

Wash cursed again as the door to the salon was thrown open and people started pouring out. Flynn grabbed for his gun and raised it, aiming and waiting for a target that wasn't wearing a dress. Wash was beside him, breathing hard and aiming his own gun with one hand.

The escaping passengers scrambled out into the main cabin and hit the curved staircase like a herd of stampeding cattle, all tied together and so frightened that they didn't even notice the two marshals standing there.

Flynn and Wash both lowered their guns and watched them, jaws lax in shock as the cavalcade of gingham and lace stormed by.

A moment later, they were gone, up or down the stairs to what he supposed they thought was safety. Flynn looked at Wash and shrugged helplessly. Even if they had been thinking to try to stop them, they wouldn't have been able to make a dent in that kind of panic.

"At least they didn't jump overboard," Wash said.

Flynn had to purse his lips to keep himself from smiling.

Seconds later, the sound of running feet shook them out of it, and Flynn raised his gun again. Beside him, Wash fired once, twice, three times in quick succession. Two men fell as they tried to escape the salon. One got back up and began limping toward the doors, trying to get away. Flynn hesitated, uncertain as to whether these were actually the hijackers or if they were escaping passengers. Even when one of the men fired back at Wash, Flynn couldn't make himself pull the trigger. If the prisoners were escaping, they could also have armed themselves, he reasoned hastily.

Then more people poured out of the doors, some of them wearing nightshirts and in their bare feet, others dressed as if for a late dinner, all terrified and oblivious to any danger as they hurtled past the marshals and their guns. Wash held his fire and began shouting for them to go back into the salon; they were safer inside, not in the midst of a gunfight. He may as well have been reasoning with a herd of buffalo, for all Flynn could see.

Several of the hijackers used the cover of their escaping prisoners to scuttle away. Flynn cursed inwardly and opened fire, aiming for those few men who were fully dressed, armed, and dusty. They headed out the doors and for the railing, leaping over it into the raging Mississippi. Flynn thought it was suicide to jump. Now that the steamer had stopped moving, the rushing water of the river was even more treacherous than it had been. A man would be swept away in the strong current and never so much as get his head above water before he drowned or was slammed into something hard enough to crack his head open. That, or when they leaped over the edge they would land on the same thing the steamer had snagged on and break every bone in their bodies.

Two more of the men dropped to the floor under their fire, one rolling in pain and the other motionless and bleeding. The rest began firing back as they tried to make their escape, heedless of any innocent bystanders whom they hit. Puffs of thick, choking gunpowder began to obscure the scene even as the moonlight diffused through the fog and gave it an eerie blue backlight.

They were all firing at sound now, rather than at men. Anyone dumb enough to still be standing would be shot. Flynn knelt behind the upturned table to reload and out of the corner of his eye caught sight of a figure behind them, running through the main cabin from the direction of the aft berths. Flynn whirled and fired. The man fell backward to the floor amidst a jumble of disturbed furniture as Flynn belatedly realized he may have just shot Rose as he ran back from the wheelhouse. Then again, it could also have been the man Rose had gone and failed to kill . . .

It was with mixed relief and dread that he saw the figure rise once more and begin limping toward them. He kept his gun trained warily on the man until he spoke.

"Don't shoot me again, you blasted Yank!" Rose shouted through the gunfire as two more wounded men managed to leap over the side of the ship and escape a bullet.

Rose slumped behind another overturned table, his back to it, legs splayed in front of him, obviously hurt. Still, he was attempting to cover the only other route of escape for the men trapped in the salon. Flynn was reloading as Rose fired off five rapid shots that dropped the two last men trying to make a break for it. The passengers had all fled. Stringer's men were all either gone or dead or dying. The movement seemed to come to a standstill with all the suddenness that had begun it. Flynn held his breath, waiting for the next shoe to drop as the smoke and fog swirled angrily.

Gradually, an unusually large shadow materialized out of the cloud of gun smoke, silhouetted by the light from within the salon. Flynn and Wash both watched from behind their protective table, vibrating with tension.

"Nice shooting," the shadow called out to them. The smoke from the guns and the fog from without swirled in the light of the salon, dissipating quickly as the wind off the river kicked up.

Flynn licked his lips and shifted restlessly. As the distorted shadow grew larger, it became obvious that it was, in fact, two men. Cage was barely standing under his own power. Wash had said the man had been sorely mistreated, and it looked like he was weakening from his injuries. He was certainly in no shape to assist them.

"Stringer!" Wash called out. "You can't win this fight!"

"We'll just see about that. Unless you aim to see Micajah's blood on this deck, you're going to let me pass!"

"You don't think I can shoot you between the eyes before you take a step?" Rose murmured in the gloom, his voice carrying eerily through the darkness and fog.

Flynn found himself shivering.

Stringer moved, pulling Cage to face where Rose was crouched. He obviously thought Rose the greater threat. Flynn heartily agreed.

"Cage!" Rose called, voice rough.

Cage jerked in response, but the larger man held him firmly, using him as a shield with his gun held to the underside of Cage's jaw.

"I'll kill him," Stringer said, though Flynn thought the man's voice wavered with the threat.

Rose answered with the very distinct sound of the hammer on his gun being pulled back.

Stringer lowered his head until he was peering around Cage, completely hidden unless Rose chose to shoot through the very man he claimed to care so much about. Neither Flynn nor Wash had a clear shot. Stringer knew where they were and he knew how to stay out of their line of fire. He was certainly no greenhorn.

Even though their numbers favored them, Flynn couldn't help but feel like they still held the disadvantage. There was no expecting help from inside. All the passengers who could escape had already done so, and none of them had chosen to stick around and aid in their salvation.

Suddenly, Rose removed himself from the darkness where he had taken cover. He stood and faced Stringer, lowering his head as he very deliberately eased the hammer down on his gun and slid it into his belt. The challenge was painfully clear. Flynn and Wash watched in morbid fascination, unable to do anything other than stare as the first rays of the sun's light began to stretch across the deck.

Cage held out his hand pleadingly to Rose, shaking his head. Flynn uncharitably wondered which man he was trying to protect. Stringer was careful not to allow him too much freedom of movement, obviously not trusting him any more than Rose did at this point. Stringer's grip on his gun tightened, but he still had it aimed at Cage's head rather than at Rose. He moved sideways, out the door and onto the deck. Rose stood stock-still as he watched and waited, his head down and his stolen hat throwing his dark eyes into even further shadow. He moved deliberately, following them outside. Flynn and Wash crept along after them.

"What are you waiting for, Stringer? Noon?" Rose finally asked with a maddeningly cocky smirk when he had reached the doorway.

Stringer moved, shoving Cage out of the way almost as if he was afraid the man would be caught in the crossfire, and he lifted his gun and took aim. Rose drew his weapon, the motion so fast and smooth that Flynn wondered if he had somehow been holding the gun in his hand all along. He fired from his hip at almost the same moment that Stringer pulled his trigger. The guns went off with resounding simultaneous blasts, echoing each other in the heavy air of the dawn.

Flynn knew that the advantage in a draw was not, as most people thought, who drew the fastest. Fast helped, of course, but you had to aim too or you were a dead man. Stringer and Rose both obviously knew that. Neither would have lived so long west of the Mississippi if they didn't.

The two men stumbled back from the showdown, both of them hit and bleeding but still very much alive.

Flynn stood and aimed his gun, but Wash stopped him just as Cage moved into his line of fire and tackled Stringer to the ground. They slid across the tilting deck of the boat toward the doors and grappled as Rose fell to his knees, stunned and bloody. Flynn could see two blood trails on his body in the diffused dawn light filtering through the skylights and the doors, one at his side as if the bullet had grazed his ribs, and one at his thigh. Flynn knew he himself had hit Rose once. He wondered which shot had been his, and which had taken Rose down this time.

As Flynn watched him, Rose kept his eyes on Cage and Stringer and raised his gun again. "Cage," he shouted in warning.

Cage turned his shoulders, abandoning the punch he had been about to land, inadvertently shielding Stringer as the man rolled to his knees and brought his own gun up. Rose hesitated even as Stringer took aim, then he jerked his gun and quickly fired two shots, missing Stringer and hitting the gas lamp hanging from a hook near the ship's hull. Sparks flew as the bullets glanced off the metal lantern and splashed the hot oil inside, and both Stringer and Cage flinched away from them. Rose lunged to his feet and held his gun in both hands, limping closer to the two men, who were both on the ground now that Rose had stolen the advantage.

"Dust the iron," he ordered in a strained voice.

Stringer glared at him, still on his back from taking cover on the deck. Flynn finally forced himself to move. He and Wash both stood, circling around the man and covering him from all angles.

Stringer looked around at them all mutinously, but then very slowly set his gun on the ground. Cage was on his knees next to him, one hand pressed to his ribs as he hung his head either in pain or defeat. Rose edged closer, his wary eyes on Stringer as he knelt next to Cage and placed a hand on his head.

"Are you okay?" he asked, so softly that Flynn barely heard it.

Cage peered up at him and nodded. "I'm sorry," he mouthed. The hard lines of Rose's face seemed to soften, and he ran his hand through Cage's hair and knelt to whisper something in his ear.

Flynn's eyes were drawn to the sight. He never saw Stringer move. Wash did, but not in time to do anything aside from shout out a warning and raise his gun.

Stringer lunged at Rose and Cage with a large knife drawn. It flashed wickedly in the dawn light as he brought it down toward Rose's back. Cage's arm shot out to block the blow, catching Stringer's wrist between his forearms and twisting it away from Rose as Rose reeled to the side. Cage lunged to his feet, Stringer's arm still in his grasp, and they wrapped around each other as they fought for control.

The knife plunged into Stringer's ribcage as the two men stayed locked in the violent embrace. Cage didn't seem at all shocked or regretful as the knife slid home, but Stringer certainly did. Cage let him go, and he staggered backward, toward the railing of the ship.

He looked down at the knife Cage had shoved into him, then up at Cage with a mixture of rage and confusion. He lurched sideways, then wrapped his arm around Rose's neck, and threw himself backward. Rose kicked his feet out, pulling on the arm that held him and struggling to get away as Stringer used his larger body mass to send them both over the railing. The two men seemed to hang suspended in the air for a moment as Rose kicked and struggled against the pull. His hands closed around Stringer's forearm at his neck, but with one last gasping breath, both men went tumbling into the darkness and swirling fog.

A splash below into the rushing waters of the Mississippi was all that signaled their passing.

# CHAPTER 16

The sun was rising toward its zenith by the time the steamer was tugged off the sandbar. The workers had been forced to bank much of the cargo, taking it to shore in order to lighten the ship enough to be able to pull it off the sandbar. Manpower was scarce, and the riverboat captain in charge decided that there was no need to post a guard on the riverbank. There was nothing left of value there anyway, and no one left to try to steal it.

Once the ship was free of the sandbar, all those boxes of fake gold were loaded back on her, along with the bags and sacks of sugar, cotton, and tobacco, and they were under way.

Bodies were lined up in the salon and covered with rough canvas as the boat limped toward port in New Madrid, Missouri. Several lawmen boarded the steamer after it began heading back up the river, including an aide from the territorial Supreme Court Justice.

"We received your telegram, Marshal Flynn," the aide told Flynn when he boarded just north of where they had gone to ground.

"What telegram?" Flynn asked.

The man produced a folded yellow piece of paper, and Flynn looked it over. It warned of an impending hijack and begged the local authorities to meet the riverboat at New Madrid to give aid. There was no name on it. How the hell had they known the boat would be stopped at New Madrid?

"I didn't send this," Flynn said as he handed it back.

"If you didn't, Marshal, then who did?"

"I couldn't begin to tell you, son."

The confused aide nodded, then thanked the marshals for all they had done aboard the ship that night and wandered away to join the investigators who were questioning the other passengers.

"You think it was Stringer who sent it?" Wash whispered just as soon as they were alone again.

"Can't imagine who else it would be," Flynn said with a frown.

"Why would Stringer warn anyone about what he was about to do? And how in the hell could he know we'd go aground near New Madrid? No way he could've known we'd be tugged here."

"Why did he do anything he did?" Flynn asked with a shrug. "He hijacked a steamer full of fake gold and did nothing but herd people back and forth and get bunches of folks killed. I'm not going to waste my brain on figuring it out. He's gone. He took a good man with him. I'm going to leave it there."

Wash nodded, but he looked troubled as Flynn turned away.

There was a lot of preening and huffing as the various and sundry law officers tried to reckon who should be in charge, and Flynn and Wash sat idly by and watched until someone decided to hear from them what had happened.

They both told their stories, as did many of the ship's officers and the passengers who had been rounded up. The authorities were still trying to decide what to do about the incident when the port of New Madrid came into view.

Wash and Flynn stood side by side, watching as the port grew larger. They were silent, unable to think of anything more worth saying after the events of the previous night. Even the elation of the few small kisses they had shared and the promise the future held for them now could not cut through the overwhelming sorrow of the loss of a man neither of them had known they even liked. Gabriel Rose had proved himself in the end, and Flynn was sorry to see him go the way he had.

Cage sat alone, his head hanging and his eyes closed. To Flynn, he seemed even more silent than usual, drowning in sorrow and pain. His wounds had been tended and his bruised ribs had been wrapped tight, so that even if he had wanted to slump as he sat, he would not have been able to do so.

They had searched the river as best they could that night, calling out for any hint of life from the rushing water below. But no sign of Gabriel Rose or Bat Stringer had been found. They had simply disappeared, like so many before them, into the muddy water of the Mississippi.

"Gentlemen," the Justice's aide said as they stood at the railing.

Flynn and Wash both turned to face him, greeting him solemnly.

"It has been determined that this was not an escape attempt on the part of your prisoner."

Wash and Flynn stared at him. Flynn fought hard not to scoff at the man, and even harder not to hit him. A day ago, he probably would have thought the same thing. Rose had tried to escape several times and in creative ways. But, at the end, he had stuck with them. He had given his life to save innocent people, even if his reasons had been selfish. That had to stand for something. The measure of a man was when he did the right thing even if no one was watching.

"We have also taken into consideration your suggestions," the aide continued officiously, "and both your prisoners will receive a full pardon for their heroic efforts."

A weight seemed to lift off Flynn's chest, and he nodded gratefully. A posthumous pardon for Gabriel Rose wouldn't do the man much good. It would probably even have irked him, Flynn mused fondly. But for Cage, a pardon would mean everything. Wash turned away from the aide and went to join Cage where he sat. He knelt in front of the silent man, unlocking his irons and telling him the news.

Cage nodded woodenly and looked over at Flynn, his eyes sad and lost. After a moment, he reached into his pocket and extracted a small, shiny object and handed it to Wash. Flynn realized it was Wash's badge, hidden away and saved from the hijackers. The gesture both warmed his heart and made him inexplicably ache all over.

They had told whoever would listen what Cage had done, trying to prevent anyone from being hurt and taking most of the punishment on himself. Flynn knew he would never really learn what had happened or what the truth behind the whole matter was. Cage was the only one who knew, and he couldn't tell them. Or wouldn't tell them.

They had neglected to mention that they'd actually had the man known as Whistling Jack Kale in their possession all this time. It turned out that Cage, aka Jack Kale, was considered dead and gone by most, and therefore was now one of the lesser wanted fugitive outlaws in the territories. There wasn't all that high a price on his head. Ratting him out wouldn't have done any of the passengers much good, but Flynn had still expected someone to talk. To Flynn's eternal surprise, not one of the passengers on board had mentioned who Cage really was. Whether they just hadn't believed Stringer or were willing to leave Cage be in exchange for what he'd done for them, Flynn couldn't guess. Mostly he figured keeping quiet about it was just the way of the West.

"Well, son, you had me fooled," Flynn said as he sat down beside Cage. The man gave him a wary look, his brow furrowing. Flynn smiled kindly at him. "I thought you were nothing but a broke horse when we picked you up. Whistling Jack Kale. Goddamn, son."

"Language," Wash said.

Cage smiled wanly and shrugged.

"I got one question for you," Flynn said to Cage. He waited until Cage nodded in agreement. "How in the hell do you go from riding with a posse like the Border Scouts to burning blankets in an Army fort?"

Cage was still frowning as he dug in his shirt pocket for the little pad of paper they'd purchased him. He scrawled a single word across it in neat letters.

*Atonement.*

Flynn stared at the word for a long time, until Cage finally closed the leather cover and slid the pad back into his shirt. Wash put a hand on Cage's shoulder and gave him a pat.

"You're a man to ride the river with, Cage," Wash said. "You done made your peace now. Now it's time for you to do right by you."

Cage swallowed hard and nodded, his eyes betraying a conflict still warring within him.

They sat with him for a long while, all of them silent and solemn.

After the ship's landing stage was secured to a particularly large tree, a bang from the hold announced the cargo being moved. Flynn edged closer and leaned over the railing to see what was going on. There were lines of soldiers on the shore, waiting for the hold to be secured so they could board and inspect the boxes of fake gold. The shipment still had to make its way to New Orleans. Flynn snorted at them in annoyance. Boxes of fake gold being transported by the Army was a new one to him. Perhaps they were a decoy, as Rose had suggested. Flynn didn't know and didn't care.

He also saw two men in impeccable suits standing apart from the line of uniformed men, waiting on something.

Flynn frowned and turned around to search for Wash and Cage. "Hey," he called to them. He gestured for them to come look, and both men shuffled over, leaning over the rail with him.

To Flynn's surprise, the soldiers began unloading the supposed crates of gold almost as soon as the gangplank was secured. Apparently, they were sending it to New Orleans in some other, more secure way. That, or they were merely unloading it yet again until the ship was inspected to make certain it was seaworthy. Why they were going to so much trouble for a load of rocks, Flynn couldn't fathom. They had to have seen the boxes he and Rose had opened. They had to know the gold was fake.

The more he thought about it, the less sense it made.

Cage nudged Wash with his elbow and pointed as two more men in suits carried a small box up the loading ramp. The soldiers were all busy with the heavy crates and didn't notice the men making away with the pallet. The box was about the size of a bread box, strapped down to a platform with handles on both sides that the men used to carry it. One of them had thrown his coat over the box to hide the stenciled words on the side that declared it the property of the army.

"What is that?" Wash asked.

"We saw that when we was in the cargo hold," Flynn said. "Rose was messing with it, talking about how he thought it was that rock the Santee were after. Had a big ol' padlock on it, and we couldn't get into it."

Cage turned and pointed at it again emphatically.

Flynn glanced at him. "What?"

"You think that's what they were after?" Wash asked as he stared at Cage.

Cage nodded and looked between them urgently, pointing at the box again.

"They were after the gold," Flynn argued. "They didn't know it wasn't real."

Cage shook his head and tugged at his ear, then pointed at the box once more.

Flynn frowned and turned his attention back to the box. Cage had obviously heard something that made him so sure of that. "You think they did all this for that one little box?"

Cage nodded and slammed his palm against the wooden railing to emphasize his certainty.

"Let's go see what the hell it is, then," Wash said. He pushed away from the railing and began jogging toward the gangplank.

Flynn and Cage followed close behind him, forcing their way down the landing stage.

"Hold on, there!" Wash called to the four men in suits as they loaded the box into the back of a stagecoach.

One of the men turned around, impassively watching them approach with his hand on the hilt of his gun. Flynn was shocked to discover it was the government man in the gray top hat from St. Louis, the one Rose had hidden from in the mercantile. Baird, Rose had called him.

"You," Flynn said before he could stop himself.

"Do I know you?" Baird asked in a deep, cultured southern drawl.

"You're Baird," Flynn said as anger and frustration welled in him. He pulled the lapel of his jacket aside, showing his badge to Baird. "Friend of mine accused you of attempted murder."

"Is that so?" Baird said, unconcerned. He mimicked Flynn's gesture, showing them his own badge. "The only men I've ever attempted to kill have been criminals, Marshal. Forgive me if I must question the company you keep in that regard."

Flynn bristled and felt his face reddening, but what could he say in response? Rose *had* been a criminal. Even now, Flynn didn't know what to believe about the man who'd given his life for a near stranger. He may have been an outlaw, but he'd also been a good man.

The other three men paid them no attention. One got into the stagecoach with the covered box, and then the other two locked him inside before taking several other seemingly unnecessary measures to secure him.

Wash didn't have his badge pinned to his vest yet, but that didn't stop him from stepping forward and pointing at the coach. "We have reason to believe that box there was what the men who boarded the ship were after," he said in his most authoritative voice.

"Yes, sir," Baird said, infuriatingly polite.

"We need to see it." Flynn came up beside Wash, face set in a determined scowl.

"I'm afraid that won't be possible," Baird said with false regret, and turned away from them.

Wash moved to stop him, grabbing his elbow. The man spun around, moving like a striking snake, and took hold of Wash's hand. The next thing Flynn knew, Wash was on his knees, twisting to keep his wrist from snapping in the man's grasp.

Flynn grabbed for his gun but Cage stopped him, grabbing his hand and shaking his head vehemently. Baird released Wash and turned away from them once more.

"You did an excellent job with your riverboat ordeal, marshals," he said smoothly as he walked past the head of the stagecoach. He patted the side of the stage, and then nodded at the driver to signify that they were ready. Then he moved to a magnificent black horse and pulled himself into the saddle gracefully. "I understand the world rid itself of Dusty Rose in the river on top of it all. Job well done, I must say. I suggest you go home and get some well-deserved rest."

Flynn and Cage helped Wash off the ground, and they watched helplessly as the stagecoach trundled away, followed by two heavily armed men on large horses. The three of them stood where they'd been left, dumbfounded and frustrated as the little caravan moved off without any soldiers riding herd for them. It was painfully obvious they'd just slipped that box out from under the army's nose.

Finally, Flynn turned to Cage and cocked his head. "You got any idea what's going on?"

Cage shook his head and flopped his arms expressively.

"You know who those men were?" Wash said distantly. He rubbed at his wrist. "Secret Service department."

"What?" Flynn asked incredulously. He'd seen the man's badge, but he hadn't recognized it. He didn't know if the Secret Service even had badges. "Nah," he added, despite his lack of knowledge on the subject.

The Secret Service department had been around for about fifteen years. They had gotten their start during the War Between the States, acting as spies for the Pinkerton agency. The Iron Brigade had dealt with a few of them in their time. They had been made official by the government after the war because the US Marshal Service didn't have the manpower to investigate everything that came under their jurisdiction. It was rumored they still performed other, more nefarious deeds.

Flynn supposed it was possible those men had been part of the Secret Service department, although he couldn't fathom what they could be up to here of all places. When he tried for an alternate explanation, he came up empty. He remembered Rose's story about the government man he'd met with, the strange object that had been so important to so many different groups, and he wondered how it all filled in. If Baird had hired Stringer like Rose had claimed, why was he here collecting the very thing Stringer had been meant to steal? How had he known it would be here?

Then it hit him, and his lips parted as he thought through it. Suddenly, the telegram made sense.

"Son of a bitch," Flynn murmured.

"What?"

"Stringer sent the telegram so there'd be enough of a fuss here in New Madrid to give Baird and his men a chance to steal away with that box. This is what they planned all along."

Wash and Cage both stared at him, then turned almost as one to look off into the distance where Baird and his men had disappeared.

"Stringer wasn't ever supposed to steal anything. That's why he did all that herding, Wash, he was stalling. He probably planned to jump ship right before they got to New Madrid, and these soldiers were waiting to attack the men he left behind."

"Damn, Flynn," Wash muttered with a twinkle in his eyes, "you're thinking a little like an outlaw."

"Shut up," Flynn said out of habit. "My God. Those coal bombs we found, they were going to blow the ship after it was all said and done, muddy the trail and make the Army think the box got lost in the shuffling and went down with the boat."

"That's a lot of people dead for one little box."

Cage patted Flynn's shoulder, then pointed off toward the horizon. He then tapped his chest where a badge would sit. He ended the gesture by making his finger into a gun, pointing it between Flynn's eyes, and shooting him.

Flynn frowned, not quite following.

"Believe it." Wash straightened his coat, nodding at whatever Cage had tried to communicate. "Whatever they had in that box? That's government business. And they'd shoot us all dead if we got into it."

"That mean Stringer was government?" Flynn asked.

Cage laughed, then clapped a hand over his mouth as if he hadn't meant to. He shook his head vehemently. Stringer wasn't government, then.

"He sure was hired, though," Wash added. "And it appears he won. But you know what this feels like? A whole lot of not our concern."

Flynn shared a look with Cage and the two men shrugged at each other. The sentiment was clear. What did they care about government business as long as they had lived through the night?

"Thank God we don't get all the government we pay for, right?" Flynn offered uneasily.

"I say we do what the . . . *gentleman* suggested," Wash said as he rubbed his sore wrist and stared into the horizon where the stagecoach had disappeared.

Flynn noticed with something like elation that Wash's hurt arm was moving even better than it had been when they had left Lincoln, his sling hanging unused around his neck.

Cage patted Wash on the arm gently. Wash turned to him, and Cage pointed to his wrist, then waved his own through the air violently and held out his hand to Wash consolingly.

"What?" Wash asked with a slight laugh.

"I believe he said at least he got your good arm and not your bad one," a cultured, accented voice translated from behind them.

Cage whirled and found himself staring at Gabriel Rose with wide, shocked eyes. The man was moving away from the crowd of milling passengers, soldiers, and dock workers with care, glancing around as if he expected to be attacked from any angle.

Flynn and Wash were silent, as stunned to see Gabriel as Cage was. They all three gaped at him.

Cage took a tentative step toward him, staring hard just to make sure he was real. He was dirty and bedraggled, his hair unruly from having been wet and then dried by the sun. He'd lost his jacket and his newly acquired hat and from his knees down was caked in foul-smelling river mud. He was a far sight from the dapper man Cage had first seen in the jail cell in Junction City. Gabriel looked every inch like he'd just swum his way out of the Mississippi River and walked into New Madrid.

"What, no hello?" Gabriel asked of the three of them with an insulted spread of his arms.

Cage impetuously wrapped him up in a hug. Gabriel's breath left him in a rush as Cage squeezed him. The hug hurt Cage's ribs like he'd been set on fire, but he didn't care. Gabriel returned the hug and laughed weakly, his filthy finger lingering on Cage's shoulders. Cage pulled back and took Gabriel's face in his hands, examining him intently.

"I know," Gabriel said to him with a small smile.

"How in the blazes did you get out alive?" Flynn blurted as he and Wash came closer. His voice was a harsh whisper, as if he was afraid one of the lawmen from the paddle steamer would overhear.

"A wing and a prayer, mostly," Gabriel answered with a wan smile. "I washed ashore on the whim of the river and started walking. I made it here to New Madrid just as I saw the paddleboat being pulled in. I want to know what was in that box," he added as he pointed in the direction the stagecoach had headed.

"What?" Flynn asked in consternation.

Cage looked back at him and then at Gabriel again with a confusing mix of emotions. He was elated to see Gabriel, almost light-headed with joy after the initial shock had passed. But he was also worried. If Gabriel had survived the river, that meant Bat Stringer may have managed the feat as well.

Gabriel's next words compounded his concerns. "I think that man Stringer made it ashore, though I can't imagine he got too far with that knife in his ribs," he said grimly. "If he did, I think he'll be headed directly for that box."

Wash moved closer and gently took Gabriel by the arm. "Forget the box, son, why don't we get you inside somewhere? We'll get us some warm food and a change of clothes and we'll discuss all this."

Gabriel shook his head stubbornly, but he didn't try to escape from Wash's grasp. "You're just trying to arrest me again, aren't you?" he said with a small smile that made Cage grin.

Wash snorted and shook his head.

"Rose," Flynn said as he held out a hand and closed his eyes. He spoke slowly, as if trying to explain the stars to a horse. "You just came back from the dead."

"I was never dead, Marshal. Just because you believe it to be true doesn't make it so," he explained in the very same tone Flynn had just used. He was smirking, his eyes dancing.

Flynn glared at him. "All the same. Aren't you ready to be done with this mess? It ain't none of our concern now. If Stringer wants to go chasing after that box, then I say let him." He paused, glancing between Cage and Gabriel. "Besides . . . I'm tired."

Cage nodded in agreement and turned to Gabriel hopefully. He wanted nothing more to do with any of it. He was no hero and didn't want to be one. He had his freedom, and now he had Gabriel back with him. That was all he could ask for. Why in the world would they go borrowing trouble now? He silently begged Gabriel to forget the whole business.

Gabriel studied him up and down. Finally, the man nodded minutely and sighed. His next words did not make Cage feel any better, though.

"Do you still plan to take me to New Orleans for trial?" Gabriel asked Flynn and Wash. He raised his chin with a hint of sadness.

Flynn stared at him as Wash shifted uneasily.

"Well." Wash glanced at Flynn, a sly light entering his eyes. "He is still in our custody."

Flynn nodded, gaze locked with Gabriel's. He shook his head suddenly, and Cage released a puff of pent-up air.

"Last I heard, dying pretty much fixes these sorts of problems," Flynn said with a slow smile. "Besides. You got yourself a posthumous pardon."

Gabriel tried to cover his shock, but he couldn't quite manage it. Cage reached out to him, ecstatic, and he squeezed his arm. Gabriel met his eyes, then looked back at Flynn and nodded his thanks. "That's quite decent of you, Marshal. I didn't think you had it in you."

"You keep talking, we'll just see."

Gabriel grinned widely, then he returned his attention to Cage and hugged him close. Cage knew what he was thinking without having to ask. They'd danced around each other for days, slowly getting closer and acknowledging the attraction they felt. They'd never had the freedom to act on it. Until now.

"I suppose a warm supper and a warm bed wouldn't go amiss," Gabriel said, and he glanced at the two marshals and smiled brilliantly.

Flynn rolled his eyes and shook his head before trudging back toward the gangplank. It seemed to Cage that Marshal Flynn had been much fonder of Gabriel Rose when he believed he was dead. The thought made Cage smile despite himself.

Wash stood with Cage and Gabriel, grinning. He reached out and took Gabriel's hand.

"I know what you done for him," he said to Gabriel. "I thank you for it."

"It was my pleasure, Marshal Washington," Gabriel replied politely.

Wash nodded and moved to follow Flynn, ostensibly to retrieve their belongings from the boat.

"Actually, it wasn't a pleasure at all," Gabriel called after them. "I don't know how you stand him!"

Wash kept walking, laughing as he went.

Cage gently touched Gabriel's shoulder. When he turned back, Cage met his eyes, unable to keep from beaming.

"You're looking a little worse for wear," Gabriel said after a slow perusal of Cage's body.

Cage surveyed himself. His ruined shirt was open, revealing the linen wrap they'd used to bind his ribs. He could feel the bruises and cuts on his face, and he knew he must look haggard and drawn. His hair was coming loose from its formerly orderly tie. But Gabriel wasn't looking much better. Cage eyed Gabriel critically, letting his gaze travel up and down with the same dubious expression Gabriel had given him.

"Don't even say it," Gabriel threatened. He pointed a finger in Cage's face. "I may smell like river mud, but I make it look good."

Cage laughed and shook his head fondly.

"Which name do you prefer?" Gabriel asked suddenly.

Cage's expression fell and he licked his lips, fighting back the nerves as they bubbled forth again. He inhaled deeply to steel himself and slowly put his hand to his chest in answer.

Gabriel nodded as if he understood. He jerked his head toward the main street and its array of hotels in the distance. "Come on, then, Cage. You can help me find all the bullet holes."

Gabriel sat on the edge of the bed, fussing with his shirt and mumbling about getting dirty after he'd just washed all the river mud off in the hotel's bath. Cage held a cloth in the washbasin and watched him worriedly. He could see a lot of wounds, though Gabriel insisted he was fine.

A bullet had grazed his arm, just enough to cause blood to well from the shallow furrow, and another had struck a glancing blow to his thigh. Cage had yet to convince Gabriel to allow him to examine it. There were also several slashing wounds on Gabriel's ribs, but Cage didn't worry about those. The thigh was what concerned him.

Cage cleared his throat and pointed at Gabriel's leg when the other man looked up at him. If the bullet was lodged in it, the gangrene would kill Gabriel quickly. He was fairly certain the bullet had gone through cleanly, though, which was a good thing. Cage had pulled bullets out of men before, but he didn't relish the idea of digging one out of Gabriel. He didn't know if he could cause Gabriel that kind of pain . . . He'd have to enlist Marshal Flynn for that job if the need arose. He might enjoy it.

"It's not your duty to tend to my wounds," Gabriel said stubbornly, as if he knew what Cage had been pondering. "And it's not that bad, I promise. If I could trudge up from the riverbank, it'll be fine."

Cage drew the cloth from the washbasin and tossed it at him, hitting him square in the face with the cold, wet rag.

Gabriel stood quickly and yanked the cloth from his face, gasping in surprise. He blinked at Cage with wide eyes, but then his lips quirked into a smile. "Temper," he said evenly. He shook the cloth and folded it neatly, then gave Cage a measuring glance. "How are *your* injuries?"

Cage shrugged as his hand went to his ribcage. He had taken a lot of punishment, but despite his ribs being bound up and sore, he no longer suspected they were broken or even cracked. He could walk and sit and bend a little, and he could carry some weight as well. Cage didn't suppose he could do any of that without being in agony if the bones were really broken. He had a thin cut on his neck where Stringer's knife had dug in too far, and numerous bruises on his face. But he would live.

He picked up the washbasin and carried it over to the bed, kneeling next to Gabriel and setting it on the floor carefully. He looked up at Gabriel and patted the mattress, requesting that he sit back down.

Gabriel shook his head in exasperation. "You are one muleheaded man, do you know that?" He undid his belt and pushed his trousers to the floor. stepping out of them and sitting obediently, offering up his thigh for Cage's inspection. He wore nothing beneath the trousers, and Cage bit his lip to keep from smiling.

"They stole my underthings," Gabriel said defensively.

Cage peered up at him, dubious.

"They did," Gabriel insisted. His expression darkened. "And my grandfather's pocket watch. A trip back to Junction City might be in order."

Cage bit his lip again and petted Gabriel consolingly on the knee. He was in for going back to Junction City for Gabriel's watch.

"Now you're just humoring me," Gabriel muttered. His shoulders slumped.

Cage nodded and took the cloth from him. He did his best to clean the wound on Gabriel's thigh, realizing as he wiped away the dried and drying blood that it wasn't nearly as bad as he'd feared. It seemed they'd both come out of the night in better shape than they should have hoped for. Cage retrieved the clean linen bandages they'd bought and wrapped the wound tightly, causing Gabriel to hiss.

Cage gave him an apologetic grimace.

"Don't. You don't have to apologize for anything."

Cage's hands slowed as he met Gabriel's eyes. Gabriel merely continued to look down at him, his eyes expressive and full of questions that might never get asked or answered. He didn't say anything further. Cage stared, letting the weight of the night slide away as he reminded himself they were both free men now, free to do as they liked, go where they pleased. And Gabriel's first act as a free man had been to crawl out of the Mississippi and trudge right back to him. They were together.

He reached up and brushed his fingers over Gabriel's face. Gabriel's eyes fluttered closed, and Cage climbed toward him, kissing him hungrily as he pushed Gabriel's back to the mattress.

Gabriel's arms wound around his neck and he made a muffled sound of surprise, but he returned the kiss wholeheartedly despite being caught off-guard. His teeth scraped against Cage's upper lip as he nipped at him. Cage's hands traveled up and down his body, appreciating the hard, lean muscles and the sinuous way Gabriel's body wrapped around him as he pressed him into the thin mattress.

Gabriel's hands were almost immediately pushing at Cage's trousers, and Cage's body responded rapidly to the invitation. He shoved himself up and stood, carefully shucking his clothing as Gabriel unbuttoned his own shirt. He just barely managed to toss it over the side of the bed before Cage was on him again, kissing him and dragging his fingers over his skin. Their bodies pressed together, hot to the touch in the cold room. Gabriel clung to Cage's neck, and he settled onto his back, obviously at ease with having Cage's weight on him.

Cage hummed appreciatively as they kissed each other, over and over.

Gabriel hooked one leg over Cage's hip. "Where's that snake oil you talked me into buying?" he asked, his dark eyes sparkling with humor and desire. He couldn't seem to pass up any chance at a wry comment on Cage's silence, and Cage found it both endearing and exasperatingly amusing. Other men who made such jabs wouldn't have gotten off so easily. It was just another twist to the spell Gabriel had cast over him.

Cage's lips twitched as he pushed off the mattress again, regretfully leaving the pleasure of Gabriel's body to go in search of the parcel. When they'd bought the bandages and other supplies from the general store, Cage had thrown in a small ceramic bottle of Minard's Liniment, "The great internal and external remedy for man or beast!"

Cage and Gabriel had both known it was just a step up from snake oil sold in the traveling medicine shows around the country. But rubbing it vigorously on sore muscles did feel good, and lord knew they would both have enough of those. They also knew it would slick up anything you wanted and keep it that way for a good long while if used in quantity. Snake oil had many uses for men like them.

Cage retrieved it and returned to the bed eagerly, missing Gabriel's touch as if he'd known it all his life. Gabriel wrapped his arms around him as soon as he was back on the bed, kissing him demandingly and arching his body to rub against him.

Cage gave him a strangled groan and reached for his hip, holding him down as the contact stoked a fire inside him. He bent to kiss the length of Gabriel's body, letting his lips linger against the heated skin of the more tender places and carefully avoiding the injuries. There were a good many of them, and Cage lifted his head to look at Gabriel uncertainly. This sort of thing could wait until they were both in better condition to enjoy it.

Gabriel's fingers drifted over the tightly wrapped linen around Cage's torso. "Are you certain you're well enough for this?" Gabriel asked.

Cage snorted at him, not surprised that Gabriel had been thinking the same thing as he.

He rested his hand on the bandaging on Gabriel's own ribs, where he'd suffered several gashes from a knife. He raised an eyebrow and let his lips quirk.

Gabriel got the message loud and clear. He tightened his knees around Cage's waist. His voice was low and rough when he responded, and it was obvious to Cage that Gabriel was feeling the same desperate need he was. "Hang the hurts, Cage, we'll get over them."

Cage nodded furtively and kissed him harder, although Gabriel's initial concerns were valid; the burning in his ribs might soon overpower the need from his groin, and Cage couldn't imagine that Gabriel was any better off. But Gabriel was right: they'd get over the aches and pains soon enough. They needed this first exploratory contact far too much to mind them yet.

Cage pushed against Gabriel and groaned as he rubbed their lengths together. Gabriel spread his legs wider and slid both ankles over Cage's calves, hooking his feet behind Cage's knees. His fingers found their way into Cage's hair and he grabbed a fistful of it, tightening his grip as he raised his hips to meet Cage's. Cage bit at Gabriel's chin, feeling like he might just explode with his desire to be closer. Gabriel's uninhibited manner was more intoxicating than any Celestial man's opium or saloon keeper's whiskey could be. It wasn't rare for men in the West to be intimate with each other, to touch each other for comfort or pleasure. It *was* rare for a man to admit he favored it and enjoyed it, though, and Cage couldn't get enough of Gabriel's enthusiasm.

"I have an idea," Gabriel gasped even as he continued to roll his hips against Cage.

Cage groaned plaintively.

"No, I know, but it's actually a good one this time," Gabriel insisted breathlessly.

Cage shook his head. He'd had his fill of Gabriel's ideas for one day, no matter how well the last few had turned out for them in the end. He took Gabriel's hands and held them down, pinning him to the bed as he continued to slowly rut against him.

Gabriel's eyes fluttered closed and his lips parted as he rested his head on the mattress. Cage took the opportunity to admire the man. His body was hard and solid against Cage's, his lean muscles well-defined, not a pound of him wasted. His dark hair had curled after bathing, and the tendrils framed his handsome face against the white of the bed linens. His tanned, prominent cheeks were flushed with desire and pleasure, and his nimble fingers clenched around Cage's hands with every movement of their bodies. Each exhale became a moan of pleasure as Cage rocked against him.

Gabriel Rose was apparently a man who liked to be held down. Cage told himself to remember it as he kissed Gabriel again.

"You don't even want to hear my idea?" Gabriel asked without opening his eyes.

Cage pressed his face into Gabriel's neck and shook his head. He released one of his wrists and let his hand travel down until he could slide it beneath Gabriel's hip. He pulled at him, clearly communicating what he did want.

Gabriel immediately had his hand back in Cage's long hair, tugging at it as he lifted his hips.

Cage reached for the ceramic bottle of snake oil and used his teeth to yank out the cork. Gabriel laughed, the sound warm and arousing in its own right. Gabriel took the bottle from him and tipped it over Cage's open palm. Neither of them wanted Cage to have to use both hands and take them off Gabriel. Cage gave himself the moment to appreciate how well Gabriel's mind worked with his own as they impatiently watched the snake oil slide out into the palm of his hand. When Gabriel judged that there was enough, he righted the bottle and held it up to Cage, shoving it against the cork he still held in his teeth to stopper it up before he tossed the bottle aside.

Cage slicked himself down hastily, taking more rough, demanding kisses from Gabriel as he did so. He didn't know if his tired, bruised body would let him do all that he wanted to do to Gabriel, but he planned to give it his all-fired best. Gabriel moved under him, obviously intending to roll onto his belly, but Cage stopped him by tightening the grip on his wrist and sliding his slick hand between their bodies. He wanted Gabriel right here, wanted to see his eyes.

Gabriel groaned and stretched his body out like a cat, pushing his legs farther apart so Cage could settle between them. Cage had rarely encountered a man so comfortable with this more intimate position. The willingness from his partner sent the already consuming heat coursing even faster through his body. Cage gripped him with his slick hand and pumped him several times, enjoying the look on Gabriel's face as the pleasure rippled through him. Gabriel's hand in his hair tightened until it was almost painful, and Cage knew he couldn't draw it out any longer without the whole thing coming to an abrupt end for both of them.

He took himself in hand, coating more of the thick snake oil on himself, and then he tugged at one of Gabriel's knees. Gabriel lifted his leg obediently, and Cage hiked it up onto his shoulder. Gabriel tossed his head to the side and moved for him with a groan, whether of approval or pain Cage didn't know. He belatedly remembered the wounds he'd just moments before been doctoring and worrying over, but if Gabriel wasn't going to complain, Cage would let it be.

He lined himself up as he held Gabriel's hips off the mattress, his body trembling with the effort and the restraint it took to go slowly.

Gabriel's hands clutched at the sparse hair of Cage's chest as Cage pushed into him, and Cage was unable to keep the moan of pleasure from passing his lips as he watched himself sink into Gabriel's tight body. Gabriel echoed the sound as he rolled his hips and his body tensed against the intrusion, his short fingernails scraping down Cage's chest. It was an easier entry than Cage had expected, and he briefly wondered who else had been riding Gabriel lately. It was a passing fancy, and an issue that didn't matter to Cage as he rocked into his newfound lover.

He began with measured, careful thrusts, trying to make sure he didn't hurt either of them or shoot off his load too soon. But the way Gabriel moved with him and the sounds he made didn't make it an easy task.

Gabriel pulled his ankle up higher to rest against the small of Cage's back, and his hands dug into Cage's upper arms as he tried and failed to make him thrust harder into him. Cage grunted and fumbled to capture his wrists again, first extricating his arm from beneath Gabriel's leg to grab one wrist and then the other as he pinned Gabriel to the bed. Gabriel linked both legs behind Cage's back, smiling as if that had been his goal all along.

Manipulative bastard. Cage huffed a fond laugh, then kissed the smile off his lips and thrust into him, hard. Gabriel gasped at the sudden change in the rhythm of their bodies. Cage continued the punishing thrusts, grunting with the effort as Gabriel moaned and tugged at his hands, trying to free his arms. When Cage's grip loosened, Gabriel wrapped one arm around Cage's neck, the other around his torso, and his nails dug into Cage's skin as Cage fucked him hard and fast for a few more torturous, glorious minutes before slowing his pace once more.

He was panting with every roll of his hips, and not merely from the exertion or pleasure of the act. Gabriel's breaths were hot against his skin, and it felt so damn good inside him.

When his rhythm began to falter, Gabriel gripped him hard and whispered into his ear, "Roll over, Cage."

Cage groaned and forced his hips to stop. He lowered his head against Gabriel for a moment of pure pleasure before he gripped his lover tightly and rolled both their bodies to the side.

Cage found himself on his back, Gabriel astride him with his hands on Cage's stomach and his chin raised as he rocked his hips and forced Cage fully back inside him. Cage watched raptly as Gabriel took himself in hand and began to stroke in time with his slow rocking.

Even being ridden by another man, Gabriel still found a way to guide the horse.

Cage reached for his hips and held on to him, enjoying the sinuous movement beneath his fingertips almost as much as the clench and slide around his dick. Gabriel's moans deepened as he rode Cage, and his hand moved faster as he pleasured himself. Cage found his hips pushing upward almost of their own accord, and every time, Gabriel would groan plaintively and his body would jerk and tighten.

Finally, it appeared he could take no more, and his body bowed forward, Cage's name on his lips as the evidence of his pleasure pulsed over his fingers and onto Cage's stomach. Cage watched him reach his end, entranced and overwhelmed by the sight. His body screamed at him to find his own release, and he gripped Gabriel's hips hard and bucked under him like an unruly mount that refused to be broken.

Gabriel called out hoarsely and threw his head back, first merely holding onto Cage as he rode him, and then regaining his senses enough to roll his hips and meet the wild thrusts. Cage would come almost completely out of him, then slam back into him with the satisfying slap of their damp bodies.

It didn't take long for Cage to break. He sat up to wrap his arms around Gabriel and kiss him passionately, holding him still as he emptied himself into his new lover's willing body.

Any hesitation Flynn and Wash had harbored over sex with each other had disappeared once they shared their first private kiss. Stepping inside the room at the hotel had offered an awkward few seconds, but Wash had taken care of that by tugging Flynn to him and kissing him greedily.

They hadn't stopped since.

Wash's lips gave under Flynn's as they wrapped around one another. They'd somehow found their way to the bed, and Flynn had come out on top, momentarily at least.

Wash lifted his knees to squeeze Flynn between them, and he pulled one hand away from Flynn's back to grasp at his neck and hair. Flynn propped his weight on his knuckles, then he slid his hand under Wash's shoulder and lifted him off the mattress. He rubbed against him slowly, knowing they'd both enjoy the friction.

Neither of them was by any means a virgin, but their first encounter with each other was still fraught with nerves and awkward first attempts. Flynn found they were able to laugh off the moments where they both turned their heads the same way to kiss, or knocked noses in their urgency to taste each other. Flynn had never done this with a man, and the thought of slipping inside Wash made his entire body tingle with both anticipation and fear.

"You done this before?" Flynn asked, surprised by how breathless and needy he sounded.

"Not . . . not like this," Wash admitted.

"I hate to lead off with caution, but . . ."

Wash nodded, somehow knowing what Flynn was trying to say. "We got time to get there."

Flynn kissed him again, harder and messier than before. Wash groaned and arched up into him, his fingers digging in as he let Flynn do as he pleased.

Flynn moved down his body slowly, pushing away clothing in order to kiss and nip at his skin, making sure he thoroughly explored all the new places and sensations as Wash squirmed beneath him. He slid his hand under the rough material of Wash's trousers and undergarments, inching them down just enough to lick at the juncture of his hip and thigh.

He looked up at Wash and smiled slightly. Wash was watching him intently, his breath short and his face flushed. He slid his fingers through Flynn's hair.

"Want me to keep going?" Flynn asked, nearly choking on the nerves that bubbled up.

Wash nodded, and Flynn pulled down Wash's pants farther and nuzzled his face against Wash's abdomen. He inhaled deeply, Wash's scent bringing back decades of memories between them, then he crawled up Wash's body to kiss him again.

"You smell right," he told his partner in a low voice.

Wash inhaled through his nose and let out a shaky sigh. "You feel right," he murmured. "I'm damn glad you got up the nerve."

"Wish I'd done it years ago." Flynn pushed down onto Wash's body and hummed as he dragged his lips across Wash's. Wash's mouth opened under Flynn's, and he slid his hands up and down Flynn's body, pressing his knees close, almost wrapped around him.

Flynn buried his face in Wash's neck and rocked against him, thinking of all the times he'd wished he could do this without shame, just enjoying the warmth and anticipation. Finally, he rose to his hands and knees and crawled backward, shoving Wash's trousers down to his thighs as he did so. He pulled them farther, managing to get one leg completely off, then he stood and shucked his own clothing.

If they were going to be rutting in bed like a couple of dogs, they might as well do it right.

Wash got rid of the garments he had left, then grabbed for Flynn and pulled him onto the bed. The iron headboard banged against the thin wall accusingly, and Flynn and Wash both snickered as they curled around each other, foreheads pressed together.

Flynn dragged both hands down Wash's chest. "C'mon," he whispered. "You're the lead bull in this herd."

Wash took one of Flynn's hands and kissed it quickly, then guided it down his body until Flynn's fingers grasped his dick. He closed his eyes and slowly rocked into Flynn's hand several times.

Flynn choked on his breath and shivered. His grip tightened on Wash, the callused pads of his fingers gliding over the contours of his partner. He was just as hard as Flynn was. Flynn shoved his hips closer, taking himself in hand as well, rubbing their dicks together as they both moved.

Wash groaned against Flynn's mouth and grasped at him to pull him flush to his chest. He grabbed out for the iron headboard with his other hand, but it was too far away to reach. He kept unconsciously grasping for something, anything, and finally he just let out a plaintive moan and curled his fingers into Flynn's hair.

Flynn rutted against him, and Wash's hips jerked in contrast to his own, sliding with him, shoving him. Flynn loved the way Wash sounded and smelled. The way he tasted. Now that he had a hint of what this could be, he knew he'd need to have it for the rest of his life.

A gasp from Wash might have been Flynn's name, but it was difficult to tell through the low moans now dragging out of Wash's chest as he shifted back and forth against Flynn. He kept trying to roll to his back, then probably remembering that he couldn't if he wanted to keep in contact with Flynn. He would kiss Flynn with a groan of complaint each time.

He flicked his tongue and sucked hard on Flynn's lip. Flynn's entire body thrummed with the desire to stop and just take Wash hard and dirty right there.

He picked up the pace with his hand, finally wrenching a blue streak of swearing and labored panting from Wash's mouth.

"Jesus *fuck*, Flynn!"

Wash's back arched. His dick was swollen and hard in Flynn's fingers.

"Please . . ." he finally whispered against Flynn's chin.

Flynn hummed in response. He didn't think he was capable of speaking.

He could tell by the sounds Wash made that he was trying desperately not to yell. Then something must have given because Wash bit down on his lip and shuddered hard, and his dick spasmed against Flynn's. Flynn realized Wash had given in to the insistent pleasure, and he closed his eyes and let go of his own control. His hand was full of Wash's seed already, and it made the slick pulls on his own dick that much better.

"Wash," he gasped, desperate to have Wash as close as he could get. Wash's hand joined his, swatting him out of the way to take over the job of milking Flynn for every last drop.

Flynn jerked his head back, pumping his hips into Wash's hand as their eyes locked. Flynn was hard-pressed not to have his way right here and now. It seemed like every muscle in him was straining, and when he let loose his soft cries of release, they were lost to Wash's kisses.

They held on to each other for long minutes, letting their bodies dry in the cold room, keeping warm by wrapping around each other under the scratchy quilt. Both of them were worn out from their ordeal, followed by such unusual exertion.

"Why the hell ain't we done this before now?" Wash asked breathlessly. He finally released his hold on Flynn and rolled to his back, shuddering and sighing.

Flynn merely shook his head, unable to form coherent thought just yet. It would take some tricky figuring, and maybe seeking some embarrassing advice from Rose, but they would figure it out for themselves before long.

"Rose suggested we use that tonic to . . . make things easier, if we're so inclined."

"Oh yeah? Guess that's one use they won't be listing on those medicine peddlers' wagons," Wash murmured.

Flynn rolled his head to look at him, arching an eyebrow. Wash was staring up at the plaster ceiling with a self-satisfied smirk. They found themselves unable to keep their high spirits from becoming laughter, and they lay together in the narrow bed, chuckling, uncaring of the world outside the hotel's doors for that perfect moment in time.

age sat stiffly in his chair, his ribs giving him a bit of trouble this morning as he and Gabriel enjoyed breakfast together. They'd purchased new clothing as soon as the mercantile opened, and Cage had to admit, Gabriel looked good. He couldn't keep his eyes from straying to the man, and almost every time they did, he found Gabriel staring right back at him and smiling.

The world that morning was a bright, friendly place, full of hope and opportunity. Cage knew it wouldn't stay that way, but he could enjoy it while it lasted.

It wasn't long before the two marshals joined them, ordering coffee to drink and bacon and eggs for breakfast. Cage was slightly surprised Flynn and Wash would eat with them, considering they'd ridden into St. Louis less than three days before, hauling them both in handcuffed to a wagon.

Gabriel smiled warmly at both the marshals and greeted them with his unusual brand of sarcastic class. "Marshals. I trust you're both well rested this fine morning."

Wash merely snorted at him good-naturedly, and Flynn glared for a moment before his lips twisted into a smile he quite obviously couldn't restrain.

"Half figured you to be gone this morning," Flynn told them as he settled into his chair.

Gabriel offered a broad grin. "I'm waiting for a newspaper. I'm quite interested to see how my death has affected the masses."

"And there was much rejoicing in the streets," Flynn intoned.

Cage and Wash both rolled their eyes and shared a glance as Wash seated himself next to Cage. "How are you, Cage?" Wash asked him as Flynn and Gabriel continued their affable bickering.

Cage pointed to his ribs and then made a so-so gesture with his hand.

"That's good. Means you can travel easier. You know what you plan to do now?" Wash asked with a nod at Gabriel.

Cage smiled fondly. Ever the optimist, the good Marshal Washington, always seeing the silver lining and expecting Cage to be able to respond. Of course, he and Gabriel had discussed their plans the night before, and they'd been in agreement over the fact that it might do them both some good to leave the country for a spell. After they retrieved Gabriel's pocket watch, that is. He gave an elegant shrug and lifted a hand toward Gabriel. And after that, they would go wherever life took them.

Wash nodded as if he'd understood.

"It's possible we may find ourselves back in England for a while," Gabriel told Wash. "To let the news of my death settle around those still trying to kill me, if you catch my meaning."

"Good idea," Flynn said. Cage was under the impression that he merely liked the thought of Gabriel leaving the country.

"Well, you ever find yourself up by Lincoln way, you just . . . tie Rose to a tree and come on into town and visit us," Wash told Cage, and he began laughing.

Cage smiled with him, nodding. He doubted they would ever see the two marshals again, and though he felt a pang of regret over it, he was sure he was the only one of the group that did.

"You got a second lease on life, Rose," Wash said as he ate. "But I get the feeling you got something bothering you still. You know what's in that box, don't you?"

Gabriel shifted uneasily and glanced between them. "I have my guesses, yes."

"It's that Indian stone, ain't it," Flynn said.

Gabriel took a deep breath, seeming to come to a decision. "Months ago, the government man Baird ordered me to a meeting with him and Stringer."

Cage couldn't conceal his surprise. He placed his hand over Gabriel's forearm.

"I know," Gabriel said to him. "His threats were real enough, and so I went more out of self-preservation than anything. He wanted us to steal a trinket of some sort from the Army, they were digging it up from the Rosebud Creek."

"Why you?" Wash asked.

"He claimed I had information that would be useful after we acquired it. He didn't tell me what, but the only thing I could come up with was my knowledge of the native tribes they talk about in those damn dime novels. They're exaggerated, of course."

"Of course," Wash said wryly. "You're no master of escape, and you aren't an ace with the draw, and you sure don't have a dog who steals keys from lawmen."

Gabriel had the good grace to look a little ashamed, but there was still a glimmer of amusement in his eyes.

"And you're no outlaw," Flynn added with a smirk.

"I'm not," Gabriel insisted.

Flynn merely smiled at Gabriel, almost fondly. Almost. "What are you, Rose?"

Gabriel returned the smile and then met Cage's eyes. He took Cage's hand in his, not averting his gaze when he spoke. "I'm just me," he said softly.

Cage's chest tightened. He gave a single nod. He didn't care where Gabriel had picked up his variety of dastardly skills. He didn't care.

"Baird wanted me to help him, and I refused. The men I killed in Junction City, they were sent by him. They'd been trailing me since Denver. I shot them," Gabriel admitted, and he gave Flynn and Wash a defiant jut of his chin. "I goaded them into a fight, and I shot them because they were there to kill me. I took their badges off them before the sheriff arrived on the scene, and I buried them. I . . ." He looked at Cage again apologetically. "It's not just my pocket watch I was going back for. I was going to go back for the badges."

Cage just nodded and smiled gently. He still didn't care. He'd still go to Junction City with Gabriel, and he'd still follow him to wherever the road may lead.

"Why'd you stick around to be arrested?" Wash asked.

"Who better to watch my back than two US Marshals who want to hang me?" Gabriel asked, beginning to snicker.

"You are something else," Flynn grumbled. He sipped at his coffee and shook his head, continuing to mutter to himself.

Gabriel cleared his throat, fighting a smile. "Yes, well . . . at least I'm on your side now, Marshal."

"God help me," Flynn said as he cast his eyes heavenward.

Gabriel laughed delightedly. Cage squeezed his hand, admiring him. He'd been through quite a thing. So had Cage. But they were together now, and even the marshals were sharing a happy ending. Bat Stringer's possible escape from the river's grasp still niggled at the back of his mind, but he pushed it aside. They'd have plenty to keep them busy without buying trouble.

"You still intend to go after that box?" Wash asked finally. "Never pays to mess with the Secret Service."

"Secret Service?" Gabriel said, eyes widening.

Wash nodded, and Gabriel paled visibly. He cleared his thoat and gave Cage a fond glance. "No, Marshal. I don't intend to pick a fight with the Secret Service over a box. I have better things to tend to, don't I?" He squeezed Cage's hand and winked.

Cage and Gabriel left New Madrid shortly after breakfast, with newly purchased horses and equipment, and several parcels of new clothing for each of them. They bid farewell to the marshals, assuring them that they would leave the badges, and Gabriel's pocket watch, in Junction City and were heading for Nashville first, and then probably a port on the East Coast from which to sail. It was quite touching, if not a little painful, to watch Flynn try to thank Gabriel. They ultimately settled on a handshake, and then Flynn and Wash were gone, heading back to Lincoln by way of St. Louis.

Cage and Gabriel hadn't ridden more than half a mile before they were joined by Gabriel's scrappy little mutt, Koda. Cage was shocked to see the animal lope up to them and bark happily, but Gabriel greeted him as if he'd known all along he would find them. Cage told himself right then that his life was about to get far more interesting than it had ever been, and he should start expecting anything and everything.

"Does it sit right with you, letting that box make its merry way on to wherever they were taking it?" Gabriel asked him as they rode side by side.

Cage glanced at him with a pointed sigh, but he was smiling.

Gabriel's eyes were shining. "I know, it's the Secret Service. That would prove . . . challenging. And I'm no thief, mind you. But I am curious. Of course, you just say the word and you and I will disappear into the sunset."

Cage's lips twitched as he tried to keep a straight face. Finally, he reached into his pocket and withdrew the small leather booklet and the length of charcoal pencil the marshals had bought for him the previous morning. He wrote his response quickly, then leaned over in the saddle to hand the booklet to his partner.

Gabriel took it and read it aloud. "The only thing a man ever got from riding off into the sunset was sunshine in his eyes."

He barked a laugh and looked up at Cage, grinning from ear to ear.

"Let's go find something more substantial than sunshine, then, shall we?"

"You know they're going after that box, right?" Flynn asked Wash as they readied the horses rented from the livery that would take them to St. Louis to retrieve their own mounts and the wagon.

"I know it," Wash said in a long-suffering tone. He peered over his saddle at Flynn. "You suppose it's our job to go stop 'em?"

"If we go according to Hoyle it is," Flynn said with a crooked grin.

Wash glared at him for a few moments, then he groaned and looked away. "Damn you and your rules, Flynn." He pulled himself into his saddle and stared off toward the south, tipping his head sideways so his hat would shield his eyes from the sun rising in the east. "I am a mite curious myself."

"Then we better get moving before they have all the fun."

Dear Reader,

Thank you for reading Abigail Roux's *According to Hoyle*!

We know your time is precious and you have many, many entertainment options, so it means a lot that you've chosen to spend your time reading. We really hope you enjoyed it.

We'd be honored if you'd consider posting a review—good or bad—on sites like **Amazon, Barnes & Noble, Kobo, Goodreads, Twitter, Facebook, Tumblr,** and your blog or website. We'd also be honored if you told your friends and family about this book. Word of mouth is a book's lifeblood!

For more information on upcoming releases, author interviews, blog tours, contests, giveaways, and more, please sign up for our weekly, spam-free newsletter and visit us around the web:

**Newsletter**: tinyurl.com/RiptideSignup
**Twitter**: twitter.com/RiptideBooks
**Facebook**: facebook.com/RiptidePublishing
**Goodreads**: tinyurl.com/RiptideOnGoodreads
**Tumblr**: riptidepublishing.tumblr.com

Thank you so much for Reading the Rainbow!

RiptidePublishing.com

# ACKNOWLEDGMENTS

Special thanks to Hugh Wells for his endless historical knowledge and for waiting until *after* the novel was finished to inform me he possessed a scale model of the steamboat *Robert E. Lee* in his basement.

ALSO BY

ABIGAIL ROUX

ABOUT THE AUTHOR

Abigail Roux was born and raised in North Carolina. A past volleyball star who specializes in sarcasm and painful historical accuracy, she currently spends her time coaching high school volleyball and investigating the mysteries of single motherhood. Any spare time is spent living and dying with every Atlanta Braves and Carolina Panthers game of the year. Abigail has a daughter, Little Roux, who is the light of her life, a boxer, four rescued cats who play an ongoing live-action variation of Call of Duty throughout the house, one evil Ragdoll, a certifiable extended family down the road, and a cast of thousands in her head.

To learn more about Abigail, please visit abigailroux.com.

# Enjoy this book?
# Find more historical romance at
# RiptidePublishing.com!